THE KNIGHTHOOD OF ZION

Return to Eden

Book 2

By
Forrest Haskell

ISBN: 1-4392-0337-7
ISBN-13: 9781439203378

Visit www.booksurge.com to order additional copies.

This book is dedicated in loving
Memory to my green-eyed beauty
Who slipped into eternity on
January 21st 2008

THE KNIGHTHOOD OF ZION

The temperature gauge on the dashboard of my Ford truck indicated I had a problem. Pulling over to the side of the road and opening the hood, I saw what little water that remained in the radiator sneaking out from under the cap as steam. My wife, our four kids and I had been on the road for eight days since we left Michigan and headed south looking for a new home. We were somewhere deep in Texas and on the outskirts of a small town. Fortunately, I could see a Texaco sign high in the air about a mile or so up the deserted two-lane road. I told my wife Peggy Sue that she and the kids should seek some shelter from the late afternoon heat under a small tree. I would walk into town for some water or help, whichever came first.

The hot West Texas sun had me sweating profusely in just a few steps. No wonder the truck engine had heated up. It must have been a hundred degrees on that road. I walked past a faded sign that read Palomino, Texas, and beneath the town's name, Pop. 1936. Finally, and not a moment too soon, because I too was running out of water. I arrived at a one gas pump service station. Sitting in the driveway was an old dilapidated pickup truck that was missing both rear fenders. Two men, one tall and rail thin the other short and heavy set had their dust-covered cowboy boots propped up on the front bumper. They were talking and spitting chewing tobacco juice into the dirt.

"Pardon me," I said humbly, "Is there a hose where I could get some water?"

Pushing his sweaty cowboy hat to the back of his head and smiling through his tobacco stained teeth, the thin one, after spitting and wiping his mouth with his hand said, "Y'all want to drink it or take a bath"? Both cow-pokes broke out into a loud roar as if the one liner was that funny.

Because they were laughing, I said with a chuckle, "Well I do need a drink and so does my truck. It's broken down a couple of miles back up the road. Say, if you men could give me a lift to my vehicle with some water I'd be happy to slip you a few bucks."

"What do ya call a few bucks, pardner?" Heavy said while still snickering.

"Would twenty dollars be okay?" I said hopefully.

"Twenty? Hey Pard, I'd tow her all the way back into town for that. Clint, get some water." Heavy said hurriedly to the other guy. "We just made ourselves some easy dinero," as he jumped into the pickup and started the engine, which knocked loudly as if it had never had a quart of oil in it.

In just a matter of seconds, cold hard cash had turned their funning me into my being their boss and it wasn't long before we were pulling up to my disabled truck.

Clint jumped from the pickup cab, grabbed the full water bucket from the truck's bed and dumped it into the sweltering radiator of my vehicle. I pushed a twenty into Heavy's sweaty palm. Just then, Peggy Sue and the kids walked up to us. When I introduced the two ranch hands to her, their demeanor changed completely from sarcastic and tobacco spitting to one of respect as if they were addressing their Sunday school teacher. "How do ya do mam? Mighty hot out cheer ain't it?" Slim commented to the introduction while tipping his ten gallon hat.

"How do you do, mister?" Peggy said hesitantly.

"Name's Clint mam and that over there is Jeb" he said, motioning towards heavy.

"Afternoon, Mam" heavy replied nodding his head.

After replacing the radiator cap and closing my truck's hood, Clint said, "There, that thar should do it. This here motor looks brand new, it sure should run. Say, we ain't never seen a truck like this down here in these parts. What ya hauling with her?"

"Oh, nothing but some footlockers full of our clothes," I said as a quick defensive response to the casual question.

I was being very careful and secretive, when talking about the load I was carrying. It was something very valuable, so valuable that I was sure it's worth exceeded that of every building in the whole town of Palomino, Texas, including all the cattle, holding pens, even the town hall. You see, I was carrying an enormous amount of money. Yes that's right, greenbacks; cold hard cash; American currency, anyway you want to put it. Concealed in the footlockers was what remained of a huge fortune my wife and I had discovered hidden in the walls of an old mansion we had bought in Michigan. You may have heard the old expression, "Take the money and run." Well that is exactly what we did.

Not wanting to carry on the conversation with my two rescuers, I walked them back to their truck and expressed my gratitude to them as they got in it and pulled away.

The wife, kids and myself piled into my Ford, where upon turning the ignition key the engine came to life with the temperature gauge back in the cool range.

Soon we were passing the Texaco where I had met the cowboys and we entered the center of town. How clean the streets and storefronts were, took us completely by surprise. The town had a friendly air about it with children playing in a park beside a large white gazebo and ladies carrying their groceries to old but highly polished station wagons. There on the town square were several small businesses. My wife saw a neat little restaurant and being it was way past suppertime suggested we should stop to eat. I agreed completely, as not only was I hungry, but thirsty as well. I drove around the square a couple of times, waiting for a parking spot to open up in front of the eatery so I could keep an eye on my load. When one opened up, I slipped that Ford into it before someone else could. Entering the crammed diner, I noticed the sign overhead that read, "Chicken Scratch Restaurant, Authentic Mexican Food". We saw an empty table at the back of the room so the six of us hurried over and took a seat.

Shortly, a nice looking young blond waitress, with her hair tied in a ponytail, came to our table and greeted us with a big smile and a hardy, "Howdy y'all, what can I git ya?"

"Naw, can't say I do, but better be careful of that salsa in the red bottle, it can be mighty brutal at times," said my food advisor chuckling.

He then held out his hand and continued by saying, "By the way, my name is Wes Johnson and I'm the town pharmacist. Some folks call me Doc, but the real doctor is thirty miles away in Weatherford.

I shook hands with him and said, "How ya doin? I'm Zack Heikel, this is my wife Peggy Sue, that's Kim my oldest, Denise, Forrest and my youngest boy Monroe. Say do you have anything over at your store to help me get rid of this heartburn? I've got it big time"

"Them peppers will do it every time. Sure, I've got all kinds of remedies. I was just fixin to leave so ya jest follow me next door and we'll get ya some Tums. Y'all plan to stay a spell or just passing through?" He said, with a big broad smile still on his face, a face that re-markably resembled my Uncle Fred's.

As we followed him to the door, we stopped to pay our check and I answered his question, "We are just passing through but I think we should probably spend the night if you could recommend a nice clean hotel in town."

"Well!" Mr. Johnson said while brushing dust from the brim of his Stetson, "Only one in town is on the south side down near the brewery. There are only six or seven rooms though. When we git to my store I'll call over there for ya, see what they got."

After arriving at the store, and placing the phone call to the hotel, Wes turned to Peggy Sue and I and said, "Nope no luck, four of the rooms are occupied, one is being painted and the other one's toilet is all plugged up. Ya know if y'all would like, ya can stay at my place. I got a big old house with plenty of room and my two boys are living up in San Antonio these days. All I got to do is call the misses so she can change the sheets. I know she would love some company."

Peggy Sue responded quickly, she knowing how hectic unexpected guests can make things, "Oh no, that would be way too much trouble, although it would be nice to sleep in a house again."

Personally, I was hoping she would want to stay with the Johnson's. I was bone tired and really needed some sleep.

"Well then it's settled, y'all can stay with us. Oh and here Zack is your Tums" Mr. Johnson said with that same friendly smile on his face.

As I took the bottle of antacid tablets from his hand, opened it and started chewing two, I said, "What do I owe you? We would also be happy to pay you some rent money for tonight."

"That will not be necessary, the only thing y'all will owe my wife and I will be a good evenin's conversation. Just bring us up to date on what's it's like to be raisin younguns nowadays and what is Michigan like in the winter. Ya know we ain't never seen snow down here."

All I could say was "Why that is very kind of you Wes. Are you sure it's okay with Mrs. Johnson?"

Wes looking at his Timex said, "I'll jest give her a call right now and tell her we are all a comin." He spoke on the phone a few moments then turning out the store lights said, "Everythin is all set, she's happy as a lark about the visit and goin ta air out the upstairs bedroom. Being business has been slow today, I think I'll close early and y'all can just follow me home. It ain't but a few miles."

As we left the store, Wes paused momentarily to lock the front door and said, "Follow me, I'll be in that blue pickup over yonder."

The six of us piled into our truck and waited for Mr. Johnson to get his cowboy Cadillac on the road and then it was off to his house.

Soon we were pulling up in front of an old, white, well kept ranch house about ten miles or so from the pharmacy. When Wes said it was big he understated it size considerably, the place was huge. The house was situated back from the road several hundred feet and was surrounded by live oak trees. Off in a distant pasture we could see several head of cattle, surrounded by men on horseback, with their lassos spinning high in the air. At any second, and to the strains of the "William Tell Overture, I envisioned my childhood cowboy hero, The Lone Ranger to come riding up on his big white horse Silver and his faithful Indian companion Tonto, galloping close behind on his horse, Scout.

Stepping out of my truck, I shouted to Wes, "Man, this is a pretty big spread you got here. How many head you got over there and how many acres do they have to roam?"

Walking towards the house he said, "There's about two hundred head out there on well over two thousand acres or so. We usta keep about five hundred head when Aaron and my youngest boy, Josiah were living here at the house, but I had to cut em way back now that the boys are gone. It's just too much work for an old cowpoke like me, what with the store and the ranch here. You know I'm nearby seventy."

As we neared the front porch, I saw a short, stocky lady standing there. She was dressed just like a woman I once had seen in a magazine about the old West. She had on a white puffy sleeved blouse, black skirt with red flowers around the bottom held up by a heavy black belt with a big silver buckle embossed with a bucking horse. On her feet were white cowboy boots. She wore rose colored tri-focal glasses, had curly blond hair and on her face, was the broadest smile which flashed the most pearly white teeth, I had ever seen on a person.

"Welcome y'all. What a pleasant surprise. Have y'all eaten?" Commented the lady and spoken in rapid-fire west Texas drawl.

Wes, climbing the front stairs gave her a peck on the cheek and turning to us as we reached the porch said, "Mr. and Mrs. Heikel, children, this here is Sandra, my bride of fifty years come next month.

As Peggy Sue approached the woman, she held out her hand as if to shake, however Mrs. Johnson just grabbed Peggy and gave her a real big hug. I was next in line to receive the warm welcome embrace and then she patted the kids on the top of their heads as we moved into the front parlor of the house.

Removing his hat and holding his wife affectionately around the waist with one hand, Wes gave her another big smooch on the lips and said, "We all ate a late lunch at the diner, but desert would be just fine, Sally?"

Before she could answer, I asked inquisitively, "Excuse me Wes, I thought you just introduced your misses as Sandra."

Wes chuckled a bit then playfully said, "Sure, ya'll got that right Zack, her name is Sandra, but so is Sally. Just in case I calls her another of her names ya'll did'nt hear before, her full name writ on her birth notice is, Sandra Joann, Ashburn, Martha Anna-Lee, Sally Siotta, Mary Texas, Whitworth Carlton. She being named after all her mothers sisters. I calls her any one of these dependin on my mood. Sandra Joann is my favorite. Sometimes in behind closed doors I calls her some of the others. Makes me think I'm a makin love to another woman," as he looked into Sandra's green eyes, who was now blushing from ear to ear.

I thought to myself, It certainly was easy to understand how these two had been married for fifty years. They were not like your typical married older couple; they seemed to actually enjoy one another and acted as if they were still on their honeymoon. Then I said aloud, "Why don't we just call Mrs. Johnson, Sandra or Joann. Is that okay with you, Mrs. Johnson?"

"It's perfectly fine with me! Whichever." She said with a broad smile.

figured out, but when I discovered a secret room in the basement of the place, it changed everything.

The room, hidden behind large sliding wine racks revealed a huge, locked, walk-in vault built into one of the basement walls. After cutting out its combination lock with a heavy acetylene torch and looking inside, we found the most amazing things; boxes of old documents, clothing, jewelry, and weapons. We also found a tightly capped glass jar of formaldehyde containing nine human fingers, all had gruesomely been severed at the knuckle from different human hands, three of which still wore silver rings. However, by far the most astonishing find was fifty-seven canvas bank bags filled with cash as well as piles and piles of additional greenbacks lining the vault shelves. With the discovery of the secret treasure trove, a completely new series of additional and baffling mysteries began to reveal themselves to us. This is when the nightmare and paranoia began for me of what to do with all those greenbacks, over *FOUR MILLION* of them, a nightmare which caused me to constantly rack my brain over whose money had I discovered and would they be coming after me?

For several good reasons, I felt the cash horde might have belonged to the modern day descendants of the "Knights of Zion." This was the reason we had to abandon the state where we were born and be on the run. Taking the cash as well as all the strange items we found in the old vault, we looked for an inconspicuous place to hide and start our new life. I was beginning to think that this quaint ranching town of Palomino, on the edge of the great plains in remote West Texas, only a few miles from the Oklahoma border and some 1700 miles from our old home, might be just such a place.

"Zack, Oh, Zack," I heard Peggy Sue's voice calling me from what seemed very far away, "You do want some apple pie and hot coffee, don't you?"

"Are you kidding? Absolutely!" I said as I came out of my stupor and hurried into the kitchen.

The eight of us sat down for the desert at a large table, so large that there were still several vacant chairs and the conversation we promised our hosts began. These two old folks were just full of questions for us ranging from; what nationality we were and if our parents were still alive, to the age of our children and why were they not in school.

We answered all the questions enthusiastically and with a smile. It was just so wonderful to see two older people still so inquisitive about other people lives. However, when Wes asked the question of why we decided to move out west I had to lie to him. It would have been super stupid to reveal the truth of why we left Michigan. Anyway, I don't think he would have believed me if I had, God forbid, mention the millions hidden in my truck and that we actually were on the lam from people who might be trying to get the money back. I was not sure this was the case, but I was taking no chances. I was going to protect my fortune come what may.

Immediately I changed the subject and just out of hand asked how the schools were here in Palomino. Wes and Sandra talked so glowingly about the school system and how well their two boys had done in school that Peggy Sue became very interested in every detail and began asking about where the grocery store was and if the town had any churches. Could she be thinking the same thought I was? Maybe this was the small town we had been searching for to start our new life?

I happened to glance over at the kids and saw that they were almost falling asleep sitting at the table. Peggy seeing this also asked Sandra where the children would be sleeping the night and she said in one of the upstairs bedrooms.

While Peggy Sue and Nancy took the kids up to bed down for the night, Wes poured me another cup of coffee and we continued our conversation. Just out of curiosity, I asked about what kind of business opportunities might be available here in Palomino and were there any nice homes for sale.

Wes seemed to get all excited and said, "Y'all not think-ing about staying are ya, cause if you are that would be just fine. We need some young folks here with new ideas. And y'all don't need to be a thinking about a house just yet, cuz you and your family are welcome to live here with us. As you can see we got plenty of room and the school bus goes by just up the road a piece."

"Hold on to your horses, Wes. We just met tonight and I am not sure what my wife is thinking. Although I must say, it is not that bad of an idea. You know I just might talk it over with Peggy Sue and then sleep on it overnight. We'll see what the town looks like in the morning."

"Aw, that's just peachy, Zack." Wes said while patting me on the back. "Ya can come to the pharmacy with me in the morning and we can talk business and figure out just what might be available for y'all. Peggy Sue and my wife can take the children over ta get a gander at the school and then spend the morning together and get good an acquainted, then we all'll meet for lunch at the diner. But you have gotta promise me that you will not try anymore of those jalapeno's, cause you almost gave me a heart attack yesterday," Wes said, laughing so hard that tears came to his eyes.

Just then, the wives came back into the kitchen. Sandra Joann had taken Peggy on a grand tour of the big old place and Peggy was saying how nice the rooms were, especially where the children were sleeping. She could not wait to show me where we were going to sleep. I countered with "I don't care where it is as long as it's in the house and in a bed." I was completely tuckered out.

"Well then why don't y'all go on ahead and git on up to bed? Mom and me will stay up a while and plan tomorrow. Y'all get a good night sleep, we got a heap of talking to do tomorrow." Wes said while cutting himself another piece of pie.

As Peggy Sue took me by the arm and started up the stairs to show me where I was going to spend the night she said, "What's this heap of talking thing, you fella's planning something we women need to know about?"

Pushing her ahead of me up the stairs, I said, "Not just yet. I'll tell you when I see what kind of surprise you have for me first, then I might let you in on our secret."

I followed Peggy up the long staircase and when we reached the top, proceeded down a darken hallway lit only by a small chandelier hanging from the 12 foot ceiling.

Peggy Sue pointed out the room where the kids were sound asleep, then moving further up the carpeted hall, she opened the door to our room.

The room was huge and had several very ornate sofas and chairs scattered here and there. On one side next to a row of tall open windows where the soft night breeze was blowing the curtains ever so slightly was an enormous bed.

Peggy Sue, like a young school kid, ran over and jumped right into the middle of it and yelled, "Look it's an old fashioned feather bed," as she sank deep into the soft feathers.

I said, "Yeah that looks great but at this stage I am ready to sleep in anything. Does this room have a John?"

"Yes Honey, across the room, that door over there." She said pointing to a couple of doors on the other side of the room.

I walked in and took a leak in the strange looking toilet, then looked for the handle to flush, there wasn't one. "Hey how do you flush this thing, or does a maid empty it out in the morning?" I said playfully

"Hon, there is a chain hanging from the ceiling, just pull it."

I did and I could hear the water rushing down a long pipe hooked to the wall and then it filled the bowl and the toilet flushed. The water closet must have been in the attic or somewhere else, this sure seemed like a lot of trouble but it was functional. I found the washbasin, threw some water on my face and headed back over to the bed. Sandra had laid out a pair of Wes's old pajamas, which I put on, and then dove head first into the pile of fluff.

The stuff was deep I will admit and I had to feel around for Peggy but then I touched her warm arms and crawled into them. The bed being next to the window gave us an exceptional view of the darkened meadow and the moon was just hanging there silent, silver and very large. The softness of the bed, the romantic moon and Peggy's tender arms seemed like the perfect setting for love, but what did I do? I simply fell into a deep blissful sleep.

I was in the middle of a carefree dream when I heard noises coming from one of the clouds upon which I was floating. As I listened intently, I realized it was nothing more than a rooster crowing in the barnyard a short distance from our room. Dawn had arrived. I had slept the night away in the same position I feel asleep, entwined in Peggy's arms. As the sun slipped silently up in the sky, its warm rays fell upon our bodies giving me a sense of complete tranquility. I lay there in the sun soaking in the sweet sensations that seemed to come at me from every direction. The morning air carried the smell of roses that were climbing up the side of the house. Out of the window, I saw a mother cat playfully rolling around in the grass with her kittens. What a beautiful way to start the day. Quite frankly, I thought I was in heaven and I never wanted this euphoric moment to end.

I looked over at my Peggy who was still sleeping. The sun gave her face a kind of golden glow and she had the most peaceful smile on her face. All of the traveling and confusion had made me almost forget how much I loved her. This gal had been through a lot with me and she was still one hundred percent behind whatever I wanted to do. I thought, how lucky can one guy get? Just then, her pretty green eyes slowly opened and looked into mine then she gave me that smile which always caused me goose bumps. I had been right, this was a beautiful morning.

After I kissed her smiling mouth we lay there discussing our future. I explained to her what Wes and I had been talking about the night before. When I mentioned that I might want to take a look at some houses in the area, she said with a sigh, "Oh, Yes darling let's stay. I can't remember having a more beautiful night and morning in a long time, even up on the hill. I think I could be happy living here. Maybe this is our sleepy little town," as she gave me another wet kiss on the lips.

It was very early in the morning and I felt everyone must still be asleep and I could feel my emotions rising when Peggy's warm lips met mine, if you know what I mean.

Then I heard Sandra's booming voice calling from down-stairs, "Y'all up? Its 5am and I got the coffee on."

I looked at Peggy Sue, she gave me a wink and said, "Some other time big boy," and then ran laughingly into the bathroom, the one with the strange operating toilet.

Feeling obligated to answer my host's bellowing ques-tion, I slipped on a robe and walked over to the head of the stairs and called out that we would be coming right down.

Returning to our bedroom I saw through the open door, Peggy Sue standing across the room in the nude getting ready to put on her bra. I stopped dead in my tracks so she could not see me and just stood there motionless ob-serving her. My God she was sexy and a beauty. I mean she was beautiful when I married her at seventeen but at thirty she was breathtaking and in full bloom. Seeing her long, smooth, slinky body and upturned full breasts gave me another surge of testosterone but I knew there was nothing doing. Then I thought, Oh! What the hell, snap out of it will you, there will be plenty of time for love making, after all we are married for life, so closing my open robe, I walked in and said nonchalantly while hop-ing to hide my,......*MANHOOD*, "The kids are up and by the smell coming up from the kitchen I guess its time to eat. Mrs. Johnson must be cooking up a storm."

I went to wake the kids and as I turned towards their door, Kim, my thirteen year old was already up, "Dad, I heard you yelling. Is it time to get up already, its just barely light outside?" She said.

I replied to her sleepy comment, "Well I guess it is Honey, life just starts early on a ranch. Wake the others and get dressed, Mrs. Johnson is making us breakfast."

After Peggy Sue and I had gotten dressed, we walked downstairs holding hands and upon entering the kitchen found the kids already digging into the scrambled eggs, ham and biscuits that had been so lovingly prepared.

"Well good morning to you both!" Wes and Sandra said simultaneously.

"How'd ya sleep in that thar feather bed?" Wes said laughingly.

Forgetting that I was in far west Texas I said, "I just crashed and burned."

"You what?" Wes said with a puzzled look on his face.

"Oh I'm sorry, that is just a northern expression. I slept fine thank you. But the morning sure comes real early down here doesn't it?"

"When you been gittin up at dawn all of your life like we have it just seems natural. Don't worry y'all get used ta it in no time. You won't want other folks gittin a head start on ya, would ya? I bet because you, howd ya say it, crashed and burned, ya didn't get a chance to talk over y'all stayin a while, did ya?" Wes said while pouring Peggy and I our coffee.

"You know Wes, Peggy Sue and I were just talking about that first thing when we woke up this morning. We both agreed we should take a look at the town, but if everyone here is as nice and friendly as you two, wild horses could not chase us away."

The kids, hearing the conversation started yelling, "Are we going to stay Dad? Are we going to school here, are we,...... are we?

While telling them to stop jumping up and down I said, "Yes we may stay, however we are not sure, but we might. Mrs. Johnson and your mother are going to take you kids by the school and see what it looks like and if you might like to attend there. I'm going to town with Mr. Johnson to look at some businesses. We will talk later on in the day and see what everyone thinks of Palomino."

Just then a plate full of the hardy breakfast was set down in front of me and Wes by Peggy who had jumped right in to help Mrs. Johnson serve.

"Aren't you two going to eat with us?" I said to the women while putting my hand around Peggy's waist and pulling her tight to my side.

"No! You boys just go on eatin and we girls will clean up then plan our day over coffee and we'll meet y'all at the diner for lunch around one," said our day's social director as if she was a first sergeant in the army.

I looked over at Wes, who had already wolfed down half of the food that had been placed before him for only a few seconds. Not wanting to be left behind and put to doing dishes, I started downing the eggs and biscuits but left the ham, which I never did like anyway. The brown sugar gravy made the meat look a little like dog food to me. I was pretty sure Wes favored it that way because he was soon sopping up the remaining brown stuff with a piece of biscuit as he stuffed it into his mouth he mumbled,

"We better git on the road it's nigh unto seven."

I took one last swallow of hot coffee, kissed my sweetheart on the lips and rushed out the door behind Wes, he already had his pickup's key in the ready position for the starter. It was not long before we were arriving in front of the pharmacy and beginning the workday. A day that I would later find was the one that changed my life forever.

There were several people milling around the front of the store patiently waiting to get their prescriptions filled. I noticed most of these folks were Hispanic, which is the norm here so close to Mexico. They were poor looking but business like, well mannered, and most spoke in Spanish so I could not make out a word they were saying.

I turned to Wes and said, "Hey Wes, how do you fill their prescriptions if you can't speak their language?"

He laughed a little and said, "Well first off Gringo, the prescriptions are written in English but if I hafta speak to them I "hablo espanol" real well, took it in school as a kid and then learned more of it talking to the Mexican cowboys over the years. The wife speaks Tex-Mex too."

"Tex-Mex? I thought you said they spoke Spanish."

"That's right Zack they do, but its so mixed up with Tex-an we just call it Tex-Mex. Don't worry yourself about it you will get the hang of it and if ya don't, and need be, they can speak enough English to let you know what they want."

"Okay, I understand that" I said. "But what was that name you called me? Gringo, I don't get it."

"Oh that, it's something Mexican folks call Northerners. It's not really a nice thing to call someone, and I guess I use it so much in a funning way it just slipped out. Sorry, and one thing fur sure don't y'all call anyone that unless ya know them real well and then in just playing."

Wes unlocked the front door to the pharmacy and he and I stepped in along with the customers who were still talking away.

I asked Wes, "What's all this conversation about anyway? Sounds like they are in an argument."

"Well it seems that some of em had a problem with the bank late yesterday and their just bitchin to one another" Wes said, already at work pouring pills into a bottle.

A short Hispanic man with skin so dark it looked like he had been in the sun his whole life, spoke up in broken English, "Ya darn tootin we got a problemo when we can't get our dinero out of old Herman Fletcher's bank when we needs it. He says that cause he's afixin to sell the bank and the auditors are there, no one can get to their money. I'm just a hopein we got enough to buy these here medcinns."

Just then, Wes piped up, "Not to worry Renaldo. I know you are good fer it, you got good kredicks here."

"But that's the problemo Mr. Wes, we don't need to be a askin ya for no kredicks. We got some money in our accounts, just can't git to it, that's all." Shorty said while kicking at a piece of paper lying on the floor.

"Ya know Zack, he's right," Wes said as he adjusted the eyeglasses on his nose. "I bank there myself only because it's the only bank in town. There is one over there in Seadrift but that's over thirty mile away. I jest hope the folks what buys the place start runin it up to date. Not the same old business style Herman has used fer over fifty years. Come to think of it, probably been running that way even longer than that. Herman's father started the bank way before the century turned. I reckon it is time for a change. I'd buy the durn thing myself but I'm too far over the hill for that thar to happen, and anyways, I hear he wants over three hundred and fifty thousand fer it. Why the building's shot and thar ain't many customers left. Who'd be stupid enough to pay that much for it?"

All the while Wes was talking about the bank the wheels were turning in my brain and suddenly an imaginary light bulb went off over my head. I began to think about the possibilities of owning a bank. What better place for all those greenbacks I have been trucking around all this time. Could this be the lucky break I've been looking for? The three hundred and fifty thousand dollar asking price was just chicken feed to me with all the cash I had secretly hidden in the truck. I knew it would be fast acting on my part. It was just the first day of looking at businesses but for some strange reason I knew this was the right thing, at just the right time.

Suddenly I blurted aloud, "Wes, is the vault at the old bank any good?"

"Why I do believe it's the best part of the old building. I've been in it several times to get to my safety deposit box. I tell ya one thing that thar vault door sure looks mighty stout. What ya askin fer, ya got something in mind?" Wes said looking at me over his bifocals.

"Oh I don't know, I always wondered what it would be like to run a bank. Seems so clean and you get a chance to help people." I said sounding a little like a garbage collector turned philanthropist.

"Are ya out of ya head, ya don't know nothing about bankin, or do ya? Anyhow where would ya get the three hundred and fifty thousand?" Wes said with a smile on his lips.

"I thought you would lend me the money Wes," I said quickly.

"Now I know ya have lost your head, I ain't got that kind'a money just a layin round. Without getting a mortgage on the store here and the ranch, I might get together fifty grand but that would just about be it. I'll tell ya what, you put up the three hundred, I'll throw in my fifty, and the two of us will buy the bank." Wes said laughing to the top of his lungs.

Thinking a second, I said holding out my hand, "Okay Wes, I'll shake on that, its a deal. I have some friends up North that I'm sure would lend me the money and I do have a rather large check that I could deposit into an account at the bank to show my good faith.

Wes, you said you knew Mr. Fletcher. Do you think you could get us a meeting with him?"

"Well I declare, Zack yer serious ain't you? Boy, ya better get a hold of yourself, you're just a talkin crazy. Do ya think ya'll can just come sashaying in here one night and the next morning tries to buy the only bank in town?" Wes said with a frown on his forehead.

"I don't know why not, it isn't that weird. Who would'a thought that I would have spent last night sleeping in a perfect strangers home and this morning my family is out shopping with his wife, and I'm here talking about going into business with the same stranger."

Wes looked me straight in the eyes and said, "Zack you are gonna have to put this conversation on ice fer a spell. I just got ta get these here prescriptions done. You know some of these Mexicans can understand what your asayin and in an hour it'll be all over town that a stranger's goin ta buy Palomino State Bank. Anyway, they along with me think you've gone plumb loco and ain't makin a lick of sense.

"Wes, I know you do not know me that well, but I am not kidding. I'm dead serious about that bank. I always move fast if I see a good deal and I think this could be just one of those crazy things that happen every now and then. Now I will let you alone till you get caught up, but to show how serious I really am take a look at this."

I pulled out of my wallet a cashier check for over eight hundred thousand dollars I had gotten from my bank in Michigan when I closed out all my accounts and left the state. The check was the proceeds from the sale of the business I was operating in Michigan. It represented all the money I had legally come by, but a pittance of what I had found in the basement of that old mansion. The found greenbacks had been looking for a new hiding place and were rumbling around in the bed of that truck for several months and the old bank vault would seem just like home to them.

When Wes got around to looking at the humongous check I held in my hand, his eyes grew large and he said. "Dadgum, if that thar thing is fer real yer not just a foolin, y'all really do want that bank and that thar just might get it fer ya. We need to do a heap of deep thinking here fore we'all go off on a wild goose chase. Anyway, I think I heard that Herman already has a deal in the works with a bank over in Austin. Let me get finished with these here customers and we'll talk this over with the wives at lunch. I'm not all that sure Herman will see us cause he may already have a done deal."

The morning went really fast with Wes filling bottles with medicines and me playing mind games with myself about the old bank and all the possibilities that might dwell behind its shabby outer walls.

When lunchtime finally rolled around, Wes and I locked the store and headed for the Chicken Scatch. When we entered the diner, which was near full to capacity, we heard a loud yell from the rear of the dining room and there sat our families all smiles. I could see in an instant that Peggy Sue and Sandra had hit it off splendidly. Arriving at their table the kids all started talking enthusiastically at once about how great the school was and Kim said she had already made a friend her age.

I faced Peggy Sue and said, "Well what about you, did you find a new friend?"

Surprisingly she said while reaching over and touching Sandra's hand, "I sure have, this lady right here. We seem to have a lot in common and I think we will become fast friends."

Wes spoke right up, "Honey, is that the way you feel about Peggy?"

"Yes Hon, it certainly is. She and I have much the same goals in life and they pretty much centers around you two old boys."

As Wes and I took our seats he said, "Well I'm real glad you two gals are getting along so well cause what we have to tell ya would not be worth a plug nickel if y'all were buttin heads."

Sandra laughing said, "Okay that thar sure sounds interesting. Now which one of you two cowboys is going to tell us just what in tarnation y'all are talking about."

Wes answered, "Well I guess I'm the one ta do it, now y'all take a good hold on to the table, cause this is gonna shake things up .... Hope yer ready? Because here goes. Zack is goin ta try to buy the Palomino State bank and wants me to be his pardner!"

"Buy the bank? Why I didn't know it was fer sale. You boys ain't been into any of that thar wood grain alcohol ya keeps over there at the store have ya? Surely y'all must be a jokin. And where would y'all get the money?" Sandra Joann pipes up.

"Zack show her that thar check in your pocket. That should convince her," Wes said confidently.

I pulled out the check and because the diner was so full of unfamiliar faces, I unfolded it so only the amount showed. Covering it with my hand, I leaned over, and let Sandra see the figure printed on it.

"Well I declare we have had a rich man sleeping at our house. Peggy Sue did you know he had that check?"

"Yes I did and if he says he's going to buy the bank we should all get ready to start calling him Mr. President, because he's just the kind of guy to do a cockamamie thing like that. He's sometimes very impulsive but usually comes out smelling like a rose. He knows what he's doing."

Just then the blond waitress who had waited on us before showed up at our table and without hesitation Mrs. Johnson ordered eight lunch specials saying, "Put it all on one check and give it to him." Pointing her finger at me, she continued, "Something tells me he can afford to pick up the tab."

Looking in my direction Blondie said, "Hey! Ain't ya the cowpoke that can't take them thar jalapenos. If it wern't fer all that iced tea, we'd have ta of carried ya over to the clinic. Ya okay with da check, Sir?"

My only spoken comment was, "That will be just fine, but please leave my jalapenos in the kitchen." My silent thought was, "I hope she is not too blond to learn."

After our lunch of chicken fried steak, black-eyed peas and cornbread, we washed it down with a gallon of iced tea. Wes and I went over our proposed plan to buy the bank with the two wives, while the kids ate their fill of key lime pie. After using the women for a sounding board and answering their questions, our ideas seemed to fit perfectly together like the pieces of a puzzle. Now if we could only get an appointment with Herman Fletcher, we could present our purchase plan.

The girls still had to shop for groceries for dinner, so gathering up the kids, they said so long. Wes went to use the phone to call the bank and left me alone at the table with the check for lunch and my thoughts.

Most of the customers had left the diner and things had pretty much quieted down. However from a back room, I saw Shorty, the Mexican man I had met at the pharmacy, shouting at an elderly gentleman sitting at a corner table eating his lunch. Shorty and another man were really giving him a piece of their minds. No, that's too mild, they were really pissed off to say the least, so I thought I would act the peace maker and just walk over and say hi to Shorty, hoping to defuse the shouting match.

As I approached the argument I first spoke to my Mexican acquaintance, whom I could see was highly agitated, but he did nod in recognition. The other Hispanic man had drawn a knife and had it menacingly close to the older man who had now stopped eating and begun to return the shouts with insults. I suddenly realized I was in the wrong place at the wrong time. I turned to exit the room and enlist a little help from some customers who were still in the diner, when I heard Shorty call out, "Herman Fletcher y'all ain't nothin but a gringo son- of- a bitch."

My God I thought, it's the guy we want to see, the old coot that owns the bank. Man! If the guy with the knife uses it, he might accidentally kill old Herman and there would go my chance of buying the bank.

I knew I had to act quickly. "Renaldo!" I said remembering the name Wes had called him and it must have surprised him that I called him by name, because he turned to face me and stood there silently. "If you will stop for a moment I have something to tell you that might solve your problem. Could you please step over here?"

He shook his head yes and said something in Spanish to the guy wielding the knife, who then slowly folded the blade and returned it to a small leather holster he had on his belt.

Both men seemed to calm down a bit and walked with me to the other side of the room. Old man Fletcher nonchalantly returned to finishing his lunch as I explained to the two Hispanic men that I understood their problem with trying to withdraw money from Fletcher's bank.

Renaldo said, "Oh ya reckin so, do ya! What the hell can a Gringo like y'all do to help me get my dinero from the bank?"

Point blank I said, "Its real easy. Wes Johnson and I plan to buy the bank and we will pay attention to our customers and their problems. Anything will be better than what you now have and don't forget your money is still in Fletcher's bank. Harming him will certainly not get you your money any faster, only a lot of trouble with the cops. Does that make sense to you?"

Shorty said with a dejected look on his face, "Well, I don't see what we got to lose, I'm willing to give y'all a chance if ya can get the bank. Anythin involving Mr. Wes is fine, cause I sure am beholding to him. He helped my family and me many times in the past with medcinns when we'all was broke. Guess we'll be on our way and good luck with buying the bank. Adios

As the men turned to leave, I tapped Renaldo on the shoulder and said, " We will probably be doing business in the future so I think it wise that you should not call me Gringo. I don't like it."

Shorty mumbled under his breath then said in a voice I could plainly hear, "Se, comprendo."

Just then, Wes walked up and said "Hi Pardner" to Renaldo as he was leaving, then asked me what I was doing here in the back banquet room. Before I could answer he noticed the old guy just finishing his food. "Hey there Herman! He said, addressing the old guy. "I was just a fixin ta call ya on the phone and all the time y'all was here in the same restaurant. Did you have a nice lunch?"

The old man spoke in a low raspy voice, "I was until those two wetback bastards started up a ruckus. One of em pulled a knife on me, but I wern't scared, I had him covered with my six shooter under the table. If he would'a took one more step at me, I would'a blown his guts out." He then laid his pistol on the table and gently lowered the hammer.

Immediately I thought, what kind of businessman is he. Man, with an attitude like that it's a wonder he had any customers at all left at the bank.

The old fella lit up a cigar, inhaled and said as he blew out a lung full of smoke, "This here stranger stepped right in and backed off those two sidewinders. Why'd ya do it? Do I know ya?"

Wes jumped into the conversation and said, "Herman this here is Zack Heilkel and he's a stayin at my place for a spell."

"Well I'm mighty obliged to ya. You some kind of kin to Wes here?"

I spoke to him respectfully, "No sir, I was just passing through and Wes offered me a place to stay the night. However me and the wife seem to like your nice little town real well. Now if I can only find a job, everything might work out and we just might stay."

"Well that's one thing I ain't got, that's a job. I plan ta sell out and move over to Austin and go to a lot of movin picture shows. We ain't got any down here, ya know. That might be a good job for y'all, open up a picture show house," Mr. Fletcher said.

This was the opening I had been waiting for so I quickly said, "Sir, Wes and I was hoping to set up a meeting with you to discuss buying your bank."

"Buying my bank? That's a laugh," was the old gun-slinger's sudden remark. Then he continued sarcasti cally, "What ya goin ta use for money? I can't make y'all no loans, cause I want out of the business. I think I'm much older than you Wes, I'm near on ta eighty, don't ya know?"

This was turning out to be a better meeting than a formal one with him in the bank boardroom. I thought I would hit him right between the eyes with the check. Pulling it out of my pocket I held it up close to his face so he could see the numbers real good as I said, "Sir, I plan on using this and would like to open an account and deposit it your bank to show my good faith."

Looking at the check and with a broad smile that spread from ear to ear Herman said, "Young man if that cashiers check is good, which it sure looks genuine to me, y'all are an answer to my prayers. Let's mosey over to the bank get this beauty deposited and then we can talk turkey."

Herman stood up to leave the diner and I noticed he was a big old boy, well over six feet tall, bald and very heavy, maybe two hundred and fifty pounds. His three-piece business suit was so wrinkled and baggy that it looked as if he had slept in it for a week and his cowboy boots were dusty and scraped up. He picked up his still smoldering cigar and clamped it tightly in his teeth. Casually he slid his revolver off the table and into his belt beneath his suit coat, buttoned it, then retrieved his dingy white cowboy hat from a hook on the wall and placed it on his head.

Somehow, his attire just did not come together at all. He looked rather comical, somewhat like a combination of a Wall Street banker and Hopalong Cassidy. We paid our checks for lunch and the three of us headed across the street to the bank.

When we approached the bank, the rundown condition of the exterior of the building gave me a slight impression of how the inside might look. The large square bricks that had been used in its construction were weather beaten, several were loose and a few missing completely. A crack ran across one of the four pane glass windows that occupied the front wall facing the street. A torn awning that looked as if it once had been a gold color flapped helplessly in the breeze above the front door, whose glass made our images appear wobbly as we came near. The wooden door, which had been carelessly painted a dark green color numerous times, squeaked loudly as Herman pulled it open. The three of us stepped into an enormous office with high twenty-foot ceilings. Our footsteps were very noisy on the bare Mexican tile floor and echoed loudly as the sound bounced around the room causing several workers to quickly look up from their tasks.

Inside the musty smelling room and sitting at old oak desks were male and female employees busily typing on manual typewriters or pulling the handles on antique looking adding machines. The interior of the office was painted a very gaudy purple color, reminiscent of the dance halls of the 1890's and the dusty drapes that hung on either side of the outer windows looked as if they had not been cleaned in years. Across the back of the bank were the teller cages with iron bars protecting their windows and directly behind them was,............ *THE VAULT* with its door swung wide open.

Even from my perspective across the room I could see that the insides of it were cavernous, easily capably of holding the load I had been trucking all around the country. I was not going to let anything stand in my way of acquiring this bank. It certainly was the answer to my prayers and I would find a way for me to be the answer to Herman Fletcher's prayers.

We immediately retreated into Herman's office, passing several employees who said hello to Mr. Fletcher as well as to Wes.

Herman sat down in a high back leather chair behind a mahogany desk the size of a Brontosaurus and we plunked down into two high back winged chairs with tufted arms across from him.

The air in the office initially was breathable, but reeked of stale cigar smoke. Soon it was filled with fresh smoke, if there is such a thing, as old man Fletcher lit up a big fat stogie, took a long drag and blew the stench out. He sat back in his chair and said, "I noticed that you two did not use tobacco, so I won't offer y'all one of my expensive Havana's. Well now Wes, let me hear y'alls offer for my bank. Y'all ain't just wasting my time, are ya?"

Wes spoke right up, "Absolutely not, that Texas size check Zack has in his pocket should speak for him and ya know the condition of my accounts, so lets get on with it. I don't want ta waste my time either, y'all know I also have a business to run. Can ya tell us about the rumor that is all over town that y'all already have a deal for the bank from someone in Austin? "

Sheepishly, Herman said, "Maybe I do and maybe I don't. Just forget about the rumor and give me the numbers of dollars y'all have to offer."

Wes, not the least bit shy, said, "Well from the git go I can tell you one thing fer sure. The rumor mill has it that a figure of three hundred thousand was being bantered around. That's way too rich for this here old place. Why the building needs almost that much in repairs just to keep it in the upright position and I don't see what else is here cepting that big old desk you're sitting behind. So we will not be anywhere nears that price."

Herman took another puff on the Havana and said in a low voice, "Three hundred and fifty thousand is the figure San Antonio was tossing in the air."

Wes fires right back, "Yeah that thar is one of them thar so called trail balloons. They ain't serious like us."

I could not help myself from laughing then said, "Wes, please excuse me but that is trial balloons not trail balloons." I then tried to straighten my face and intelligently inquired, "Mr. Fletcher could you reveal to us some private information that I swear to you will not leave this room? Like what is your cash flow and how much does the bank have on deposit from customers? And lastly, does your accountant's figures have you earning a profit for the year?"

Herman was not shy either. He had after all managed to stay in business for many, many years so certainly was no push over and knew exactly what he was up to and how to get it. He came right to the point with his own proposal, "See here young man, y'all may be a friend of Wes's and probably saved my hide a little while ago, but in order for y'all to get that kind of information from me, ya need to at least deposit your check. We'll wait until it clears and temporarily ya put down some money for good will. If we all can't come to terms y'all will forfeit that good will amount. It's goin ta cost ya something, so y'all won't take these negotiations lightly."

His conditions really woke me up and I had been right; Herman was not a small town hick. He was a very shrewd businessman but in a crude way. He had however just earned my respect. I would handle any further meetings just as if I was in New York closing a big deal with the stock exchange.

"Alright Mr. Fletcher here is my check for you to deposit and what amount would you consider enough for my good will?"

Herman took the check from my hand and while making out a deposit slip, said, "Oh! I won't hit y'all too hard, say five thousand. That should keep ya quiet. Here's a blank check ya can fill out for the five thousand and as soon as y'all's check clears, I will cash it and then we will talk figures."

Wes broke his silence and said, "Hold on to your horses there Zack! Ya just make out that check of y'all's for twenty-five hundred and I'll throw in one for the difference. I'm in this with ya all the way."

I did as Wes said and wrote it out for the twenty-five and commented, "Thanks Wes, I was hoping you were really in on this deal. I need a man like you to steer me around. I'm beginning to get the impression West Texas is almost like a foreign country."

Herman spoke up as in a huff, "Well if he didn't come up with a check I ain't goin ta tell him nothin, just you. I don't want any of this to be made public." Hesitating a moment he continued saying, "Ah! On second thinking, I probably would have told you anyway, Wes. I know that yer a straight shooter and a man what keeps his word."

As we stood up to leave, we shook hands and agreed to meet again later in the week. I was tickled pink to hear Mr. Fletcher speak so highly of Wes. Even though I felt he was a righteous guy, one can never be too sure. He was going to be something I had never had in my life, except for my wife, and that was a business partner.

In just a few short days, I had become quite fond of Wes. Not only did his face remind me of my Uncle Fred but also I felt very comfortable with him almost as though he was family. He was friendly, sincere, and funny at times and seemed to be a wonderful husband, always loving and placing kisses on the wife.

His personality was a far cry from some of the men I had just left behind in Michigan.

One of the men I was thinking about I had buried in a private gravesite on my property only a few months before I left the state. He was a sad old guy, a hunchback with a very bad harelip and speech impediment. Truth was, Wes sure did scramble the English language but that was his upbringing in the west Texas not a physical problem. Anyway, the old hunchback once had saved my life so I felt obligated to him and took it upon myself to give him a decent burial. He lived in a small two-room shack on a back road in the hills of Southern Michigan and even though he was scary looking as hell, he was a good neighbor. However, just before he died, he confessed to me that he once killed some men, *NINE* to be exact, not in a World War but as a member of a ruthless gang in Detroit.

The other person who came to mind was also a criminal and a confessed murderer who committed suicide by hanging himself at age eighty-two. He was in the State of Michigan witness protection program for turning state evidence on several mobsters in Detroit.

Now I don't want to give the impression that I associated with hoodlums, because I did not. These men came into my life indirectly because of the old mansion I bought in the hills of Michigan. Neither of these two guys ever exhibited the tenderness, kindness, and downright decency of Wes Johnson. Somehow, I just knew he was a man I could trust.

Over the next few days while I waited anxiously for Mr. Fletcher to get back to us, my family and I were in a kind of limbo, not knowing for sure if we were staying or leaving. But, one thing was for sure, Peggy Sue and Wes's wife were constantly together, taking the kids shopping for clothes or visiting several of the Johnson's friends. They just seemed to mesh perfectly.

Wes kept me busy helping him to repair broken fences around the ranch and showed me around town. On Sundays he also introduced us to several of his friends at the Baptist church. They were mostly hard working ranchers or farmers who all seemed to be pillars of the community. One couple was Palomino's Sheriff, Billy Flynn Barrett and his wife, Kati McAdams Barrett, who was also to be our Sunday school teacher. What an interesting couple they were, he was tall, lean and all business, while she was cute, petite and full of humor. After church one Sunday and over coffee in the social room, she told us an amusing story about when they first met. It was at a country western dance where Billy spotted Kati across the room and swaggered over pushing his cowboy hat to the back of his head and asked if she cared to dance.

"Why yes!" Kati said, looking up into the tall man's baby blue eyes as she felt herself swoon, and a small voice inside her whispered, "I can't explain this funny feeling, but I'm quite sure I see myself married to this cowpoke."

They danced the night away and were an item from then on. It was love at first sight however Kati was in for a few surprises.

One afternoon a few days after they met, Billy had to make a stop by his house in the country to pick up some things and decided to show Kati around the place. As they entered the front door of the old two-room farmhouse, Kati noticed that the boards on the walls were a few inches apart and sunlight passed through them and cast itself onto the dusty kitchen floor. She could also hear the wind whistling through the openings as it made its way around the small kitchen. Thinking she might lighten the moment, she said, "Sounds like the breeze is playing us a tune."

Billy, not one to miss a chance to also be funny said, "Why it sure is. Can't you tell, its whistling Dixie." They both shared a good laugh and Kati knew for sure that she had found the right man and he came with a sense of humor. Life with him could be one continuous happy time.

Billy asked if she would like a drink of water or a sandwich. She said that a sandwich would be nice, Billy put together a few slices of bread with some cheese and tomato in between and served that to Kati along with a Mason jar of milk.

When they had eaten their fill of most of the food, Billy, nonchalantly lifted the oilcloth on the table top and scraped the left over food they had left on their plates into a hole in the floor directly under the kitchen table which Kati had not seen when she first sat down.

Suddenly she heard hoof beats and snorting, coming from under the floor. Looking into the hole, she could see the ground under the house then two big pigs came into view and began fighting over the scraps. Kati could hardly believe her eyes. However, when Billy took a broom and started to sweep the floor and push the debris into the same hole that was too much for her, so she asked him to take her home immediately.

A short while later when Billy popped the question, Kati's answer was affirmative, but came with a qualifying attachment. She would marry him but there was no way in Hell she was going to live in a ventilated musical shack over a pig's troth. Billy took the hint and they were married soon after, but moved into *TOWN*.

Not only did we burst out laughing when we heard Kati's tale, but Billy grabbed his stomach and was laughing so hard he had tears in his eyes.

After hearing Kati reveal this personal adventure she had with Billy and enjoying their friendly attitude toward us, I was convinced that with friends like these, who were so unusual, what would be a crying shame, was that if we could not come to terms with Mr. Fletcher on the purchase of the bank. Peggy Sue and I were just crazy about this little town and the people in it, because they were so uninhibited and down to earth. Anyway I was dead set on getting my hands on that bank and just about ready to make any kind of a deal.

Almost two weeks went by and I was beginning to think that Herman was getting cold feet about talking to us or was busy closing his deal with Austin. One day at the pharmacy with Wes the phone rang. It was Herman Fletcher.

"Howdy Wes! Sorry I took so long to give y'all a call but I was out of pocket for a few days. Next time y'all see that Yankee, Zack, tell him his check cleared and he's got some real money here at the bank. I know most of y'all's cash is already on deposit here so the three of us can get together fer our talk. How about tomorrow morning here at my office, say around eight."

Wes said into the phone, "Just a minute I'll ask Zack he's standing right here." He covered the mouthpiece of the phone with his hand and whispered to me, "He wants ta meet with us tomorrow at his bank around eight, okay with you?"

"That's good news, sounds like he didn't make the other deal. Yeah, tomorrow is great with me. I'm just happy to be getting the meeting I've been holding my breath for over a week."

Wes uncovered the mouthpiece and said, "Okay yer on fer the morning at eight. Do we need to bring anything or anyone, say like a lawyer?"

Herman jokingly said, "Nope just your check books and a smile will do just fine."

I did not sleep well that night because I spent it thinking about a fall back position that I might take in case Herman turned down our offer. It also came to my restless mind that I might want to consider becoming a rancher myself. It seemed like a good life and appeared to me that a good living could be made raising cattle. But then I realized what did I care about making money, I was trying to hide the millions I already had and just spending it was becoming real difficult. All kinds of thoughts were running through my mind and I couldn't seem to get to sleep. Suddenly, I heard my friend the rooster crow. It was dawn and the beginning of a very important day for my family and me. I hit the floor with a bang and was raring to go. I could already smell the coffee that early bird Sandra was brewing downstairs. I threw on my clothes, kissed Peggy and hurried down to the kitchen. Wes and his misses were up to their usual chore, making a huge breakfast.

"Ready to eat some of this here ham and eggs?" Wes asked after he said good morning.

"No thanks, none for me this morning, even though it smells wonderful. All I need is a cup of that coffee. I'm feeling a little up tight about the meeting with Herman this morning."

Wes made a comment which reinforced a thought I had earlier when he responded with, "Well I can see why y'all might be tight, that thar belt is just cinched up too taut again yer belly."

"Yeah right Wes" is all I wanted to say in return as I loosened my belt. I was just too confused to explain a slang term that was commonly used up North. I had to keep reminding myself that I was truly making a new life for myself in what seemed to be, to me anyway, a foreign country. They just did not speak English as I did. I only hoped that in my dealings with Herman Fletcher I would not have a language barrier in discussing business terms. I also hoped I would not somehow irritate him and blow the whole deal.

I did not have to wonder very long about the speech difference because Wes and I were soon walking into Herman's office and receiving a greeting from him, "Well lookie here at these two sidewinders all coiled up and ready to strike. Come on in here to my house, kick the mud off y'alls boots, brush the hay out of y'alls head and pull up a seat. We all need to do some real horse tradin.

Sitin thar on the desk are two folders with all the figures Zack asked fer. I guess y'all know how to interpret them."

Picking up one of the folders and looking inside, I found that to my amazement the reports were well prepared and very professional. A CPA certified the profit and loss statements, the asset sheet was up to date and the three previous years tax returns that were enclosed showed a very nice profit each year. With the completeness of the reports it was very clear to me I would not be buying a pig in a poke. This was a very profitable operation.

I turned to Herman, complemented him on his record keeping, saying nothing about the pig in a poke so as not to confuse him, and asked if he owned all the bank stock. He shook his head in the affirmative. I also asked where the record of bank liabilities was.

Herman stated rather proudly, "There ain't a sheet cause there ain't none of them thar debts. We don't owe anybody, nothin."

I think that said to me that the bank was free and clear of any debt, quite an accomplishment nowadays. I would have to be real careful with this old guy because he acted kind of stupid and backward but these reports indicated a very smooth running bank with him at the helm.

I had run a very successful business for several years and then sold it to a company listed on the New York Stock Exchange a few years earlier, so I was very familiar with the numerous reports that were required to run a corporation and was very knowledgeable as to how purchase deals were structured. I only hoped that these same rules and terms applied to business transactions out here in ranch country.

I asked Herman if I might have a few private words with Wes he said he had to use the toilet anyway and left us alone in the room.

I turned to Wes and before I could say a word he said, "Well what do ya think? Looks ta me that he sure pays a lot of taxes."

I was happy to see that Wes had picked that out of the reports and then I explained what I thought of the banks financial condition. "Wes," I said "This balance sheet shows hard assets of nearly one hundred thousand bucks, and with profits like these and no liabilities, even if we gave him the three hundred and fifty thousand dollars he has been mentioning we'd have our money back in less than three years. I even saw the deed to this building in there, which by the way if he goes for our deal, I will need the title to the building in my name only. I hope that's alright with you, Wes. I'd call this a mighty good deal, if he still wants to take that amount for the bank.

"Are ya sure Zack? I'm not real up to date on this kind of figurin, but seein as yer puttin up most of the cash, ya got to have the final say. As fer ya having the building in your name only, if that's the way ya wants it, I don't have no fuss bout it."

I told Wes I was sure it was a good deal and for him not to worry about losing his fifty grand because I would guarantee he would not lose anything. Even if I ran the bank into the ground and lost everything, I would see to it that his money would be returned to him. Little did he know what kind of financial firepower I had hidden in that truck in his barn, only Peggy Sue and I knew that we could buy the whole town if it were for sale.

After letting out a big sigh Wes said, "Hew, that thar is mighty nice of you Zack. I sure hope ya know what yer doin, but I'm right thar with ya. I can't figure on how we is to lose no how."

About that time, we heard a slight rap on the outer door and Herman's voice, "Okay if I come back in?"

"Yeah ya can come back in, we's though talking about ya anyway." Wes said with a laugh.

Herman returned to his desk and in a serious voice spoke right up, "Well, did ya see everthin ya need ta?"

"Yes we have!" I responded. "We like everything we have seen so far. How would you like to proceed?"

Herman acting real business like said, "I'd like to proceed with y'all telling me how much of that thar money ya both has in yer accounts, wants to be in my account."

I took that to mean, what our offering purchase price was to be and said, "Sir, Wes and I will pay you in cash, after we certify these figures, three hundred and seventy five thousand for all your bank stock and all its assets including, of course, this building. We will assume no liabilities because you said there are none. This is just a straight forward deal. I know it's a bit more than what you said Austin might go but Wes thinks it would be better if the ownership of the bank stayed in local hands so we're offering to bump up the price. Ain't that right Wes?"

Wes, looking a little befuddled by my offer of twenty-five thousand more than the asking price, which he at first thought ridiculous said, "That's right Herman, we think that we can help our community better than those over thar in Austin. You know we hear first hand what our town folks need. We keep our ear to the horse"s mouth so to speak."

For some reason the offer we made seemed to hit Herman just right. So he smiled broadly and said, "Ya know

I think you boys are right, there was somethin a botherin me. Those boys up there in the big city don't have a lick of sense bout what we all even do down here in Palomino. How was they a goin to take care of our needs from way up thar. They all didn't offer me no cash deal either, called it some kind of thing like an earn-out. Why I didn't even like the term. I already earned all's I wants from this here old bank. I think its now bout time for y'all to take it under arm. Y'all got yerselves a deal." Herman held out his hand which Wes and I both shook vigorously.

After asking us for our complete names and addresses, (I used Wes's home address) Herman said he would have his attorney draw up the necessary papers for the state to transfer ownership of the bank charter to Wes and me and make out a simple bill of sale for the assets. After talking over the transfer and getting Wes's okay on how the bank stock should be split up, I asked Herman to have his attorney re-issue to me fifty one percent of the bank stock, Wes twenty percent and my wife Peggy Sue Heikel twenty-nine percent which, he said should be no problem. A friend of Herman's in the real estate business would do the title work on the building and transfer it into my name. Herman said he would put a rush on all the paper work and everything should be ready for signatures and our exchange of checks for the balance of the purchase price in about two weeks. Just like that, all in just one morning, Wes and I appeared to be the proud future owners of The Palomino State Bank.

All we had to do now was wait for the documents to be transferred, the CPA we had hired from San Antonio to do an audit on the books and assets of the bank. Herman eventually agreed to let our auditor rummage through the books and records only after commenting that he hoped we did not think he had anything to hide. He said business transactions here in Palomino were done a little differently than up North. They were normally sealed with a verbal commitment and a firm handshake. I assured him this was just my way of showing any future investors that our deal was fair and above board and the audit had nothing to do with his honesty or integrity. I believe the grumbling was his way of hiding his coming to grips with the fact that he would soon be out of the job he had held for over sixty years. I was certain of one thing, he would be feeling very comfortable when he would be up in San Antonio attending all the picture shows his heart desired. I would probably not be seeing many movies any time soon myself, as I had a lot of planning to do setting up my new life as a banker and resident of Palomino.

Another thing I did not see much of over the next few weeks except over dinner and to sleep with, was Peggy Sue. She and Sandra were constantly on the go, looking at houses for us to purchase, getting the kids enrolled in their new school and something Peggy Sue loved to do, shop for a new car.

Sandra and Wes knew from church a gentleman, Bryce Brown, who owned the only auto dealership in town, a Ford sales outlet. Even though Bryce was also a displaced Yankee like me, Wes and his wife did not hold that against him. They considered him an honest man and a good Baptist.

It was at his dealership that Sandra had purchased her new Lincoln the year before, so she took Peggy in to see him. Peggy Sue loved her previous car, a Cadillac and was a little skeptical looking at a Lincoln. However, when she saw the selection she could choose from in such a wide variety of colors and body styles. The two gals had a ball putting together all the features, exactly as Peggy wanted the car equipped.

After the better part of the day, the girls finally had chosen the style of car, color and all the accessories. Of course, something this varied had to be ordered directly from the factory, but Peggy Sue was willing to wait and was informed that the vehicle would be delivered in about three weeks. The sales price was thirty seven thousand five hundred and fifty dollars. As Peggy Sue signed the sales order for the car, she nonchalantly asked Mr. Brown if she could pay for the car in cash when she picked it up?

Mr. Brown said, "Why sure, we accept certified checks or cashiers checks here all the time, just the same as cash. No problem at all."

Peggy Sue handed Bryce the signed sales order and said, "No Mr. Brown I mean cash, like greenbacks. Is that okay?"

Somewhat startled he said, "Well I don't see why not, although I have never had anyone pay that much in cash, I think it will be acceptable. What did you do, hold up a bank?"

Peggy Sue remembered that we wanted to use some of the cash horde we had hidden in the truck. She also thought about the problems we had encountered in Michigan buying items for cold hard cash. She then told Mr. Brown a big whopper of a lie when she said, "Why No, I have been saving money over the years on my grocery shopping using coupons, and thought this would be a good time for me to spend it and not have to ask my husband for one red cent."

Bryce said laughingly while scratching his bald-head, "Cash will be just fine Mrs. Heikel, but could you please tell me where you shop and got coupons that were that valuable. I need to tell my wife about them."

As Peggy Sue and Sandra said goodbye to the still smiling Mr. Brown, Peggy thought, "Well so much for buying a car! I wonder what kind of resistance we will run into when it comes time to purchase a house using cash money."

With everyone being so busy, we just lost track of time and before we realized it, three weeks had passed since Wes and I had agreed to purchase the bank from old man Fletcher.

The two of us were in the Palomino Diner for lunch one bright sunny day and ran into Herman who was eating his lunch at his customary table in the back room. He motioned for us come over to eat with him.

The place was crowded as usual so to save time Wes and I always had the special. When the blond waitress asked, "Whattle y'all have?"

I piped up with, "Two specials," and before I could say another word, she stated flatly,

"Yeah! Yeah! I know! I know! No Jalapenos!"

As she hurried away into the kitchen to place our order, I said to the guys, "I guess in her case I was wrong, she was not to blond to learn. She has finally gotten my order right."

After the snickering died down Herman said, "Y'all's spy, that thar CPAs, he beat it out of town a couple of days ago and left ya a sealed envelop, probably his charges. The state bank regulators are just about ta finish up their work this afternoon, so we all can git on with da signings tomorrow, that is if y'all two big shots ain't got more important things ta do."

"Well that's just great. The usual time about eight at your office." I said as I saw our lunch arriving at our table.

Herman said, "Fine we all need to git an early start. I'll have everythin arranged, y'all just bring your own pencils.

Then I heard Wes say, "Ach! Oh!"

I looked at him expecting a problem. "What?" I said and saw him pointing to my plate. There sat the Blue Plate Special and on the side were two of the biggest Jalapenos I had ever seen.

After pointing them out to Blondie, she barked at me, "Oh! Shit! Yeah I see them, I ain't blind you know. So I made a mistake, just don't touchem, especially with your tongue." In one quick motion she reached into my plate with her fingers, plucked up the little green devils, and scampered away from the table flipping her long blond hair.

The next morning Wes, Peggy Sue and I were at Herman's office just as he arrived at eight o'clock and the three of us went directly into his office. Every document needed to complete the bank sale and the transfer was laid neatly on a long table. After a few minutes of discussion between us, we looked over the material our CPA had left and then examined the figures covered in the forms. Finding everything in order, we three commenced to signing them. A few moments later Herman did the same. Wes and I made out our checks for the balance of the three hundred and seventy-five thousand purchase price and handed them to Herman. He asked us if the three weeks time, spelled out in the sales contract for him to help us with the transition, was long enough and we agreed it was. The four of us shook hands and that was it. Wes, Peggy Sue and I were now the official owners of the Palomino State Bank.

The final meeting was quite anti-climatic. I had thought it would be a long drawn out negotiation, when in reality, the whole transaction took less than two hours.

In the next several weeks with much help from Herman, Wes and I settled into our roles of bank officers, I as president and chairman of the board of directors and Wes, as a member of the board and special advisor to the president. The board consisted of three other people, Peggy Sue as Vice-President, Mr. Bryce Brown, (the Ford Dealer) and the banks chief loan officer, Mrs.

Martha Salazar rounded out the board of directors. Fortunately, for me, Mr. Fletcher had hired the best that the town had to offer in the way of employees. Everyone right up to Mrs. Salazar really knew his or her stuff. At the end of the three weeks that Herman was scheduled to help us assimilate the chores of the bank, I felt there would not be any problems that the staff or I could not handle for ourselves. Therefore, Herman said his good-byes and headed up to San Antonio and started his new life going to the movies.

Now that I was in charge of the bank and alone to make decisions, the very first thing I knew I needed to do in the worst way, was to check out the soundness of the banks vault. Inspecting it from top to bottom, I changed the combination sequence on the doors huge locking mechanism and finding everything else in good working order, it was finally time to somehow and with the utmost secrecy, transfer the heavy load of greenbacks the truck had been carrying around for months into the sanctity of the vault.

I wasted no time. The next Sunday, late in the afternoon, told Wes I thought it might be a good idea if I started up the truck as it had been sitting for so long and take Peggy for a ride. Then I'd drive over and while the motor was warm, have the engine oil changed, and afterwards park it behind the bank building, giving him back the use of his barn. He said this was perfect timing as he had a large order of grain being delivered and he could now store it where I had the truck parked.

Peggy and I hurried over to the bank and I backed the truck up to the back door. Using the hand trucks the bank employees used to move large bags of coins, we slid 6 large steamer trunks as well as 14 footlockers, all full of the green stuff off the truck. We then rolled them into a remote corner of the bank vault and behind a set of steel cage like doors, which was a kind of extra secure place inside of the vault. We put old clothes and boxes of documents on top of the footlockers giving everything the appearance of just a pile of old belonging we were storing. I carefully removed the strange old black book, the one with the pistol in its center, as well as the jar of severed finger from one of the lockers and locked them all in the largest safety deposit box available in the safe and out sight of prying eyes. In less than an hour, everything was safely secure in the confines of the bank. I moved our now empty truck over to the side of the bank building and locked the doors.

When I returned to the bank's office, I was surprised to find Wes standing there with Peggy Sue and he said to me, "When ya told me you were goin to leave your truck here, I figured y'all might need a ride back out to the house, so I come to fetch ya. Did y'all get the oil changed?"

Not wanting to be caught in a lie I simply said, "No, we went for too long a ride so we just came back to the bank and parked the truck."

As we pulled away from the now dark and silent bank, I said to Wes, "Thanks for doing a little brainwork for us, somehow I never thought about how we were getting back out to your place."

Changing the subject, I said, "Peggy Sue, when is your new car being delivered?"

"Oh, anytime now! I think I will check tomorrow, because I hate to keep asking Wes's wife to drive me around," she replied.

I closed my eyes and thought about the main reason I had wanted the old bank. It was for the vault. It was a place to safely store my millions and give us a chance to spend some of it, however I had also acquired a good running business in the deal along with a prestigious position in the community. Everything was working out much better than I could have planned and on top of getting to buy the bank, Peggy Sue and I had found us a nice sleepy town to live in and made us some wonderful new friends in Wes and his wife. I just hoped and prayed that the money would not come between us and ruin our new-found friendships.

Monday morning right after Wes dropped me off at the bank on his way to the pharmacy, Peggy Sue called on the phone to tell me her car was in and she needed the money to purchase it with. "No problem," was my answer to her.

She then said she would need a ride to the bank. I asked Mrs. Salazar if she would not mind going to pickup my wife and bringing her back here to the bank. She said she would be more than happy to do so. I purposely asked her in order to get her out of the bank because she was the only one, other than me, who knew the combo to the vault's door lock. I wanted to make a withdrawal, so to speak, from one of the cash laden footlockers, without raising any suspicion. When I saw that everything was clear, I stepped into the vault and slightly closed the outer door. I went over to one of the top footlockers, moved some of the clothes from atop it, opened the lid and slipped out over sixty thousand bucks, all in hundreds. Putting the cash in a brown paper shopping bag, I carried it back into my office and waited for Peggy Sue to arrive.

When I saw Martha and Peggy coming through the front door, I asked my secretary if she could take us to the Ford dealer, which she agreed to do. Arriving there and getting out of Martha's car I told her to pull up to the dealerships gas pumps and that I would like to repay her by buying her some gasoline for her trouble. She happily agreed to take the fuel, so an attendant filled her tank.

Mr. Brown, seeing us arrive, met us at the door of his office, "Come on in Mr. President and make your self comfortable. Hello Peggy Sue, ready for your new wheels?"

"Yes Bryce I sure am." Peggy said with a smile.

"Well I got you all set up and ready to go. You know Zack you should also be thinking about a car for yourself."

"Okay!" I said. "I'll take that white Ford two door you have right there on the showroom floor. How much is it?"

Bryce said with a laugh, "You're not kidding are you? Man, you move fast. I'll let you have it for twenty thousand and I'll pay the taxes and title transfer, seeing that you are buying two cars today."

"Good deal Bryce, Let's see, Peggy's was thirty seven five fifty plus twenty for the white one, that comes to fifty seven five fifty." I said as I lifted the shopping bag from the floor and poured the contents on Bryce's desk.

Bryce smiled and said, "I was kind of expecting something like this when Peggy asked me if she could pay in cash. That much money sure makes a rather large pile, doesn't it?"

"Yes it does, you got no problem taking the cash do you?"

"No sir, coming from my bank's president anything is fine with me. Just give me time to count it"

"Bryce, there should be about three thousand over what I owe you, could you please let us go and then bring the change over to the bank tonight when you make your nightly business deposit?"

"Sure Zack, can do, here are the keys to your Lincoln Peggy Sue and yours are in the one on the show room floor, Zack. Do you want me to go over some of the features on your new automobiles?

"No I don't think so, I really need to get back to the bank. We have purchased so many new cars we are quite familiar with how they operate."

"Alright you're the boss. I'll have one of my men bring the cars around to the front of the building for you."

"That will be just fine Bryce. You know you can move pretty fast yourself if you have to. You're my kind of guy. Thanks for everything. I know I can trust you to keep our dealings private.

"Sure you can trust me. Business is business, and goes no further than me. Of course, I am confident my bank will not question this large cash deposit anyway, he laughingly replied.

Going out to our new cars, I gave Peggy a kiss and told her to drive safely and that I'd see her at home in a little while.

As I pulled away from the showroom and out of sight, I let out a hell of a big laugh. I had just passed over fifty grand from my cash stash with no trouble or questions at all. I had found my Valhalla, the land of milk and honey. Living in this town was going to be like living in heaven, or so I thought. As in life, things just somehow do not always work out smoothly. In the coming months, many strange and mystifying things would begin to happen, not from the town or anyone in it but from something I had brought with me from Michigan.

I did not have to wait long for bizarre things to start happening. One of them I met head on the very next week.

On Monday morning, driving through a blinding thunderstorm, I arrived at the bank. Mrs. Salazar greeted me at the office door and after wishing me a good morning said, "Mr. Heikel there is a terrible odor coming from one of the safety deposit boxes in the vault and a sticky fluid is running down onto the floor."

"Oh that's odd, please show me." I said wondering what it could possibly be.

When we stepped into the vault the stench was almost overwhelming and smelled like something dead.

Reaching over I quickly flipped the switch that turned on the vaults ventilating system.

Following Martha further into the safe and approaching the row of boxes where I had put the book and glass jar, I saw a putrid looking yellowish liquid dripping down the face of the boxes and forming a small puddle on the floor. I was quite sure it was coming from the one with my secret articles in it.

I asked Martha if she would get me the mop and bucket with a little water in it along with some paper towels from the storage closet. When she returned with the cleaning items I insisted she go back to work and I'd clean up the mess. I knew I would have to open the box and did not want to take the chance she might see the jar or book.

I quickly mopped the floor a little and used the paper towels to wipe the goop from the boxes. Opening the safety deposit box with my key I immediately saw where the liquid was coming from. The seal on the top of the glass jar had deteriorated badly and the jar laying on its side permitted the formaldehyde to spill, dumping the foul smelling fluid all over the place. I righted the jar, tightened it's top and wiped up the interior of the box with the paper towel.

With the air being circulated, the lid tight on the jar and the fluid cleaned up, it was again bearable to be in the vault. I realized that I would have to replace the formaldehyde in the jar quickly or the contents would deteriorate rapidly. Now that the rain had stopped, I decided to take a walk over to Wes's Pharmacy about two blocks away and get the chemicals.

The air had a sweet smell after the heavy downpour and it cleared my head of the bad odor from the vault. Dodging a few water puddles and arriving there, I asked Wes for a bottle of the preservative, telling him I was picking it up for my daughter Kim for a class project.

"No problem, pardner. How much do ya need?" he asked.

"Oh, how about a quart," I said casually.

"Y'all must be coverin something pretty big," he commented

"No not really," I said trying to hide my white lie. "Maybe some of the other kids will need some."

Even though Wes wanted to visit a while, I lied again and said I had to get back to the office. Taking the paper bag he handed me containing the chemical, I hurried back to the bank, slipped into the vault, opened the safety deposit box, removed the lid from the jar and poured the entire quart into the jar, refilling it to the top and replaced the lid.

In doing so, I noticed one of the old ornate rings had fallen off its bony finger. I reached into my pocket, got my pen, removed the top of the jar, and reaching in with the pen retrieved the ring.

I left the bank vault carrying the silver ring in my handkerchief and went to my office, where I rinsed it off under running water in a small sink, and then sat down at my desk to dry it off. Examining it more closely, I could clearly see the words "Shalom" engraved in the polished silver. The ring, made for a finger much larger than mine, was unusual and quite heavy and gleamed brightly in the glare of my desk lamp.

Slipping it on my finger, I held it up to the light to admire it, when suddenly the ring begun vibrating and my whole hand seemed to be on fire and in extreme pain. I jerked it off as quickly as I could and the next thing I remembered was Martha shaking me and asking if I was all right. She had rushed into my office when she heard the thud of my body hitting the floor. Obviously, I had passed out from the pain.

Dazed, I drank down the paper cup of water Martha handed me, thanked her for her concern and said I was feeling much better now. But my finger hurt like hell. She asked if she should summons Wes to look at my hand, but I assured her I would be okay.

When she returned to her office, I searched under my desk and found the ring lying there. Using my handkerchief again I picked it up and placed it in the far back corner of my top desk drawer. Very shaken I left the office for Wes's house where we were still staying. I had to have time to figure out just what had happened to me. I surmised I had fainted from the effects of the formaldehyde fumes or contact with it on my skin. However, I distinctly remember washing off the ring before placing it on my finger which now was very red as if burned and some of the skin was beginning to peel away. I took two aspirins and applied some first aid cream, which helped to alleviate some of the pain. My severe reaction was either from the chemicals or from something unknown and mysterious, the later would prove to be most accurate in describing just what had happened to me that morning.

Over the next few months' business at the bank just exploded. I was so busy that I did not have much time to dwell on the incident with the ring and other than my hand bothering me occasionally, I completely forgot about what had happened.

We were opening up several new accounts every day. People seemed to have a newfound confidence in banking and the money that they had hidden at home in their mattress, they brought in to deposit. I was beginning to think they liked the way we were running the bank because of all the bright smiles I would see in the outer lobby. With all our new friends and the fresh cash inflow, we were making more loans, so the bank became a beehive of activity.

One busy weekday afternoon a man approached my desk. I looked up to see Renaldo standing there with his hat in his hand.

"Buenos tardy, Senor Zack. Remember me?" He said respectfully.

"Why I sure do, Renaldo. How are you?" I said as I rose and shook his hand.

"I have been fine, gratis. I would like to say many thanks to you for making my money easier to get to, and how nice I find banking here, but I have a problemo. I am told by Mrs. Salazar that I am no good for a loan I need for seeds for my fall crop and I hoped you could help me. I really need to get them in the ground because I have a wife and seven children to feed."

"Well I will see what I can do Renaldo but I usually do not override my loan officer's decisions. Have a seat and

I will go talk with her." I walked over to Martha's desk and asked about Renaldo's loan application and the reason it was denied.

Martha, handing me his folder said, "Sir, He usually pays his notes on time and is currently up to date, but our loan funds have just about been depleted and we are now only making loans to our very best customer's who have sufficient assets."

"Boy I can hardly believe that. You mean even with all those new accounts we are running short on money to make loans? I knew we were doing a lot of business but I never thought we would run low on loan funds so quickly." I said astonishcd.

"Well sir, most folks are depositing hundreds but needing loans in the thousands. I am sure they will all be repaid timely, but we are just running low on cash at this moment. Mr. Fletcher always operated this way. I don't know what else we can do, unless you have a source for some federal or state funds," Martha said shaking her head.

As I handed back to her Renaldo's' loan application I said, "Let me think about that for a while. Maybe I could make a few phone calls and roundup some additional cash."

When I got back to my desk, Renaldo was still sitting there wringing his hands together. He looked up at me and said, "Mr. Zack please, you just have to help me. I have no one else to turn to. You know I am good for the loan."

Seeing that the poor guy was desperate I asked, "How much do you need to get you by?" All the time feeling guilty and thinking about the millions I had stashed just a few yards away.

With a very sad expression on his face he said, "I think I could make do with twelve hundred dollars. With that amount, I could plant enough to feed my family and make a little profit after I repay you in the fall. You know I own all my land, three hundred and seventy five acres. It was my fathers and his fathers before that. I will not run away. You can trust me."

His pleading went straight to my heart, if I could not trust a guy like this, who can one trust. The man was hard working, dependable, a good husband and father. I felt I had to give him a hand and told him to sit tight I would be right back.

I slipped into the bank vault, unnoticed, went over to one of the footlockers and without anyone seeing me, re-moved twelve one hundred bills, then took them straight over to Martha's desk. Handing them to her and lying through my teeth I said, "Martha, go ahead and process Renaldo's loan using this cash. It's from some federal funds we are holding overnight for shipment up to San Antonio tomorrow. I'll replace them with some State funds we are receiving in the morning. If a situation like this arises again, see me and we will just take them one at a time. This way maybe we can help out some of our less fortunate depositors."

Surprised, but doing as she was told, she opened her loan file and went right to work.

Arriving back to my desk I told Renaldo his loan had been approved and to see Mrs. Salazar for the proceeds. I don't know how many times he thanked me or pumped my hand, but I must say I can't remember feeling that good in quite a while. My hidden cash had finally helped someone who really needed it.

That evening when I arrived at Wes's house I was in a very happy mood and it must have shown on my face, because Peggy Sue, after giving me a big smooch, said I looked extra handsome. I told her I had a great day at the bank and everything was working out really well. She said she had just as good a day and that after dinner, she had something to talk over with me.

After a most scrumptious meal prepared by my love and while the kids were doing their homework, Us four adults retired to the big front porch to watch the sun go down. What a perfect ending to a perfect day. Or so I thought.

Sipping on a cup of freshly brewed coffee I said, "Now, what is this something you need to talk over with me?"

Peggy Sue piped up, "Something exciting."

"Yes, real exciting!" added Sandra with a broad smile on her face.

"Uh Oh! When you two get together it could be anything. Wes you're not part of this conspiracy are you?"

"Nope, I had nothin ta do with it." Wes said sheepishly.

"Okay come on out with it. What's the big secret? You're not pregnant are you?" I said to Peggy Sue with a comic look on my face.

"Heavens no! Nothing like that. Now there you've done it, gone and spoiled the moment with that comment. Its just that we have found us, that is you and I, a *HOUSE*!" Peggy said as if disappointed because I ruined her surprise.

"Sorry Honey, go ahead and tell me all about the place." I said rather apologetically.

"Well its about ten miles North of town on the old road that leads out past the abandoned oil fields. Its an old place but fairly well kept. Nancy and I would have a blast redecorating it. You know, I think that Wes could tell you more about it than me. He knew the owner. Go ahead Wes you tell him."

I laughed and said, "I figured he was involved in the scheme of things. Nothing much happens around here that he don't know about. Is there any land connected to the place?"

"Ya darn tootin thar is, I'm not all that thar for sure but I recollect there being over fourteen hundred acres," Wes added.

"Fourteen hundred acres, Man! You have got to be kidding. What in the world would I do with all that land?"

"Why y'all always said ya would like to try ycr hand at cattle ranchin, now heres yer chance. I could show ya a few pointers, get ya a small herd goin and the rest is easy. Nature takes over and before y'all knows it ya got several hundred head. Ya never know, I jest might get my boys ta come back home and give y'all a hand. I also heard tell that some oil companies are trying to buy up some leases over in Seadrift, won't be long fore they'll be over here. Y'all wants to move to yer own place so ya may as well get somethin with possibilities," Wes said enthusiastically.

Not one to pass up a good deal and starting to show my interest I inquired, "What would something like that cost and is the house livable?"

Now it was Sandra's turn to speak up. "Zack, that thar old ranch house may be over a hundred years old but its still very stout and y'all could move right in. The place has been empty for several months, so I know fur a fact y'all could get a good deal."

Wes stepped a little on the tail end of his wife's sentence and said, "Right, I think John, our realtor said the owner would take two hundred thousand cash fur the whole kit and kaboodle."

When I heard Wes utter that I could pay in *CASH*, I was really interested and said, "That's a steal at that price. Sounds pretty good to me. When can we take a look at the spread?"

Peggy Sue jumped at my question and said, "Tomorrow morning, if you are not too busy at the bank."

"Hey I'm never to busy for a deal like this."

"Neither am I," Wes said enthusiastically. "I'm a takin the day off and a goin with ya'll."

Smiling and looking at his wife he said, "Well it's a gittin late. Come on Sally, we should be headin up ta bed anyways. Tonight's Tuesday and ya knows what ya always gives me on Tuesday night."

"Oh, you dirty old varmint, watch your mouth in front of our friends. Well, you are right, it is Tuesday. Okay come on, Red Ryder, you are overdue for one of my famous back rubs and pony rides."

The dirty old man took her by the arm, headed towards the stairs, then looked back over his shoulder and winked at us.

Upon seeing the wink I laughed and said, "Oh, Oh! Peggy we better go take a long walk and check out the livestock. He's calling her Sally again and you know what that means."

Peggy just smiles slightly and says under her breath, "You men, sometimes you are just like dogs."

The following morning right after the school bus picked up the kids, the four of us hopped into my Ford and we took off to look at the old ranch.

It did not take long to drive the twelve miles to the house. Even though we were traveling on a dirt road, because it was straight, and sat high and dry, so it would be passable most of the time even in bad weather.

The home was large and similar to Wes's ranch house, but older, much older. It was a two-story place with huge weather vanes attached to tall chimneys and had a large veranda style porch across the entire front of the house.

The wood appeared to never have had a coat of paint and was weather beaten and cracked. All the windows were intact, as were the doors, so all in all it seemed to be sturdy and definitely had possibilities. There was however something that bothered me deeply. I had a feeling of de-javu about the old place. I remembered another old house that also was a good deal, isolated and remote just like this one. I was thinking about the old mansion up in Michigan. I bought it on the spot and then spent the next eight years trying to get over the serious life threatening effects it had on my family and me. I sure was not going to let that happen again. So needless to say, I was very skeptical and made my feelings known to all, especially to Peggy Sue, when I said, "The place does not look too bad and I'm sure you two women could make it look like a palace. I'm also impressed with all the land but something just don't feel right to me. For all I know the place might be haunted."

"Ah! Zack don't be so silly" his wife quipped, I knew the housekeeper at this here house and visited many times, this is a wonderful old home. Y'all will love it here.

Sounding inquisitive I said, "Housekeeper? And did you say you visited here, why whose place was it anyway?"

"Why Zack I thought you knew. Well then, maybe we did not mention it but it belonged to Herman Fletcher. I have been here many a time myself and thar ain't a dang thing wrong with da place, and you remember Herman said he had no family, that's what the housekeeper was fer. Be sensible, use yer noggin, this is a real deal." Wes said.

Trying to contain my surprise I said, "Well maybe you both are right, but I have been burned real bad on a very similar deal like this before and it is not going to happen again. I guess being that the place is vacant we could take our time and go through it extensively and maybe it will be all right. That sound okay to you Peggy?"

Peggy nodding her head said, "Sure Honey you're absolutely right. I never thought about any connection between the two old homes, but if it makes you feel better about the place, lets go over it with a fine tooth comb, and check every nook and cranny. Maybe we'll grab some blankets and even spend a night or two out here with the kids, if its okay with the realtor."

We did just that, but not for two or three nights, instead we stayed for over two weeks. I mean we checked out every room, closet, attic and especially the basement which really was nothing but a glorified root cellar on one end of the home, nothing like the 22 foot deep basement at the old house on the hill. I even went so far as to knock on all the walls in the whole house with a small hammer to see if I could find any hidden rooms or hollow spaces.

At the end of the two weeks, we were convinced that the house was not hiding any secret rooms or escape tunnels or creepy crawl spaces. I drove over to John the realtor's office and signed the papers to purchase the ranch and it's fourteen hundred and seventy seven acres. The price was two hundred and sixteen thousand dollars. Knowing how large a pile of greenbacks this amount would make, I did not attempt to pay for the place with cash, instead I wrote out a check from my account, which contained the balance of the money I had legally brought down from Michigan. At closing time on the deal, I never even saw Herman; he had signed all his documents through the mail. I guess he could not make it all the way down to Palomino because he was too busy at the movies. At last, we had our own home and Peggy Sue and Sandra Joann were raring to go with the re-modeling.

As for Wes and I, it was back to the old salt mines, he was at the pharmacy and I was at the bank.

In the ongoing several months, the girls really had the old home spruced up, with a complete new paint job outside and in, new rugs, appliances and curtains. You name it and they had it replaced including all the bathroom facilities, namely the toilet, which made me very happy. We soon moved into the place and my family and I started attending the Baptist Church with Wes and Sandra. The kids were happy at their new school, Peggy Sue kept busy puttering around her new kitchen and I even had a new horse given to me as a gift from Wes. I spent a lot of time on the animal riding throughout all the land included in my purchase. I came across several old outbuildings, old farm implements, all rusted and entangled in sagebrush, and even some broken down windmills connected to now dried out wells. It's amazing what stuff accumulates and gets abandoned over a hundred years of operations, but now the place was still and desolate. However, I was in my element and just loved the adventure of what I might find just over the next knoll. It seemed like old times to me again straddling a muscular horse, very similar to the one I had loved to ride in Michigan, but had to give up because of its mysterious behavior.

Life for us had turned into the dream we hoped for and everything went humming right along. Until one night, when our phone rang at three o'clock in the morning. I knew it was trouble. Good news never comes in the middle of the night, only bad.

It was the sheriff, Billy Flynn Barrett on the end of the line with the bad news. Someone had broken into the bank and the front door was standing wide open. Billy Flynn and the other two members of our police force had the place surrounded. Their old police cruisers were parked in front and the rear of the building, but they did not want to enter until I came down and shut off the burglar alarm which was screaming so loudly that no one could hear orders being barked by the sheriff.

As I hurried to get dressed, I thought, "Oh no! The money, not the banks mind you, that was insured, I was worried about my millions just sitting there for the taking in those footlockers inside the vault. Hopefully, the old safe had stood its ground and its door had not been breached."

I took off in my Ford, the wheels throwing rocks into the air as I peeled out and the tires screeching as I turned corners. Driving like a speed demon, I got to the bank in about twelve minutes. All the cop cars had their flashing lights on and the flashes of yellow, red and blue, lit the front of the bank in an eerie cascade of colors. As I approached the crouching Billy Flynn who had drawn his revolver and clinched it tightly in his right hand and in the left he held a flashlight he yelled loudly, "Zack! Can y'all get that darn clanging shut down, I can"t even hear myself think"

"Sure I can, but I need to get up to the door. The shut off is just at the entryway," I said with a stammer

Billy Flynn cocking the hammer on the gun said, "Come on, I'll cover ya" and we both ran towards the front door.

When we got to the alarm box I was almost out of breath and trembling with fear, but managed to shove my key into the switch and turning it plunged the area into an immediate spooky silence. The sheriff, who did not even hesitate, continued running straight into the darkened bank, playing his flashlight beam on the doors and windows.

I did not know what to do so I pressed my body tightly up against the front wall of the building, hoping that no one would be chased out of the bank by the sheriff and run right in front of me. If they did, I was sure I would mess my pants. I was that scared!

Looking at the front door of the bank, I saw that it was heavily damaged and appeared as though someone had used their car or truck to ram it open. Just then, Deputy Ray Stokes, another friend of mine from church came crawling up beside me, took me by the arm and pulled me over behind his police cruiser then told me to stay put for my own protection. He then jumped to his feet, drew his weapon and ran headlong into the dark, toward the bank and disappeared into the building.

It took the two police officers about fifteen minutes of searching through the building before Sheriff Barrett finally emerged and announced, "Okay, everythin's all clear. Dadgumit, it sure looks like they all made a clean gitaway, we musta missed'em by only a couple minutes. Mr. Zack, it looks like they'all done ram sacked yer office and one of them thar teller cages. If ya flipps on them lights, y'all could determine wats all missin."

At about this time Wes, who had received a call from the sheriff about the same time as I had, came rushing up to the bank and the two of us went inside to see what had been stolen.

Turning on the office lights we could immediately see that several of the desks had been overturned while others had their drawers thrown about and papers and office machines were scattered everywhere. File cabinets lay on their sides and their contents had spilled out covering the office floor with a layer of white papers. One of the teller cage's cash drawers had been ripped out, dumping all its coins on the floor. Its paper money was also missing and with it, a package of fake bills that when the wrapper was removed, could explode, spraying the robbers and anything around them with a deep purple dye.

Not wanting anyone to enter the vault if, heaven forbid, it was open, I sent Wes to check my office while I headed toward the vault. The moment I saw the safe, I let out a sigh of relief, the door was closed and trying it, found it remained locked. However, and lucky for me, the real money trove had been overlooked by the crooks and was still safe and untouched.

I then went directly into my office and found Wes picking up papers and documents off the floor. My desk had been torn apart and all it's contents stolen which included a customer's late deposit of over three thousand dollars in cash, which I had carelessly left in one of the top draw-ers, never dreaming that our small town bank would ever be the subject of a late night burglary.

After about two hours with Sheriff Billy Flynn and his two deputies going over everything for any kind of a clue and taking fingerprints from the teller cage drawer, my office desk and the front door, they called a carpenter for me. When he arrived, he nailed some boards over the door to secure the bank, vowing to return in a few hours with a new heavy-duty door.

Wes and I, having prepared a list of what we thought was missing for the police, as well as answering all their questions, went home to wash-up, shave and grab an early breakfast. Sheriff Barrett and Deputy Stokes re-turned to the station house leaving behind one officer in this patrol car to stake out the bank just in case the burglars made a mistake and returned to the scene of the crime.

Just as dawn was breaking and not more than thirty minutes after we had left the bank, the phone rang, I blurted out as Peggy Sue handed it to me, "Oh, No! Not right in the middle of breakfast. First no sleep, now no food." I was right, it was Sheriff Barrett again and in a very official sounding voice said, "Mr. Heikel, I was just returning to ma office when I gets a call from Alice Crutchfield, who'all lives out on old route 20 saying that she sees a fire aburning out in the woods just south of her ranch. I'm over here now at the scene and wants y'all to come on over to identify some of yer properties. We'all is about 500 yards south of the old grain silo on route 20."

Excited I said, "Yes I know the place. Do I need to hurry or should I just drive normal?"

"Nah, y'all just mosey on over here, take y'alls time ain't nothing gonna leave."

I jumped up from the table, took a big swig of my coffee, gave Peggy a peck on the cheek, grabbed my keys and was off again, like a bat out of Hell.

I knew Billy Flynn told me to take my time, but I was curious as the dickens about what was on fire in the woods and did not want to waste any time getting there.

When I got near the widow Crutchfield's home I could see way off in the woods the flashing blue and red lights on the sheriff's patrol car. I drove toward them on the old dirt road that led to the grain silo, pulled up, and parked behind the cruiser. The sheriff was standing beside a white four door Buick with the driver's side door open, but I saw no fire. I asked him what this was all about and he told me to look inside the car and see if anything in it belonged to the bank.

Looking inside the vehicle it was unmistakable that something there belonged to the bank, the purple dye. It covered the whole interior of the car and sitting on the front seat was the night deposit bag, with "Palomino State Bank" printed on its side and next to it, my set of expensive Mount Blanc fountain pens, both of which had been in my desk drawer. Bills of all denominations were scattered helter-skelter about the floorboard and the 38 caliber automatic pistol I kept in my desk was under the front seat. I instantly recognized it by its pearl handles.

In the back seat was a duffel bag, some dirty rolled up shirts, a pair of old shoes and an empty bottle of cheap whiskey.

Turning to the sheriff I said, "Yeah, this stuff is all from the bank. That's pretty obvious, but what's this about a blaze? It's apparent this is the burglars Buick but it don't look like it caught fire."

The sheriff motioning over towards a stand of tall grass said, "Whatta Y'all make of that over thar?"

Walking with the sheriff to the area he was pointing to, I saw it. The scorched skull of a human skeleton lying in a large patch of cinders. The body was so completely incinerated that I expected to see a gas can or some other inflammable liquid nearby, but saw nothing.

"I don't see how a body can burn that completely without gasoline or something else being poured on it. Although he probably was drunk as a skunk and even with his bloodstream full of alcohol it certainly could not cause this. Could there have been two bandits? One of them could have killed this guy, and then he took off with the gas can?" I said to Billy.

"Naw, ain't nothing like at happened. There ain't no other footprints ceptin his'n. This is our man and he did the burgalin by himseff!"

Just then, the radio in the patrol car squawked the sheriff's name and he walked over to answer the transmission. This gave me an opportunity to look over the corpse more carefully. Kneeling down I picked up a stick and began looking under some of the ashes when suddenly something shinny caught my eye. Moving more of the ashes, I saw it, *THE RING*.

It was lying next to a seared bone that once had been a finger. Then I remembered that it had been in the back of the top drawer of my desk and this joker must have picked it up when he spilled the contents on the floor. Quickly, before the sheriff returned, I used my hankie to pick up the ring, rolled it up in my nose rag, put it in my overcoat pocket and stood up. I knew this would be tampering with evidence from a crime scene but I just had to keep that ring out of the hands of the police. At this point in time, no one but Peggy Sue and I knew the strange ring even existed and I would do everything in my power to keep it that way.

I walked over to the patrol car where Sheriff Barrett was still in deep discussion with the police dispatcher. After a few minutes, of his himin and hawin and a final, "Y'all sure?" he returned the microphone to the dashboard and said to me, "Well I declare, this here auto belongs to one of y'all's countrymen!"

"What the hell does that mean?" I said rather bluntly.

"Just y'all take a look at that thar plate on da rear of this thing, tha'll speaks fer itself."

Doing as he suggested I stepped behind the car and looked down at the rear license plate. The plate holder covered the state's name, but I could clearly see the words, "Land of a Thousand Lakes" on its bottom. The white Buick was from *MICHIGAN*.

"Well whata y'all think bout dat? Not onlys this here car from y'all's home state but that thar pile of bar-b-que over thar probably hailed from thar too, dont ya reckon?"

The sheriff was right. If the car was from Michigan, chances were good that the dead man was also. I once knew a man that drove a car very similar to this one but he was dead. I was sure of that, so *WHO'S* body was laying over there in the weeds?"

I asked the sheriff a very pointed and direct question, "Billy, I know you know your stuff, but did you have your dispatcher contact Michigan and inquire as to whom the plate was registered? You did do that didn't you?"

"Sure nough, dat thar was first on ma list."

"Well don't just stand there. Tell me the name!" I said frustrated.

"Man's named Charles Christensen. Dat mean anything ta ya?"

When he uttered the name, I felt like a knife had just been plunged into my stomach. Sure, I knew the person. He was the guy I had hired to use an acetylene torch to cut open an old safe I had found in a hidden room in the basement of the mansion where we used to live in Michigan. The one that was rumored to have belonged to the mob. Why he had come to Texas to rob me, I could only guess and how he found me was another question. I needed time to think this out, so I responded nonchalantly to the sheriff who was waiting patiently for my answer, "No can't say that it does. I don't understand why someone would come all the way down here from Michigan to rob a bank, they do have a lot of them up there." My last remark was a feeble attempt at trying to cover-up my shaky voice.

"When I told them thar State Police that the auto was implicated in a bank breakin and death, they all said they'd be a sendin two dicks down here to look over da case. I'm just glad y'all didn't know da deceased. They all might need to visit with ya, anyhows, dat Okay wit ya?" the sheriff said putting me on notice.

Just then, a wrecker from the Ford dealer arrived to tow the Buick with its contents intact back to the dealership to await the arrival of the cops from Michigan.

A few minutes later, a hearse from the local funeral home came on the scene to remove the remains. Two big burly men managed to slide into a black body bag the remains of the burnt corpse of the Michigan burglar, my old acquaintance, Chuck Christensen.

I overheard one of the morticians telling Sheriff Barrett, that the body was in such a deteriorated state that this was looking increasingly like a Federal case. They were going to have to drive it straight up to the pathology department at the University Medical Center in Austin. There it would take forensic experts a couple of weeks to determine the cause of death.

My mind started to whirl I'd have to think this through very carefully and try to position myself whereas I would not be implicated in any way to Chuck's death. I was sure I could pull that off, because I wasn't involved at all. I was as surprised as everyone else about the identity of the dead man, but I had lied to a police officer and had removed what could have been, for the cops anyway, a very vital piece of evidence from the crime scene, *THE RING*.

Yeah, *THE RING*. Immediately I thought about how it had seared my finger the time I slipped it on for just a millisecond. I could only imagine what would have happened to my body if I had not managed to pull it off as quickly as I had. Then another thought struck me right between the eyes as I remembered what the old hunchback caretaker back in Michigan had told me about the condition the body of his employer was in when he found it, all charred and burned, like a piece of toast, he said. The body was also wearing the Knights of Zion's silver signet ring on its index finger.

I was convinced the ring had something to do with these men's gruesome deaths, on second thought, probably not something but, *EVERYTHING*.

I wondered what the pathologist would think when he looked at this body and what kind of weird results his autopsy would turn up. I was certain of one thing, I would have to be one of the first people here in Palomino to see the report so I could get all the lies I was going to have to tell straight. Not only did my life as a free man depend on the right set of lies, but quite possibly the fate of my hidden millions. I was prepared to defend my golden booty, even if killing was involved. "My God," I thought, "What am I turning into?"

I figured I had two weeks before the pathology report got back to Sheriff Barrett, so I thought I would do a little research on the ring. Possibly the old black book that was locked in the safe deposit box back at the bank might provide some insight into the weird piece of jewelry. Telling the sheriff, I was going to work and if he needed me for anything, I would be at the bank. I left in a hurry because suddenly I was very curious about the black book and what it might tell me. I had not opened it but that one time when I first found it years earlier in the old library in Michigan.

When I arrived at the bank, Martha was waiting for me. She had four more ranchers who needed loans, which she could not approve because of their lack of assets. I wanted to keep her and everyone else in the office busy because I needed to get into the vault and look at the book and I did not want to be disturbed. I had been dipping into the footlockers quite often for money for her to loan out and I was not about to stop now. I really felt I was doing some good by helping out these hard working people and I was making a good return on the loans. Asking Martha how much she needed to fund all these requests she said, one hundred and sixty eight thousand dollars.

My only inquiry to her was, were they all good customers of the bank and did they pay their notes on time. Her response was that everyone was timely in his or her payments; they just did not have much in assets other than their land, which they were putting up as collateral. I told her to wait at her desk and I would get the funds for her. I was so wrapped up in thought about the ring and getting to that book, I quickly slipped into the vault and went to one of the lockers and counted out the amount she needed. In doing so noticed, the footlocker was almost empty; taking money out of them whenever Martha had asked for it, was empting them rapidly. However, I was not alarmed but very confident in her judgment, so closing the locker I took the needed funds to her to disperse. I then hurried back into the vault, opened the safe deposit box, took out the black book and headed into my office, closing and locked my door behind me.

I sat the old volume on my desk. It was heavy, maybe thirty pounds in weight. Its wooden cover was dried and cracked with age and the forged iron hinges and clasp were rusted and bent. On the front and attached side by side with rusted square headed nails were two triangles forged in solid gold. The hammered gold metal still gleamed brightly in the sunshine streaming through my office window. It was apparent to me; the book was indeed very old and had to be extremely valuable.

Slowly I lifted the wooden cover and glanced at the first page. On it was displayed the same two golden triangles as on the cover and boldly engraved above them and in heavy old English style writing was, "The Knighthood of Zion." I began thumbing through the pages of the ancient script where additional pages were written in English. Further on the writing changed to what appeared to be German and English mixed together. Then continuing on the writing was all in German. Near the center of the book, the script turned to what I surmised was Hebrew.

Thumbing through the pages, I came to where there was the hollow area containing the German Lugar pistol which rested on a hammered metal plate.

Lifting the pistol out of the book, the plate was exposed to full view, revealing that it was beautifully etched and handsomely engraved with the Hebrew word "Shalom." On the left side of the plate was a long slot running from top to bottom and on the right a hole with a notch in it about the diameter of a thick pencil. At first, I thought the plate was the back of the book but noticed when I tapped on it, it sounded hollow. Then it dawned on me that I was looking at the front cover of a book inside of the larger book. I tried to open the metal plate but it would not budge. Realizing the front cover was locked, I speculated that the hole on the right side could actually be a keyhole.

Sitting there for some time contemplating what I might use as a key I tried some things from my desk. A fountain pen as well as my letter opener but neither seemed to fit. My eyes fell upon the gun and I noticed that the end of the barrel seemed to be about the same diameter as the hole. Picking up the pistol, I tried it in the keyhole and the gun sight on the end of the barrel fit perfectly into the notch in the hole, then slid right on in. I pushed on the handle until I felt it bottom out then turned the gun to the right and heard a faint "Click" and with that, the plate popped open. I had actually used the pistol barrel as a key.

Amazed, I lifted the plate and encountered an even older text than the front sections of the book. Depicted on very brittle parchment like paper were strange inscriptions and written in bold gold leaf letters at the top of the page were the words, "*URIM THUMMIM*" in what I again thought to be Hebrew. The border around the edge of the page was decorated with small nude, curly haired children with wings, seemingly in flight. The following few pages were filled with nothing but the apparent Hebrew writings. Then on one of the pages, there were diagrams of several rings hooked together forming a small circle. Also pictured were two separate types of rings, one larger than the other and with a precious stone set in the center and on either side an upright triangle that was much bolder than the smaller rings.

One of the circles was composed of six rings another eight and the largest circle consisted of twelve. Each ring depicted, as well as the circles of rings, had written beneath it Hebrew script, seeming to explain the illustrations. However, I had no earthly idea what I was looking at or what the inscriptions meant.

If only I knew somebody who understood Hebrew, he or she might be able to shed some light on what these writings were explaining. I certainly could not think of anyone who fit that description down here in Cowboyville and anyway I didn't think the translation would do me any good whatsoever, because I only had three rings and six was the least number shown needed to complete a circle.

I thought for a moment about the three rings I had, the ones that were in the glass jar of formaldehyde, well only two were in there now, one I had taken out and had left it in my top desk drawer and later found beside the incinerated bank burglar the night he broke in and eventually died horribly.

Suddenly, I remembered another ring I had found in Bruno's old shack in Michigan, which I surmised once had belonged to his employer, a mysterious Judge by the name of Seymour Levison. Also in the briefcase was another ring Bruno gave me on his deathbed.

More amazingly still, I had thrown them both into an old leather briefcase with some other items found in the shack. I remembered that I had placed the briefcase into one of the footlockers with the greenbacks, the same footlockers that were sitting in my bank vault at this very moment. The fourth and fifth rings were right here in this building. I had to find that briefcase.

Leaving my office and locking the door, I had to resist running through the bank to get into the vault because I was so excited about remembering the rings. The first footlocker I opened looking for the briefcase contained only money and old canvas bank bags with Detroit Bank & Trust printed on their sides. Searching through several more, I finally found the old briefcase. Opening it, I saw several old and tattered documents as well as a six shot revolver with Police Special stamped along its barrel. Reaching into the bottom of the bag I felt a leather box, picking it up I opened it and there they were, The Rings.

I closed the box containing the rings and slipped it into my pocket, replaced the briefcase in the footlocker and hurried back to my office to get a closer look at them. Closing my office door and again locking it for privacy, I removed the box from my pocket, took out the rings, and sat them on my desk. I then went over to my overcoat and removed the ring I had taken from the dead body. Still rolled up in my hankie, I carried it over to my desk to compare it to the other rings from the briefcase.

As I placed the rolled hankie on the desk and slid out the ring, three paper clips that were sitting close by instantly shot toward the ring and stuck to it, the thing was magnetized.

Looking at one of the rings I had taken from the briefcase, I could see that it was much larger. Peering closer, I saw a small hook on one side as well as a small slot on the other. There also was a stone resembling a Ruby set in the center with the word "Gad" engraved below the stone. On each side were the upright triangles. I picked up my metal letter opener and touched the ring to see if it too was magnetized. Surprisingly, it was not.

Something very strange was going on here, what I could not be sure of, so I again consulted the old book with the illustrations.

I could clearly see by the depictions that I had both types of rings. In the picture of the circles, I could make out five smaller rings and one of the larger types all hooked together in a small circle. The writing below the pictures was certainly some type of explanation and some of it resembled Egyptian Hieroglyphics, I just had to find someone to decipher it for me, but who?

I sat there thinking; Just as my life had finally settled down to a high degree of happiness something like this comes up and rekindles all the memories of the strange happenings I experienced on that hilltop in Michigan, an experience I certainly did not want to ever endure again as long as I lived. It was that terrifying.

Looking at the rings on my desk and knowing that two others rested in my bank vault I had a good notion to gather them up, throw them into the ocean, and eliminate any further involvement with them. My life could return to the happiness I had found here in Palomino, but something had intensely aroused my curiosity.

Reaching over, I pulled the paperclips off the small ring, and found that it took quite a bit of effort to remove them, because they were being held so tightly. It was apparent that the magnetic force was very strong.

Suddenly I remembered someone I knew at the University Of Michigan who was an expert on magnetism, and who had worked with NASA trying to develop an anti-gravity flying craft utilizing the earth's magnetic field, a Professor Otto Schweitzer. He, along with another of his colleagues; Professor Joyce Hoover, who incidentally helped to develop a propulsion system for Mag-Lev

Trains using super magnets, helped find the cause of some of the weird phenomena that were being created by a magnetic force, which encompassed the hill, and old mansion where we had lived. If I could only reach him, he may have a suggestion on why the ring may be magnetized and with a name like Schweitzer may even be Jewish and able to read Hebrew thereby shedding some light on the inscriptions.

Without hesitation, I picked up the telephone and dialed information asking the operator for The University of Michigan, Department of Weather Phenomena and was promptly given the number.

My fingers trembled with excitement as I dialed the number and my voice cracked when I asked the person who answered if Professor Schweitzer was located at this number. She said, "Yes he is. Could you hold for a moment?" I could hardly believe my luck on finding him so easy.

After a brief pause a familiar sounding voice said, "Hello, how may I help you?"

"Professor Schweitzer, its Zack Heikel calling, do you remember me?"

"Do I remember you, why of course? You are the man who lives on the hill with the reversing natural magnet.

How could I ever forget you. I received a lot of praise from the scientific community on the article I wrote about the atmospheric conditions surrounding your home. What good fortune do I have in hearing from you? Are things still calm on the hill?

"Professor I'm sorry to say that I no longer live on the hilltop. The house burned down almost a year ago and we now reside in Texas and think we have come up with another mystery and I need your advice. Do you have a little time to talk with me about it?"

"Do I ever, take as long as you like. It is terrible to hear that your home burned down, that is too bad. Now please explain to me what you are troubled with in Texas."

"Well Professor its magnetism again. This time however it is involving a strange ring I found at the mansion and an old book which seems to describe how the ring is used. Most of the words I think are written in Hebrew or some other biblical script. Some of the inscriptions are more like Egyptian Pictor-graphs. Do you read or under-stand either language and if you would also permit me to ask if you are Jewish?"

"Yes, I am Jewish and I do speak and read Hebrew flu-ently. Could you please spell out a few of the words or describe what they look like? Possibly I can tell if it is indeed Hebrew?"

I said, "Yes Sir," then struggled with the strange inscriptions as I attempted to explain them to the professor. "Sir, under each ring shown in the book are a few words. Written under the small ring is, "Ma'agar Energiya" and under the larger one is "Rashee" does this make any sense to you?"

"Why Zack it sure does. The writing is definitely Hebrew. Ma'agar Energiya means something holding electricity like a capacitor. Rashee, could mean several things, like teacher or master."

"Well Professor, I guess you have determined what the language is and that helps a lot. Here are another couple of words that are capitalized and underlined, Zehirut, Mesukan and Gorem Ma'vet." I spelled them out for him.

Professor Schweitzer said rather startled, "Hold it right there, you're not touching anything are you?"

Nervously I said, "Why no! Why do you ask?"

"Those words absolutely mean Careful, Dangerous, and Fatal. I would strongly suggest that you put away under lock and key whatever you have before you and then send me a copy of everything else printed or written about the rings. Now until I interpret it and find out just what you have discovered, Please don't touch a thing. Do I make myself clear?" the professor stated plainly.

"You sure do! Just the word deadly is enough to make me put these articles away. I don't know if this is anything you want to get involved with because one of the rings have already been linked to a man's death by burning. His whole body was completely incinerated," I said rather hesitantly.

After a long silence on the other end of the line, I heard the professor say, "That settles it. What you are playing with is deadly. Please get to me that writing as soon as you can. I will look it over and get right back with you by phone."

"Thanks you so very much Professor Schweitzer. I'll overnight it to you today just as soon as I can get it copied. Thanks again, and you may have just saved my life."

"I would not be a bit surprised that I have. I will be anxiously waiting your overnight package. Just mail it to me here at the university. Good bye and good luck," the professor said as he hung up the receiver.

I had to wait almost two hours for the office to clear out for the night. As soon as everyone left for home, I took the old journal out to the copy machine and copied the pages depicting the rings as well as the weird inscriptions on several of the pages. Having finished my copying I carefully placed the rings as well as the book back in the safe deposit box, locked it and then hurried to our post office and mailed, by special over night delivery, the copied text to the professor.

That evening when I got home from the bank, Peggy Sue was her usually jovial self. Not wanting to worry her about what I had discovered about the rings I sat rather stoic at dinner and then after a sleepless night returned to the bank. Late that afternoon I received a phone call from the professor, who had received the package that morning, had quickly read the pages, and felt it was imperative that he contact me immediately to report his findings.

Picking up my phone as it rang I said, "Hello professor! Man that sure was a fast turnaround," I said into the mouthpiece.

"Well I felt it very urgent that I speak to you. The writing is Hebrew, very ancient Hebrew. In fact, it is a language called, Afro-Asiatic and not used in the vernacular since about 100B.C. Zack, where did you say you acquired this book?"

"I found it in the old dusty library at the mansion on the hill in Michigan. The one you and Professor Hoover visited in regards to the unusual things that took place there.

"Sure that's right, how could I forget that. The report I gave to the scientific community about my findings made me somewhat of a celebrity. Now about the pages you copied and sent to me. They contain some very technically advanced information and I don't see how they could be outlined in a book as old as you say it is. However one thing is clear, whether old or new, the writings indicate that those rings you have in your possession are very dangerous. I am not at all sure what their main purpose is without reading the whole book but I am fairly certain they are part of some type of machine or apparatus that utilizes static electricity and some form of primitive microwaves. I am somewhat confused because the pages mention guards called "The Knights of Zion" so until I look at the whole manuscript I cannot help you with that. The pages did indicate that someone who was not informed about how the rings operate and inadvertently slipped one on a finger, thereby completing the electric circuit, could be severally injured if not electrocuted or burned to death by some sort of microwave.

Those rings that are marked "*MA'AGAR ENERGIYA*" are actually better described as being more like a condenser, which are capable of accumulating and storing minuscule amounts of static electricity from the atmosphere or during thunderstorms until they contain a tremendous amount of stored voltage. Although this would be an excellent power source, however when touched or placed on ones finger they could discharge their whole electric current into the unsuspecting person. These rings would have to be occasionally discharged by touching a metal object or they may become overloaded. Only persons that were members of the knighthood which was mentioned would know about this hazard, others who were not authorized to wear the ring would probably be severely shocked or possibly even electrocuted."

The professor continued as if giving a lecture, "The larger rings seem to be some type of master link that appears to be a sort of key which uses magnetism in setting up a means to somehow communicate with the capacitor rings using a form of microwave. I can't imagine what else they would be capable of producing. You see when you have high voltage electricity and magnets you could get microwaves like in today's ovens.

These so-called master rings also act as a master link in forming these circles, which when a minimum of six are linked together do something. I can only guess what this function would be but I suspect one thing, something possibly not of this world because the word, Triangulum kept cropping up in the text, which I think is a constellation or a mythical place somewhere. The pages go on to read that the more rings in the circle the clearer the Xenon. I am assuming it is referring to the gas Xenon that is described in the dictionary as a heavy colorless chemically inactive non-atomic gaseous element, which is present in the atmosphere in the proportion of one volume in 170,000 volumes of air. It is also used to fill radio, television and luminescent vacuum tubes.

Zack what you have discovered in this old book is very, very interesting to me.

Is there anyway I could take a look at the whole manuscript? I could be on the next plane to Texas, just say the word."

I hesitated, trying to make some sense of what he had just dropped into my head which was so mind-boggling. Then realizing the line had been silent too long I said, "Sure Professor Schweitzer you can study the book, all I need is a few days to get my affairs in order so I can take the time to be with you. How about I call you back in a couple of days and we can then make all the arrangements. Does that sound okay to you?"

"That would be just fine with me. However, in the mean time, please for your own safety, don't touch any of the rings until we can get to the bottom of this mystery."

"Thanks again Professor for all your help and I will be calling you in a few days, Good Bye." I said as I hung up the phone.

My head began swirling in complete confusion and uncertainty. Just what the hell did I stumble onto. I was not sure I would be calling the professor back to discuss the rings or anything else and thought for a moment I might destroy them or at least bury them so no one could again be injured or killed. I worried maybe even someone in my family. I knew that I did not want to open up another Pandora's box and relive the nightmare I had experienced on the hill in Michigan, but that is what I was afraid was about to happen. As much as I wanted to rid myself of the burden of the rings and old manuscript, something seemed to be drawing me into the strange vortex and mystery surrounding the rings of Zion. I was helplessly captured by the intrigue. I felt compelled to call the professor and delve deeper into this paradox.

Several days would go by before I gathered enough courage to make the phone call to the University of Michigan and strangely, just before I decided to do so, in through my office door walked Sheriff Billy Flynn Barrett carrying a sheet of paper. He plunked down hard in a chair in front of my desk and said, "Y'all ready to hear what kilt our burglar? This here is the report from Austin on what did him in and it's a good one. Seems as though he all was spontaneously combusted. I ain't never heard that one before, but that what is said right cheer on this here paper. What y'all think of dat?"

Curious I said, "Well Sheriff would you mind if I took a look at the report?"

Handing me the paper he said, "Sho nuf! Go head and take a look for yourself and see what y'all can make of it."

Glancing down at the report, I found the examiner had determined through military dental records, probable height and weight, as well as age. He had definitely identified the dead person as a Charles Christensen and further down the page had listed the cause of death as a rare case of spontaneous human combustion.

I knew I had to urgently make the phone call to Professor Schweitzer. His deciphering of the old text was right on and we had our first confirmed kill caused by one of the rings. He had to unravel for me the whole mystery before another person died. I also needed his input to conjure up a story that I could hide behind for the detectives from Michigan, who I was certain would be arriving to investigate soon.

I handed the report back to Sheriff Barrett who as he left my office said that he would be seeing me around town or at church on Sunday.

As soon as the door closed behind him, I pounced on the telephone and dialed the professor. "Hello Professor Schweitzer, it's me Zack Heilkel calling you."

"Well hello there! I was getting a little impatient and was about to call you. I hope this is about my being able to study your old book."

"Well Sir, yes it is!" I said emphatically. "When would you like to fly down?"

The professor answered quickly, "Would tomorrow be too soon? I am quite anxious to delve into the writings. I also have gathered some books on ancient Hebrew, which may help me in the translation. Oh! I was wondering if I flew into San Antonio would it be too much trouble for you to pick me up at the airport?"

"No trouble at all professor," I said, "And you can stay at the house with me and my family as you did on your previous visit in Michigan."

"Well then it's settled. I will call you back with my arrival time and then I will see you at the airport. I must say Zack that I am very excited and can hardly wait to see the old manuscript for myself. So until tomorrow, I'll say goodbye," the professor said as he ended the call.

I arrived the next evening at the airport in San Antonio at the time the professor informed me he would be landing. I met the old gentleman just as he was picking up his suitcase. We shook hands and he gave me a big hug as if he was genuinely happy to see me once again. I knew I was certainly happy to see him, as he was the key as far as I was concerned, to unraveling the writing in the old book. Without him I was totally helpless and at a loss of what to do with the rings as well as the book. I was also depending on him and his findings to relieve the complete state of mental obsession I had with the artifacts.

In the three hours it took to drive down to Palomino we talked excitedly about the articles. I also told the professor about the autopsy report on the dead burglar who had broken into the bank and stole the ring and that it confirmed he had died from spontaneous human combustion. I also admitted to having taken the ring from the dead body unseen by the police and said that I was a little worried about being in trouble for tampering with the crime scene.

The professor said he thought I did the right thing in taking the ring which he was certain had caused the guys death, because the cops probably would not have understood the bizarre situation surrounding the piece of jewelry. They would have just confiscated the ring and possibly the book and then they would have lingered for years in a police evidence room and never have been studied. He said he felt I had done him a favor in picking up the ring which he was quite sure would prove to be very helpful in his studies on magnetism.

He and one of his colleagues had gone over the copies I sent him which contained examples of events that could take place in the atmosphere related to static electricity, Xenon, as well as microwaves. The two scientists had a million questions on how these things inter-related and he hoped the book contained the answers to several of them, which he found were very perplexing.

He was further intrigued about how a text as old as the one I had could contain scientific information and applications that NASA and himself were only now beginning to understand.

We finally arrived in Palomino around midnight and I drove straight out to the house, even though the professor at this late hour wanted to see the book. I told him it would just have to wait until morning because I was so bummed out with the drive as well as the mind blowing the conversation had put me through.

Peggy Sue, who had waited up for us greeted Professor Schweitzer warmly. The hour being so late, she ushered the professor to his room all the while reminiscing about how his past discoveries had saved us from some very severe mental anguish.

In trying to keep her in the dark and uninvolved with what was going on about the rings and the death of the burglar, I had not told her the real reason for the professor's visit. Only that he had requested it just to clear up some of the finding he had discovered on the hill.

The next morning after a good night's sleep and one of Peggy Sue's fine country breakfasts, the professor and

I headed out to the bank to examine the mysterious old texts.

Arriving, I took the professor into my office and made him comfortable. I knew I would have to spend some time with Martha discussing bank loans, which I was not the least bit interested in these days. She was doing a fine job and helping a lot of needy people and I felt a need to keep her enthusiastic about her work because she was practically operating the bank single-handedly of late. After taking care of business with her I hurried into the bank vault, retrieved the book, and then joined Professor Schweitzer in my office.

The moment I entered with the heavy book he could not take his eyes from it and when I sat it down on a large table in front of him he began to immediately study the cover all the while under his breath muttering, "Oh my! Oh my!"

He was quite impressed with the cover and the workmanship of the person who fashioned the golden triangles and was intrigued as to why they were so prominently displayed. He admitted to not being a metallurgist, but thought that whoever had made them used a very high purity metal.

He stood there examining the binding for some time then stated that he thought it to be made of blackened cedar wood. The design and type of iron hinge used gave him the impression that they were forged well over a hundred years ago and by a very skilled blacksmith at that.

The professor examined the exterior of the book and explained his thoughts. Then he stopped, stood straight, pulled up a big easy chair and sat down. Taking a deep breath, he lifted the cover opening the book and said, "Now let us began!"

His eyes opened wide as he saw the first page and then exclaimed, "The Knighthood of Zion, this looks like its written in Old English script to me and on very thin paper. Actually, it's not paper at all, but animal skin. The ink also appears to be very old, see the brownish tint to it, that's from the materials used, a form of clay containing a lot of iron. The brown tint is caused when the iron in the ink turns to rust on the paper. This particular ink is called, iron gall ink. Carefully turning the page, he encountered paper that appeared to be similar to the kind used today and looked to have been added to the book in the recent past.

Reading and then turning pages for over an hour, he glanced my way, looked over his glasses and said, "So far all I've learned is how to put together a crime syndicate and where a bunch of Jewish gangs are located in the Eastern United States. This writing is from the 1920's thru the 40's and not of much interest to me, however it does mention the rings, but nothing specific about them, other than that persons who wore them were members of this knighthood thing. One fact I am certain of is that these sheets are very new in comparison to the book and have just been inserted behind the old cover sheet for some reason."

Diving back into the book and resuming reading for another hour or so, he then surfaced once again saying, "What we seem to have here is a random diary of several people and their notations spanning different times and places. For instance, some notations are written in German and definitely about a crime syndicate. There are references to World War 2 as well as World War 1 in Germany.

The deeper I look into the book the writings seem to be layer upon layer and getting progressively older as it goes further toward the back of the book. I'm now reading in the English language about incidents taking place in the late eighteen hundreds in England. One thing in particular that keeps popping up throughout the writings is the phrase, "The Knights of Zion". So I am assuming all of the writers were knights and definitely Jewish. I think I will turn to where I see some older pages sticking out and see what they reveal."

Gently turning over several more of the newer pages until he came to the old leather like ones once again he then said, "Now we are back into the Old English style of writing." He stopped to read for several minutes then continued on turning the pages. I had pulled up a chair beside the professor and was doing some reading myself, although some of the old words seemed peculiar, and used thee and thou extensively, I could understand what they were describing. The office was deadly silent and nary a word was spoken between us. We were so mesmerized by the written stories.

After scanning several more pages we came to a part where I was sure the writer was telling about an eye witness account, during medieval times, describing groups of warriors on horseback in bloody and brutal hand to hand combat with swords, mace, lance and battle axe. When the carnage was over, the victors were awarded by their King, land and precious jewels for having fought so bravely protecting the throne and the countries riches. The battle took place in Saxony in the year 1286. There were additional notations of major engagements as far South as The Mediterranean Sea and Northern Africa in what the book described as "The End Crusades."

The eyewitness recorded these events almost seven hundred years ago. The professor was right; the book was old, very old indeed.

Another hour passed when suddenly the professor stood up from his chair and breaking the silence complained that his eyes were getting tired. He said he needed to take a break and give himself some time to think about what he had just read and put it all in perspective. He admitted that one thing was a certainty, particularly because of the date mentioned, the book was old, at least several hundred years, except for the few dozen pages that had been inserted recently.

Just then, there was a knock at my office door and I heard Wes's voice say, " Hey! What y'all doin in there? Playin cards? How bout lunch?"

I unlocked and cracked open the door ever so slightly and told Wes I would be right out and that I had a visitor, then once again closed and turned the lock in the door. I just did not want anyone, even my friend Wes, to see the book or get any impression of what we were up to here in the office.

Hearing Wes mention lunch the professor commented that he thought better on a full stomach so I unlocked the door and the both of us joined Wes in the outer office. I introduced Wes to Professor Schweitzer while locking my office door behind me, and the three of us walked across the street to the Palomino Cantina for lunch. I was certain the professor would keep quiet about the book, as he was becoming as secretive about it as I was.

On the walk over to the diner, Wes said he had wanted to have lunch so he could tell me directly some very good news before it came out in our local newspaper, "The Palomino Colt," which had a bad habit of stretching the truth.

The three of us pushed our way into the crowded caf□ and took a seat near the window. After I had gotten the professor's permission to order for him, I did as usual and told the waitress three of "The Blue Plate Specials." I then turned to Wes and asked him, "Now what's this big good news thing you have for me?"

"Well I hope the Professor here don't mind me talking business in front of him, but Zack do you remember some time ago that thar oil company who wantcd to look for oil on my spread?"

"Yes I do, and you gave them the go ahead. So what's the big deal?"

"Zack, the big deal is they drilled one and it hit oil and it's makin over two hundred barrels a day. Now they want to drop down another un. I guess I'm gonna to be rich. The geologist fella asked if I knew you, seein they want to look on your place too. What y'all think of dat?"

"Wes, that's great news and I'm happy for you. As for them drilling on my property that's okay too but they need to contact Peggy Sue, I've got my hands full right now on a research project I'm doing with the Professor here."

Shaking his head Wes said, "Ya know y'all seems to be takin this bird's nest on the ground deal as if its no count, I aint never seen ya act this way before, specially about business. What ever you and the prof are searchin fer must be mighty important."

All the while Wes is telling me the good news about his oil strike, my mind was constantly thinking of the book and its mysterious writings. Through the remainder of lunch hour, I thought about how my personal life had been almost non-existent for the last few weeks. I had been so wrapped up in the ancient book that I had lost all interest in my wife, my kids and my bank and even worse, had not had a sexual thought in a long time. My personal appearance had suffered too; I was not shaving everyday and wore the same clothes for a week. It almost seemed as though I was living on another plateau of life, high above the one that existed before I opened the book or found the rings. The thought of getting rid of the book and rings again flashed in my mind. I bet the old professor would just love for me to turn over to him the artifacts. But there was no way I could see myself ever parting with them, it was almost as if I was mesmerized or in a constant trance-like state and I was dead set on getting to the meaning of the old writings spelled out in the black book.

"Well I guess its time to mosey on back over to the pharmacy," Wes's booming voice said waking me from my daydream.

Then the professor added his voice, "Yes, I believe you are right. I am anxious to get back to Zack's office and resume my research."

As we left the diner Wes waved to us as he walked away and said, "I hope you boys find what y'all are searchin fer."

Not stopping to answer any of Martha's questions, we eagerly returned to the office and locking the door behind us began to again read from the book.

We proceeded downward through page after page of fascinating stories told by various authors about ancient England and The Knights of Zion. They chronicled the major events where the knights were involved and the numerous times they had to fight, always being victorious.

Another date seemed to jump out at us from the written page, October 14th, 1066.

It was the time of a major battle in a place called, "Wood-hedge" where King Harold was killed by Zion Knights while fighting for the Norman Empire's King William the First of Normandy and more or less setting off the time known as the "Holy Crusades" which began in earnest in the year 1070.

The book took us back in time 900 years and the next few pages proved to be even more wondrous they went back even deeper in time to around 500 AD, an age of tranquility and peace. A time of hunting wild boar and playing the lute during a seemingly golden and happy age set in the hills of Glastonbury. Perched on a peak several hundred feet above sea level, surrounded by dense woods and in spring time fields were full of bluebells and primroses there sat a castle called Cadbury. The book told about a king who reigned over his court of legendary knights and fair ladies. A king with such a mysterious and powerful personality, that it created a special aura of high romance, chivalry and courage.

Professor Schweitzer, looking up from the pages, over his glasses, and into my eyes exclaimed, "Oh! My God! Could this be THE King Arthur and his Cadbury Castle? If it is, then it confirms he was a real person and not a myth as some believe today. This book, no doubt has the power to rewrite history."

Quickly returning to the page and reading on he said after a several minutes, "Zack, they are all in here, The Knights of The Round Table, Sir Lancelot and Lady Gynaver, Galahad and Sir Gawain. This book is talking about King Arthur and Camelot. This is unbelievable."

Taking a deep breath he returned to the written words and read aloud, "At Glastonbury Abbey a man named Myrddrin, the kings wizard and alchemist, who could turn lead into gold by blending several metals together, made a magic sword that had special powers. It would not bend or break in battle and when swung made a loud singing sound.

Zack, this has to be describing the sword, Excalibur. It is written here that Myrddrin said he had obtained the knowledge of working with metals from an ancient sect known as the Druids. These people taught of the transmigration of souls, about the stars and their motions and the nature of things. They also were knowledgeable about the power and attributes of god. Myrddrin also believed these priests of high knowledge built the temple of huge stones on Salsbury Plain to study the stars.

Zack, this Myrddrin person mentioned here, he had to be the man Merlin the Magician. In addition, the temple that Merlin is referring to is a place that still exits today in England called, "Stonehenge." This is utterly fantastic."

He turned another page and staring at it for several minutes said, "Listen to this! It is unbelievably! It's about Sir Galahad one of the knights from Cadbury Castle. He was on a quest in the holy lands for religious articles and actually found several pieces. They were discovered in an old deserted hilltop Mosque near Jerusalem, after a desperately ill and dying priest told them where the treasures were hidden within the cathedral. One article was a gold vessel with inlaid precious gems that the priest vowed Jesus Christ had eaten from at the last supper he had here on earth.

It says here that tired and exhausted from the long campaign, Galahad sat down to eat one evening in his tent and looking around for something to hold his wine, used the gold bowl and drank deeply from it that night. The following morning he awoke completely rejuvenated and never felt so fit. In the following days he continued to drink from the vessel and at times could not remember even pouring any wine into it, it just never seemed to be empty. After a while he noticed that an old wound he had received in battle had completely healed and disappeared from his arm. Galahad continued to supp from the vessel and to flourish. His servants noticed that he rarely ate the food that they prepared for him and each time they commented on it Galahad would say that he was filled with food from the golden bowl.

Several months later he returned to Glastonbury Abbey and presented the religious artifacts, including the golden bowl, to King Arthur. Galahad said he had been having strange visions of God and Heaven and that he did not desire to live on earth any longer because Heaven seemed so beautiful and in his dreams he saw himself going into the sky to live with Christ. Eight days after his return to Camelot, he gave all his personal possessions to Arthur and members of the king's court. The following morning, Galahad was nowhere to be found. He had suddenly and mysteriously vanished from the face of the earth.

Zack, do you know what this script is describing? That gold bowl? Zack it has to be the Holy Grail we talk about so much nowadays. It was real, Galahad found it and King Arthur had it last. It is probably buried somewhere in present day England under an old building or something. I can hardly believe what I just read. If its okay with you I think I will spend the night here in your office and re-read the whole book up to this point. Tomorrow you and I can look at the pages under the metal plate that explains the rings and get into the real meaning of this whole enigma."

I said that would be fine with me and I would go home and get some sleep. I then locked the bank leaving the professor reading intently while reclining on my office sofa.

When I arrived home, it was late. However Peggy Sue had my supper in the oven keeping it warm for me. I sat down to eat and Peggy tried to engage me in conversation, but I was still going over in my mind the staggering revelations the professor had read from the book. Not only did I not hear her comments, I did not respond to her in any way. She sat there with such a dejected look on her face as I struggled with a few sentences trying to lighten her mood. I knew I had not been very attentive to her in a long time and attributed my feeling to being so preoccupied with the book and rings. I was sure I still loved her deeply, but I just did not feel my heart strings playing the same tune they once had when she looked at me. Could it be I was becoming mentally depressed or just obsessed? I was not sure what was happening to me, but something was. What I did not know. To make matters even worse, I went to bed right after dinner without kissing her goodnight. I could not ever remember doing that.

I left the house early the next morning before anyone was out of bed. Jumping into my Ford I raced to the bank eager to find what the professor may have discovered from the old book.

Dawn was just breaking over the horizon when I opened the front door and stepped into the empty semi-darkened outer office. Without wasting any time, I hurried to my office, opened the door and found Professor Schweitzer busy at work.

He had papers with notations on them scattered everywhere on the desk and a large English language bible open to Genesis.

When I said "Good Morning" to him and asked how he had slept on my sofa, without even looking up from the old text he said, "Didn't sleep at all! Things are way to interesting. Those Knights of Zion have turned out to be like today's mercenaries. They seem to have hired themselves out to various kingdoms for the protection of its royalty and the crown jewels and treasures. They did not seem to have a loyalty to anyone in particular. Maybe they just worked for the highest bidder. They were ferocious fighters and did seem to be almost invincible. No where in the book does it say they were ever defeated in battle. That is hard to believe because sometimes they fought against overwhelming superior numbers and won. It's almost as if they had a secret weapon."

I listened intently as I made a pot of coffee. When it had finished brewing, I poured the professor and myself a cup. Handing his cup to him, he drank down half of it and continued his reading never once even flinching from the steaming hot fluid. I thought to myself, "Man is this guy focused or what?"

Gazing into the book he said, "Zack I think I may be able to shed a little light on what the knights were all about. But I would dearly love to get into those pages under the metal plate in the book. They may explain some of the questions that are still nagging at me. Could we do that before I try to explain my theory?"

I was as anxious as he was to delve into the works and said, "I'm all for that!" Opening the book to its center where the pistol lay, I picked it up and using the barrel once again, as the key, pushed it down into the keyhole and turning it heard the pop that indicated it had come unlocked.

The professor scratching his head said, "That's quite an unusual key you have there. I'll tell you one thing right now, the ancients that opened this book in the distant past certainly did not use a German Luger pistol as the key. Something else had to have been used, like a key made for that exact purpose. Well at least we got it open without breaking anything and that's the important thing. Now let's see what we have under the plate."

Lifting the highly embossed, aluminum-like metal plate, his mouth fell open when he saw the first page with its little angel like figurines hovering around the borders on a sheet of thin shiny paper. In its center were the words, *URIM THUMMIM*. The professor said, after thinking for several minutes and referring to a small book of translations, "This is very ancient Hebrew wording and trans-lates loosely into English to mean something like, The Curses and the Perfections. That sure sounds strange doesn't it? Another thing, look at this paper. I have never seen anything like it before. It feels just like plastic. Who in the world could have made such a material so long ago? The ink also is very unusual. Its not the iron gall type, its more like the type one would get from a laser printer today, very sharp and jet black. And you know Zack, if I did not know better, and mainly because of the age of this book; I would say this metal cover was Tita-nium. I know that would be impossible because we have just recently manufactured it. It's a super strong alloy used in our new fighter planes. Just think what it would mean if my assumptions were correct. Although, quite frankly at this point in our research, I would not be sur-prised by anything."

Scratching his head, he turned to the next page and see-ing only Hebrew writing said, "It is going to take some time to break this all down into English, so let's just thumb thru a few pages and see if anything jumps out at us."

After turning over several he abruptly stopped and said, "Now here is something about the rings, I'm going to be slow in deciphering this, its old and very unusual, but here goes. Yes, I see we have large rings depicted with various precious stones embedded in them labeled

Rashee. Zack, to keep it simple for us, lets just call them Masters. The smaller ones with the Hebrew word Shalom, meaning Peace or Hello in English , these are labeled "Hashmalee, Ma'agar Energiya." Again Zack these are the capacitors. I really do not understand how the ancients knew this word or anything about something like a capacitor, which as far as I know is used today to store electricity."

Thumbing through several more pages he again stopped and read for several minutes then spoke, "If I make this out right it seems to be saying that there are a total of twelve of the larger Master style rings and one hundred and forty four of the smaller "*EVED*, Ma'agar Energiya" rings, which means in English, slave. They still are probably referring to the capacitor rings. Each of the twelve Master rings have their own separate precious stone. It reads that these stones are; ruby, topaz, beryl, turquoise, sapphire, emerald, jacinth, agate, amethyst, a chrysolite, an onyx and a jasper. I guess that is twelve, however I have never heard of some of them. The inscriptions go on to say that beneath the stones and engraved on the rings are these various names, Ruben, Simeon, Levi, Judah, Issachar, Zebulun, Gad, Asher, Dan, Naphtali, Joseph and finally, Benjamin."

No sooner had the professor mentioned the name Gad when I shouted out, "Hey, I got that ring. Its in the briefcase in my vault along with the others."

"Right, I remember you told me that. Do you realize that all twelve of these names are biblical. I can't just off the top of my head remember what the significance of this list is but there must be a connection here somewhere. Let's go on and maybe it will come to me," he said as he turned more pages.

He again stopped and exclaims, "Now this is more like what I am looking for. It seems to be an explanation of how the rings go together. Let's see here. Yes, this is the section that you copied and sent to me. It explains how the capacitor rings gather small amounts of static electricity from the atmosphere until they are fully charged, Uh Oh, I have not seen this before, a footnote, Lets see, oh! Here it is, Extreme care should be taken as residual charge could be as high as 12,000 volts. Aw! This has got to be wrong! I can't comprehend how something as small as those rings could retain that much voltage, And for the love of Mike, what is an old time book like this talking about electricity for anyway. It wasn't discovered until the late seventeenth century. Well, by us anyway. This completely baffles me. Give me another cup of that coffee will ya Zack? Maybe it will wake me up. I seem to be dreaming."

The professor, after drinking down the whole cup in one big swig said, "I was just thinking about the power of 12,000 volts. Man, that is a hell of a wallop. Surely if a person had that amount of juice shot into him, I guarantee to you he would be incinerated. Right there is the reason for your burglar friend being turned to toast. The ring he stole must have been fully loaded and discharged right into him when he put it on his finger, which completed the circuit. It's a good thing you did pick up that ring after it released its charge and hid it. Why the cops would have went nuts trying to figure that one out. I'm going mad myself trying to comprehend how an old civilization could have known about such things, and I have been studying electricity and its behavior most of my life. I have read that the ancient Egyptians made small batteries that could generate a very feeble current. But 12,000 volts, that is completely ridiculous. Putting several of these small things together you would have one hell of a powerhouse, enough to supply power for several of today's homes.

Let's move on here to the explanation of the Master rings. The writings are somewhat vague. They describe the rings as a kind of master switch that when linked together in a circle and supplied with enough electricity," he paused, "Well, they refer to this not as electricity as such because there was no word for it back then, but anyway enough light flow they called it, from the slave rings a viewer can see,……. what's this? An image in the Xenon Plasma! This, I don't get at all. Also, the term light flow, if that is not referring to electricity, could they mean lasers? Naw, Couldn't be!

It also mentions here a very detailed description of how a,…….. can't quite make this out, but I think it might be referring to……Oh! My, a microwave. This all sounds so unbelievable! Anyway it goes on to state that these waves can be sent out through the atmosphere to the slave rings by the masters for a type of communication. And again, sprinkled throughout the text are the words, Careful, Dangerous and Fatal. The scribes who wrote these pages knew what they were dealing with and that it was extremely lethal. Especially during sever lighting storms because of the tremendous amount of high voltage electricity in the atmosphere that might be captured by the Slave rings and could instantly charge them to full capacity."

"You know Professor that reminds me of the house on the hill. Remember you and Professor Hoover discovered that thing you called an oscillating magnet brought on when strong lightning strikes hit nearby. Could there be some kind of connection there?" I said rather confused.

The professor answered quickly, "Zack you may have a good point there and we need to one day research that further. However, right now I have my mind full of all this fascinating material. I am sure I will need every ounce of gray matter I have to figure out what this all means. Some of these explanations are already beyond my mental capabilities I'm afraid."

Turning pages until he neared the end of the book, the professor begin to read sporadically, "Can't quite make this out. It says something about when all of the pieces are inserted into the, Shvill Afar which translates into something like our word Pathway, that's with a capitol letter so it must be a proper name of something. Contact could be made. Contact with what or whom I can only guess but whatever it is I am positive we would be dealing with a very advanced intelligence, light years ahead of our own.

Zack, do you have any whiskey around here? I need a drink desperately. I feel just like a young school kid getting his first taste of advanced electronics."

I mixed the old guy a nice hi-ball which he drank down just as he had the coffee. Flopping down on my sofa and placing his glasses on his forehead he said, "So far the book has not explained just how these electrical pieces actually work. Just how to use them. Kind of like an operators manual. You know what? I think that is just what the metal-jacketed book really is, an explanation on how these rings operate. The big old wood covered book seems to have been fashioned, more or less, to protect the metal one and then it was used to hold eyewitness notes and accounts of feats accomplished by the Knights of Zion.

The two books are actually separate and don't seem to be all that connected. I would be willing to wager that if we did a carbon dating test on them it would prove that the metal one is the oldest and I mean by centuries. After all, it is referring to names that appear in the Old Testament. Now I'm not saying definitely that it is two thousand years old, but it could be. On second thought, it's just possible the Knights of Zion were protecting the metal book, not so much as whoever had it in their possession. I think it would be safe to say the Knights were guardians of that fascinating metal book. It seems to be almost as if their entire knighthood were assigned by someone or something to protect it by any means necessary.

I know that is a pretty vague explanation of the books, but it's the best I can put together at this time. Now just as soon as I can catch my breath, let's take a look at those rings and see if I can determine where they fit into the scheme of things.

I made a fresh pot of coffee and after we each had a cup, he seemed refreshed and ready to continue and said, "Zack, now could you please bring in all the rings you have. I might also add, without touching them directly, so I can examine them?"

"Will do," I said as I scampered into the vault and retrieved the briefcase with the three rings, the jar of formaldehyde containing the severed fingers that still wore two more rings and brought them in to the professor.

Who upon seeing the jar and the petrified digits commented, "That certainly is a grizzly sight. You sure have a propensity for locating bazaar articles. Where in the world did you get them?"

Caught off guard by the question, I was just ready to blurt out about the safe in the hidden room, at the old mansion where I had found the millions in cash, when I caught myself. Even though the money now meant nothing to me whatsoever because not only had most of it been loaned out to poor people to better their lives, I was deeply involved with something much more important, that was the contents of the jar I held in my hands. I also did not want the kindly old professor to know anything about the money's existence for his own good, so I lied when I said, "The jar came from the same dusty shelf in the library where I found the book. As for the fingers it contains, I have absolutely no idea who or for what reason these ring fingers were cut from someone's hand."

"Can you remove the fingers with the rings from the fluid?" the professor asked.

"Sure I can," I said as I removed the tape from the jar's lid and lifted it.

"Ye gads that smells awful. Hurry up and get that lid back on before I gag," the professor said while holding his nose.

I moved as quickly as I could and plunged my hand down into the formaldehyde, and pulled out the two fingers that held rings. Grabbing each ring and giving it a twist, removed them from the bony appendage. I soon had both rings resting on some tissue, then quickly put the bones back in the fluid and replaced the top back over the smelly chemicals. Washing my hands thoroughly with soap and water at my office sink then drying them, I opened the briefcase, removed the three rings from it, and placed them next to the ones on my desk.

The old professor approached them, lowering his glasses from his forehead his eyes were fixed in a tight stare at the five rings. "Yes its easy to see there are two different style rings here, the so called master ring and the other a capacitor or slave ring. I must say the master ring is much larger than the others and that ruby, it is the most haunting blood red color I have ever seen in a stone."

Sliding his glasses down to the tip of his nose for better focus, we studied the master ring while moving it around with the wooden pencil and he said, "Yes you are right Zack, I can make out the word, *GAD* just below the ruby. In addition, cut sharply into each side are two triangles, which I still can't quite figure out their meaning. I can see the small hook on one side and like the slave ring, he paused ....there on the other the small loop, these are definitely designed to latch onto each other."

Using the pencil to roll over one of the smaller slave rings he said he could see the word Shalom etched on it and the same as the master ring it also had two triangles, just as was described in the book. Also on either side of this ring was the hook and eye for attaching them together.

Curiously, he slid the pencil into the slave ring, picked it up, and walked over to one of the heavy iron radiators that heated the building in the winter and touched the ring to it. Instantly there was a loud, snap, as a long blue spark jumped from the ring to the radiator. The professor speaking so matter of factually said, " This one seems to be working just fine. Now that it is discharged, I should be able to handle it with no trouble at all." As he took it into his bare hand and squeezed it, he said, "See perfectly harmless, that is for the time being."

Placing it back down on the desk, he put a paper clip about five inches away from the ring and instantly, the clip was pulled to the ring and stuck to it.

"Yep, she is still highly magnetized, even without an electrical charge. The ring designer must have used magnetic metals of some kind," the professor said continuing his experimenting.

With absolute confidence, he picked up the master ring and the slave ring he was working with, holding them both in either hand managed to fit one rings hook into the other rings eye and they were both securely attached. "Well that settles that, they do fit perfectly. I wish every other piece of this puzzle went together as easy."

Taking the other three slave rings, one at a time, with the pencil, he touched them to the metal radiator and each discharged on it with the same loud snap and blue spark. However, one of them zapped the radiator so strongly that where the spark hit it left a small hole and a singed spot. Acting rather satisfied with the demonstration, the professor said, "There that should render them harmless for a while, although I would still be careful around them because I do not know how fast they may recharge. I would say a lot depends on how much static electricity there is present in the atmosphere."

I happened to glance at my office wall clock. It read 7 o'clock, and not only had everyone left the bank for the day, but we had worked straight through lunch hour. I asked the professor if he would like to come to my home for dinner, but he said he would rather stay in my office if I did not mind. He wanted to complete the translation of the rest of the Hebrew texts and he would just get a snack from the bank's office break room. I could tell the old guy was mesmerized by his findings and extremely interested in the books and rings.

I said good night to the professor and headed home for some of Peggy Sue's great home cooking. All of a sudden, I was utterly famished.

After a wonderful meal and fun with the kids, they were off to bed as it was quite late, near midnight. Peggy Sue and I were alone in our bedroom sitting on the bed after a nice hot shower, and I noticed how beautiful she was. I laid her down on the cool sheets and kissed her and then placed my head on her chest. The next thing I knew she was shaking me to get up, it was morning. Would you believe that, I had fallen to sleep with one of her breasts in my mouth? That takes the cake. And I thought that the professor was the only one mesmerized by the books and rings!

The next morning after my coffee and a couple pieces of toast, I slithered out the front door, like the low down dirty snake, Peggy Sue had called me that morning after I had left her in such a heighten sexual state the night before. Pledging to make it up to her, I gave her a hot kiss on the mouth as a prelude of things to come. With that promise lingering on her lips, I hurried away to the bank and the day's mysteries.

Driving through a light rain and arriving there at opening time, I was surprised to find a rather large crowd of people waiting to see me. Martha had already given them coffee and doughnuts as if she knew the group was coming. They had made themselves comfortable in the outer office near the front door so it was impossible for me to get by without them seeing me. What the professor had discovered during the night would just have to wait until I could get rid of the visitors.

I noticed Renaldo sitting next to Martha. When he saw me walk in, he rose up and headed in my direction with a wide grin on his face. I readied my arm for a good pumping as thanks for the loan that Martha had surely given him and very surprised when he said, "Mr. Zack, I come here to speak for the poor people from the small village of Vera Dulche, in Mexico. Just then, all of the visitors, upon hearing their village name, jumped to their feet and started to cheer as loud as they could.

Renaldo raised his hands for quite then motioned to an older couple standing respectfully just behind him and said, "Pedro, Maria, por favor." The couple approached me each holding items in their hands, the lady, Maria spoke first in her native tongue, Spanish, "Patron Zack, **por favor,** (acepte esta colcha de cama, tejido y hecho de mano, y dado por la gente de Vera Dulche con el deseo que la colcha le trae a usted el mismo cari□o que usted a dado a nuestra aldea. Muchas gracias.)

Bowing slightly she hands me the handed me a beautifully quilted blanket. Before I could say a thing, Renaldo proceeds to interpret what was just said, "Mr. Zack, Maria hopes that this hand woven quilt will bring you as much warmth as you have shown to our small village of Vera Dulche.

Now Pedro would like to say a few words to you, Pedro,"

The old guy dressed in Mexican style ranch clothing stepped up to me, removed his hat and said slowly, **"Por favor,** Senor Zack, Los mayores de la aldea escribieron un proclamaci□n y yo, el alcalde, soy orgulloso presentarle, Senor Heikel, el proclamac□n por el pr□stamo que le dio a Renaldo y los otros Mexicanos que viven en Palomino, Texas. Nuestra aldea ser□ siempre agradecido. El dinero, sesenta y seis mil dolares Americanos, fue usado para construir una refiner□a de agua tratamiento nuevo para nuestra aldea. Ahora, todos podr□n gozar agua pura, sin germenes y bacteria, que mas antes la gente tuvieron que aguantar. Muchas gracias y que Dios le bendiga."

Renaldo wasted no time and went right into his translation saying, "The village elders of Vera Dulche have written this proclamation and I, the mayor am proud to present it to you, Senor Zack Heikel for the loan of money to Renaldo and other Mexicans. Our village will be forever grateful. The money, sixty six thousand American Dollars was put to good use building a new water treatment plant for our village. Now every person enjoys pure drinking water free from all the germs and bacteria, which they have had to endure in the past. Muchas Gracias and God bless you."

As Renaldo was translating the Spanish into English, I was completely confused, and did not remember making any loans to Mexico. Just then Martha came to stand by my side and placed her hand on my shoulder. The moment Renaldo finished his recital, Martha spoke even before I can utter a word, "Mr Heikel I can explain everything. My parents are from this small village in Mexico and I was very aware of their plight. Every year several children would come down with diseases caused by water born bacteria and some die. One of which was my cousin. I knew they needed a new water treatment plant but they did not have access to the money, although they owned plenty of land. I saw how generous you have been about loaning money to some of our Hispanic farmers. So I took the liberty of making loans to Renaldo and three other Latino farmers under the false pretense of making improvements to their farms, when the money was really earmarked to be sent to Vera Dulche for the treatment plant. Please understand that I realize I was beyond my authority but I knew if you understood their situation, you would approve the funds but I could not take the chance you might say no. Please do not worry about the money. You can put your mind at ease because all the loans have been re-paid with interest. I do want to say personally that I think it is just wonderful of you to loan out your personal cash that you have in those footlockers. Its quite unusual for a rich person like yourself to have any concern about poor people. I too would like to say, God bless you, Mr. Zack. Now do with me as you will, I'm ready to face the punishment for my actions."

For a moment, I could not speak and was breathless It was as if someone had punched me right in the chest. I looked around at all the smiling faces, and then at my hands holding the proclamation and the quilt.

Inhaling deeply, I smiled and said to Martha, "First of all I did not know you were aware I had cash in the footlockers. All the time you went right along with my flimsy excuse of using federal overnight funds to grant some of those questionable loans. I want to thank you for that. I really do want to help those less fortunate than you or I. As for you facing any punishment, forget about it. You are the one who should have been given these gifts. Now that all the loans have been repaid, I only ask that you promise in the future, please don't make any international loans. I'm not sure our bank charter allows us to do so, lets use the money here in Palomino, where plenty of folks need a helping hand. Do I have your promise?...... Martha do I?"

Hesitating a few seconds, Martha wiping tears from her eyes, smiled and said, "Yes Mr. Zack I promise." In addition, she proceeded to throw her arms around my neck and plant a real big kiss on my cheek. Then as if embarrassed she said, "Oh I'm sorry for that Sir."

I just smiled back at her and patting her on the back said, " You needn't be.

Now if these festivities are over, could we get back to work?"

As she hurried towards her guests she said "Yes Sir, right away!"

Still carrying my gifts from the villagers, I staggered into my office overwhelmed by the tribute the villagers had paid me.

The professor, as usual, was sitting at the desk working on the book. He looked up from his task and said, "Good morning, Zack! I hope you have not had your coffee yet; I sure do need a cup. Say! What's that you have there?"

Placing the quilt and proclamation on a corner of my desk I said, "It seems I have been made an honorary citizen of a village in Mexico. I never even heard of the place before today. It's a rather complicated story I will have to tell you some time. But right now, I think I could use a cup of java myself. I'll make a fresh pot. Did you discover anything exciting last night?"

The professor had walked over to my desk and was admiring the hand stitched quilt, "Mighty nice work and what beautiful colors.

Yes, I did do a little experimenting with the slave rings, those babies do charge up quite rapidly. Late last night after I had discharged one of them, a mere twenty minutes later it had regained enough power to make a small spark when I placed it against the radiator. I would say however that to build up a charge of twelve thousand volts it would take maybe a couple of days. That's really all I got done last night. I worked a little on the translations and wanted to finish the rest of the Hebrew but I wound up falling asleep on the sofa, I guess I was just mentally exhausted. That loud cheer I heard coming from the outer office woke me from my sleep. Coffee ready yet?"

I did the honors and poured each of us a hot cup. The professor, sipping his, walked over to the desk where the rings lay, sat down his cup and with the pencil picked up one of the rings and headed toward the metal radiator saying, "I wonder how much she is holding now after sitting most of the night?" Having said that he touched the ring to the metal and sure enough, there was the customary snap and blue spark.

"I still can't figure the mechanism involved here to enable this thing to gather electricity. Maybe you and I could do a few simple experiments with them, which may help me to better understand their function."

"Sure if you think its safe. I sure as hell do not want to get zapped again. I know how it feels, hurts like crazy. I did mention to you that I did get shocked by one of those things when I inadvertently slipped it on my finger, didn't I." I said looking at my finger where a small scar remained.

"No Zack, I don't remember you telling me that. Could you please explain exactly what happened?'

"Well professor, several months ago while I was cleaning up some fluid that had spilled from the glass jar containing the severed fingers, I was curious and took one of the rings from the jar. I went into my office and after cleaning it off, just slid it on my finger to see how it looked on my hand. All of a sudden, the ring became extremely hot and I felt a tremendous jolt in my arm as I jerked it from my hand. The next thing I remembered was Martha standing over me offering a sip of water. I think I passed out. Here, take a look at my hand you can still see the scar on my finger."

The professor shaking his head from side to side while looking at my hand said, "Zack, you are luck to be alive. You managed to pull that ring off just in time, another second or so and I am sure you would have suffered the same fate as the guy that broke into your bank The one that wound up dead.

Now we know why the inscriptions in the book caution the users constantly about being careful. Something we will definitely be during our experimenting."

The professor as if thinking about his work last night and somewhat changing the subject said, "Some of my work last night was in a section written in a very old Hebrew dialect, which I had trouble deciphering. It kept referring to six different shaped triangles, right angles, isosceles, equilateral, obtuse, acute and scalene. I know what these are, but I still can't understand how they were written down in this book, because there was no way the people of that era could have understood what the words represented. However, there they are in bold print and appear to be used in some very advanced mathematical equations. The term, ein soff, which means infinity also was mentioned. Again, I am not sure in what kind of application.

You see back in Old Testament times, the Hebrew language did not have words for numbers instead, they used individual letters of their alphabet as numbers. For example using English, A would represent 1, B would be 2 and so on. Zack look in the Bible and you will find a whole book devoted to Numbers and there are several examples of how the ancients used words as numbers.

I know it sounds complicated and to many of us it is, however another Bible verse, Genesis 11: 1–9 about the Tower of Babel pretty much sums up Gods intensions about confusing man and language.

I bet you did not expect a Bible lesson today did you. However, the deeper I go in your old book the more I am convinced these writings and rings are somehow Biblically connected."

Picking up my bible and reading the verse in Genesis, I said, "Yes I have read this before but it never had the impact on me it just did. I guess this explains why there are so many different languages spoken today. I am sitting here thinking that if it wasn't for you and your understanding Hebrew, I would never have been able to realize what I had found. You certainly have shed a lot of light on the books meaning and the rings functions but we still don't know what the rings are capable of doing."

"You're right Zack, we don't, but we have a pretty good idea. I think its time we did a little experiment. My curiosity is going wild anyway," the professor said as he walked over to the table were the rings lay. Taking the wooden pencil, he carried each ring over to the metal radiator and touched them against it. Each time he did they made the blue spark and sound. He then felt each ring and deemed them safe to handle. Taking the master ring and one of the slave rings, he hooked them together, then adding the remaining three rings by connecting them with their hooks and eyes. He lay the almost formed circle the rings made on the wooden desk.

The professor acting as if he knew exactly what he was doing took four paper clips from my desk and after straightening them twisted them together and said, "I think we will have to improvise a little here. I will use these clips as a homemade heavy wire and connect the rings with it, completing the circle. All we have to do is stand back and see what happens."

The rings formed a neat circle held together by the paper clips taking the place of the missing link. We stood a safe distance away and waited......and waited, and waited. Nothing happened. Twenty or thirty minutes went by and still nothing. The professor quipped, "I must have done a good job of discharging them, they're dead as a door nail. Zack, why don't we go get a bite to eat and give them a chance to charge up a little. Maybe when we get back something might take place."

As we neared the front door of the bank, Martha, who is always on the ball said, "Mr. Zack you better take the umbrella it's supposed to rain quite heavy." I did as she suggested although I felt I did not need it as it was only sprinkling. The professor and I walked quickly across the street to the cantina.

Finding seats at an empty table, I gave the waitress an order for a couple of roast beef sandwiches and iced tea. Just as our food arrived a few minutes later, I felt someone pat me on the back and heard a familiar voice. Looking up there stood Herman Fletcher, who said with a smile, "Well I see ya'll are still in one piece, those crazy Mexicans ain't tore ya up yet. Ya'll must be doin something right cuz ya looks pretty healthy."

"Well hello there Herman, what are you doing in town?" I said standing and shaking his hand.

"I'm on my way down to Brownsville and thought I would pay a visit to my old hometown. I see nothing has changed, cepting when I passed Wes's ranch I saw a couple of big oil rigs a pumping like hell."

Sitting back down to eat I said, "Yea! They have hit a nice reservoir. Wes told me one of them is making over several hundred barrels a day. I think they should be drilling on my place in a few months. Oh! By the way, this is Professor Schweitzer, Professor shake hands with Herman Fletcher the man who used to own my bank"

The two men shook and I asked Herman to join us. He declined, saying he had already eaten and should be getting on his way but inquired if the doctor was a geologist with the oil companies.

Not wanting to let the cat out of the bag, about the real meaning of the professor's presence, I hurriedly said, "No, he is an old friend from Michigan."

Herman taking his Stetson from the hat rack and placing it on his head said, "I thought he might be from Mobil Oil here to tell you about all the oil they had discovered on my old place. Maybe I sold it too soon, hey Zack? Well I best be moseying along. It's a mighty long haul down to the border. Say howdy to Wes fur me when next ya sees him. Ya'll take care now, ya hear" he said as he turned and walked away.

I told the professor that not only had I bought the bank from Herman I had also purchased his old homestead where the professor had been staying.

Laughing he said, "What do you mean, has been staying! Why I haven't been out there in three days. I'm beginning to smell like an over ripe banana and need a bath in the worse way. Some of your wife's good home cooking would be great too. This restaurant food is killing my stomach and so is that damn stuff out of the vending machine in your banks break room. Tonight I'm going home with you."

The professor and I finished eating our sandwiches then had a nice piece of key lime pie and more coffee. We then spent the next thirty minutes or so talking about, what else, the book.

Thinking it was about time to get back to the bank, we paid our lunch tab and headed for the door. Opening it, we found dark overcast skies and it was pouring like hell. Martha was right as usual so I unfurled the umbrella and holding it over our heads, we raced through the downpour back to the bank.

Walking through the bank lobby we noticed all the lights had been switched off because of the storm. When I unlocked and opened the door to my darkened office, the professor and I were astonished to see a red haze filling the room. Stepping in we saw the source of the haze. It was coming from a ruby red, plasma-like bubble of pulsating light, emitting from the circle of rings.

Fascinated, we carefully approached the quivering red orb, which was hovering about twelve inches over the circle of rings. Peering closer into the bubble we saw a blurry image begin to take shape. We stared down in amazement at what seemed to be a hazy landscape suddenly materializing before our eyes in the floating crimson plasma.

Gazing as if transfixed we began to make out something else taking shape on the landscape and in a few seconds we saw the outline of a bearded MAN dressed all in black sitting in a chair looking down. As he came closer and more into focus, we saw his face and his eyes were looking down into his hand as if he was studying something, then we saw it, *A RING*.

It was exactly like the master ring I had in my possession except the stone was different. The dark stranger looked up from what he was focusing on and with his bearded face looming much larger, stared right into my eyes. Instantly, the hair on the back of my neck stood straight up because the smirk in his gaze scared the hell out of me.

Suddenly there was a loud pop and a blue spark emitted from the side of my circle of rings, our makeshift connection, the four paper clips had shorted out and just as sudden the red bubble holding the image of the man evaporated instantly into thin air.

The professor and I stood there as if hypnotized, wondering what had just happened.

"My God! Professor what the hell was that," was all I could get out of my mouth.

The professor being more observant and analytical than I said, "That is incredible! All the while we were looking at that guy in the bubble, he was looking at us in his ring. This whole scene is bordering on the occult or something meta-physical. It is possible however, that a high voltage plasma may have formed over the rings and its static force field could have temporally disrupted our brain waves and made us hallucinate.

"Professor, you know that's bullshit, you saw it and so did I, and it was real. We have discovered something other-worldly! What or who I don't know, but I'm so scared right now I have a good mind to get rid of these damn rings and that god awful book for good.

Just then, the professor said, "That would be a very foolish thing to do. Who knows how this may help mankind if we can only figure out just what it was. They could somehow be very beneficial. Here let me show you they are not dangerous at this time, they have been completely discharged." While saying this, he proceeded to pick up one of the slave rings to demonstrate that it was harmless, and it was. He held it in his hand and said, "See completely neutral. It's so docile I could even wear it," and he nonchalantly slips it on his finger. All the while, I was yelling to him not to do it.

It was the worst thing he could have done because at that precise moment, a loud crashing lightning bolt struck nearby and instantly charged the ring to full capacity. It lit-up with a very bright orange glow and began to smoke and so did the professor's hand. In a second, sparks were shooting out of his nostrils and his hair caught fire. Suddenly his whole body was illuminated as it turned a brilliant red and became transparent. I could see his bones and internal organs as he shook violently. His mouth was wide open but the only sound emitting from it was a hissing made by a stream of steam-like vapor. He fell to the floor and his entire body burst into flames and in a few seconds became nothing but bones and a bubbling mass of boiling bloody ooze.

It happened so fast I could not move a finger to help my friend! I just stood there paralyzed. All that lay on the floor was a pile of smoldering ashes. When my thought processes returned, I realized I had just witnessed a human being, spontaneously combusted, obviously the same thing that killed the bank burglar and probably old man Levison at the mansion in Michigan. What a hell of a way to solve a problem, giving your life. My friend, Professor Otto Schweitzer was dead. He died proving a point, a scientist to the very end.

I looked around the room nothing was singed or damaged by the flames and even the cement tile where the body had fallen was not burned. The only tell tale sign left that a person had been electrocuted was a pile of ashes and the nauseating smell of burnt flesh that still lingered in the air. Opening one of the office windows, I then fell into a chair racking my brain for an answer of what to do now. Then I suddenly realized what a horrible episode had just happened right before my eyes. I had actually seen someone die. Someone whom I was having lunch and laughing with only an hour before and who was now dead. I felt something warm fall onto my hand, it was wet, and then I realized I was crying.

I sat in that dazed stupor for a long time and when I heard the bank employees starting their auto engines and leaving the bank parking lot. I looked at my office clock it was after five. It was still not clear in my mind what my next move would be. One thing was sure, I had to clean up the ashes from the floor, if I could stomach it.

Walking out to the broom closet I grabbed a mop, dust pan, broom and several plastic bags. Then went into the safe and retrieved one of the empty footlockers to use as a receptacle for the professors remains.

Reverently, I approached the now cool pile of ashes embedded with small pieces of bone. The blackened skull's empty eye sockets seemed to peer hauntingly into my face, sending shivers up my spine.

To steady myself and to show respect, I bowed my head and said a silent prayer for my friend who had just given his life in the pursuit of scientific answers into the unknown questions of ages past.

Carefully I put the skull into a plastic bag and rolled it up, then swept the remaining ashes into the dustpan and placed them gently into other bags. After filling several,

I set them in the footlocker as respectfully as possible. I was just about to complete the gross task of putting the ashes into the make shift crematory container when my broom pushed a small remaining pile of soot, and sent an object bouncing noisily across the concrete floor, it was the *RING*.

Walking over to where it lay, I stared down at the shiny and still beautiful piece of jewelry. It was difficult for me to believe that it was as lethal as it was. It looked so harmless when in reality it had killed at least three people that I knew of, to date, old man Levison, the burglar and now the professor. A thought crossed my mind that flushing it down the toilet would do away with it nicely. Them I remembered the professor saying the rings might be of some unknown benefit to mankind and he was right. As bad as I wanted to get the artifacts permanently out of my life, I resisted the urge. Not taking a chance with my safety, I used the wooden pencil to pick up the ring and place it with the others on the desk. I closed the footlocker containing the ashes, dragged it into the vault, placed it in a corner, then marking it with a yellow check mark so I could identify it at a later time, piled several of the empty lockers on top of it.

The cleanup, which I considered more of a burial, took me about two hours and it was getting late. Peggy Sue would be expecting me home for dinner by now. Picking up the phone I called her. As I listened to the telephone ring and waited impatiently for her to answer, I knew I was going to have to lie to her, which I hated to do in the worst way. However, revealing how the professor had died would certainly cause her to grieve for the nice old guy but would also cause her to question my keeping the killing jewelry in my possession. The professor's death and now my own fascination with the mystery of the artifacts, made me more than determined to continue the research into the meaning of the book and the rings, if for no other reason than that the professor would not have given his life in vain.

"Hello," Peggy Sue answered.

"Hi honey, its me. I guess you will have to go ahead and eat without me. It seems that the professor has to return to Ann Arbor tonight so I am taking him up to San Antonio to catch the nine o'clock plane. Please don't wait up for me, if I am too tired to drive back I may get a room at the airport and spend the night there."

"Oh! Zack! I fixed your favorite meal. Well if it can't be helped, okay. Nevertheless, please drive safety and I will probably see you tomorrow. I know it's a long drive." Peggy said as usual worrying about my welfare as she hung up the phone.

The first thing I did when I got off the telephone was gathering all the rings and placed them in the old leather briefcase. Taking the book as well as the case, I put them both back into the safe deposit box and vowed not to remove them again unless I had a damned good reason to do so.

Returning to my office and turning out the lights I sprawled out on the sofa and waited for sleep to come, which it did almost instantly, I was so completely mentally and physically exhausted. However, my sleep was very fitful and suddenly I woke wide-awake screaming aloud. I had been in the middle of a bad dream where I could see the professor inside the red bubble wrestling with the mystery man who was laughing loudly, while attempting to attach two high voltage lines coming out of a huge machine onto the professor. Then suddenly touching the professor with both of them, he burst into flames and I could once again see him burning horribly.

Shaken, I lay there sweating, hoping and praying that I would never have that nightmare again. But I knew that was next to impossible. The image of the professors' death was so imprinted on my brain that I was afraid I would be seeing it for the rest of my life.

Sometime in the night I must have fallen back to sleep because a loud knock at my office door woke me from a deep sleep. I opened my eyes and saw bright sunlight coming thought the windows. It was morning. When I sat up and went to answer the door I almost fell on my face. I was extremely dizzy, and felt as if I might throw-up.

Staggering to the door and opening it, I found Martha standing there asking why I had come in to the office so early and could she do anything for me. As I reached out toward her, I saw the floor coming up to hit me flush in the face, knocking me unconscious. When I came too, Wes was applying wet towels to my forehead and working over me.

"Boy, y'all gave us quite a scare. And that bump on your head is goin to be ahurtin fur some time acomein. Whats a puzzelin me is why yer face is so red. Kind of like a bad sunburn."

Grabbing him by the arm I said, "Wes please get me home as fast as you can, I need to get in bed. I have got the worst headache I have ever had and feel like I'm going to die."

"Ya needin be worry bout that. I took y'all blood pressure and its okay. I'm a thinkin y'all just needs some rest. Here take these two aspirins." Wes said.

I did as he asked and swallowed the aspirins, then heard him call out to Renaldo who was in the bank making a deposit and he asked him for a hand in getting me out to Wes's car.

Arriving at the house, Peggy Sue came running out to the car all in a panic while asking Wes about my condition and wheather I had been in an accident. I heard Wes tell her he thought that I had just fainted from overwork, but he had no explanation for my very red face.

The two of them managed to get me into the bedroom just in time because I fell spread eagle across the bed and passed out again.

When I regained consciousness, I was nicely tucked into bed and in my pajamas. Peggy Sue was sitting by my side and there were several medicine bottles and a pitcher of water on the nightstand. She smiled at me and asked if I was hungry.

"Hungry? Are you kidding, I'm famished. What time is it anyway?" I said trying to sit up.

"Now don't you worry about what time it is. Here, try to swallow some of this tomato soup I've made for you," Peggy said while holding a spoon full to my mouth.

When that soup hit my tongue my taste buds went crazy, I can't ever remember tomato soup tasting so wonderful and told Peggy Sue to please give me more. Eating the whole bowl, I asked her what she had put into the soup because it was so tasty, or was it because I was just so hungry that anything would have tasted really great.

"Well Zack, honey! You are hungry because you have not eaten for four days."

"Four days!" I said startled, "What the hell happened to me?"

"Well we are not sure." Peggy continued to tell me. "When you did not wake up the day after Wes and I put you in bed we became very concerned and Wes called Seadrift and got Dr. Edwin to make a house call.

The first thing he did was take your blood pressure because he was puzzled by the redness of your face, but it was fine. He then took some blood from your arm for him to analyze when he got back to his office. He gave me these pain pills for you to take and ointment for me to apply to the small sores on your face and hands. He said he could not make a diagnosis until he ran the tests on the blood, but seemed to think you had been exposed to some kind of very high heat source or, possibly x-rays or maybe even radiation. However, he did question how this could even be possible because nothing like these sources existed anywhere in this area. When he called me back two days later, he told me that your red blood cell count was very low, and you were anemic, just as the blood would be if you were exposed to something radioactive. When I told him you were still out cold, he became very concerned and said if you are not awake by today he would have to place you into the hospital.

Honey, its so wonderful to have you back with us again. You had me so worried. When you feel better, you will have to tell me exactly what happened to you that night. Now you rest, I am going to call Dr. Edwin and tell him you are awake and talking."

When Peggy returned to my bedside, I felt wide awake and asked for more food, she hurried to the kitchen and retuned in no time with a nice tuna fish sandwich and hot tea. After I had wolfed those down, she sat on the edge of my bed and asked me the question I was afraid she would, "What happened to you?"

I was however ready for it, because I had been thinking up another lie that I could make sound believable.

"Well Honey." I started out, "You see when I took Professor Schweitzer to the airport they did not let the passengers use the boarding ramp, instead they had to go out onto the field to board. I was allowed to be with the professor because he was not feeling well. Anyway, when the plane started one of it's engines I was just coming down the stairway from helping the professor to his seat and I felt this awful blast of hot air from the jet engine and I think this is what could have possibility burned my face and maybe even somehow damaged my lungs. I remember being a little out of breath as I drove home that night. Then not wanting to disturb you and the kids went to my office, fell asleep on the sofa, and woke up the next morning sick as hell. That's when Wes had to give me some help."

Suddenly, the hot soup and tea hit my bowels and I had to use the bathroom. I was so unsteady when I stood that Peggy Sue had to help me into the toilet. After taking care of natures business, I passed the bathroom mirror and glanced in, my god I thought, is that me. My appearance scared me almost out of my wits. My face was still full of small running sores and was beet red. My hair was stiff and standing on end. My eyes were bloodshot and had dark circles under them. I actually felt like I was looking into my very soul and seeing some kind of a demon peering back at me in my mirror. I turned away in horror and stumbled back into bed where I would stay for six more days, my precious wife tending me all this time.

More than two weeks had passed since the professor's violent death and my fainting incident before I could return to work at the bank. Even though I was weak as a kitten, I felt it imperative that I return to the office. Martha, even as efficient as she was could not run the bank by herself. Wes had been super busy at the pharmacy and could not look in that much on the bank's operations and Peggy Sue had been preoccupied with caring for me, as well as talking with Mobil Oil surveyors about drillings sites on our ranch.

Arriving at the bank about an hour late, I was overwhelmed by the reception I received. All the employees were standing inside the front door and clapping as I entered. There was a huge sign hanging on the teller cages stating, "Welcome Back Mr. Zack." Several of the office staff shook my hand and Martha escorted me into my office where a large chocolate cake she had made and three urns of coffee sat on one of the tables.

Everyone was milling around pouring coffee and cutting the cake. I thought how wonderful it was to return to work and the real world, not the one I had been living in for several weeks studying that book and those rings. Then it hit me, those rings, they had been sitting on this very table where the chocolate cake was now resting and exactly where the red ball had formed. The office staff was all laughing telling jokes and having a good old time, standing on the very spot where the professor's body had fallen on that fateful night.

Hoping that if I focused my mind on work I would be able to forget about that dreadful night, I turned to Martha, who as usual was right at my elbow and asked her, "Well Martha, how have things been going?"

Smiling, which she always did, she said, "Everything is under control, I've made all the loans that I could but there are several that need your approval. Cash flow has been excellent and we have acquired about two-dozen new depositors in the last week. Oh, I did spend a little money and had the drapes taken down and dry-cleaned and I had the crack in the front window repaired. Other than that everything is going well."

I thought to myself, "This women is too good to be true." Then speaking out loud I asked her, "Martha, how long have you been employed here at the bank?"

She hesitated momentarily as if in deep thought then said, "Well let's see I worked for Mr. Fletcher for over twenty one years and now for you for almost two, so I guess it is just about twenty three years. Why do you ask?"

"Oh I don't know. You just seem to be so competent I was sure you had been here a long time but I was uncertain about the exact number of years. Something else I would like to know is when was the last time you had a raise in salary. In fact, I don't even know what you earn, seeing that you sign all the employees pay checks as well as your own."

"Why Sir, its three hundred and seventy-five dollars a week. I recollect the last time I had an increase was about four years ago. But I must say I get along quite well on my present wage."

"Oh! Is that so! Well starting next week you make your payroll check out for six hundred dollars. A good hard working person like yourself needs to be compensated for all her efforts, not to mention you bake a great chocolate cake. By the way, the bank can afford to pay you that increase, can't we?"

Her smile got much bigger and she said, "Why thank you sir, very much. I have been envying those new Fords at Mr. Brown's, maybe now I can get myself a new car. Oh, also we certainly can afford my raise in salary we are doing more business than we have ever done. Whether you realize it or not, people in town like you very much. You and your generosity are the cause of the banks tremendous improvement."

Her generous compliments, the friendly atmosphere here at the bank, plus all my great employees things were wonderful for the first time in a long while. I felt terrific. My bank, as Martha had just told me, was doing fine. My kids were doing well at school, my friend; Wes had oil checks coming out of every pocket. But most of all, I had my Peggy Sue. A person could not ask for a better life than the one I had. I just wished I was enjoying it more and vowed to do just that, starting today I would forget about those evil things I had locked in the safe deposit box and just let them rust and decay and hopefully turn to dust. However, I did not really believe my vow would ever come true, because those rings were here to stay and someday I would have to face them again.

Over the next several weeks my life could not have been better. My health improved and I was again enjoying my job as the president of the bank. I was back to having my customary lunch at the Palomino diner with my friend Wes, who was now occasionally picking up the check he was so flush with money.

Peggy Sue and I had even started talking about a vacation for just the two of us, down to some romantic island in the Caribbean.

I should have known that things could not have stayed that way for very long.

One day when I had just returned from lunch, Martha came into my office through the now continuously open door and told me that a man had been at the bank asking for me. When she told him I was out, he said he would be back that afternoon. I asked her what did he look like and she said he was elderly with a long beard, wore a long black robe, a black hat with a wide brim, and walked with a cane. Somehow, her description of the visitor did not bode well with me and I sensed problems. This guy could be a private detective from Michigan dressed as a priest or someone else looking for the professor, maybe even the cops in disguise. After all, he would have been missing from his job at the university for over several weeks. Even though the professor did not have any family, people just do not disappear into thin air. Someone up North had to be getting suspicious.

All that afternoon I thought about the old guy and he kept popping up in the back of my head and it was difficult to do my work properly, but I stumbled through the day. It was just before closing time when Martha came into my office and told me the stranger was here again. I asked her if he had given his name and she said he had not, but mentioned that I would know him. This really puzzled me, so I told her to show him into my office. I knew I had to confront this guy head on and not act as if I was guilty of some offense, because I was satisfied in my own mind that what had happened to the professor was in fact an accident. Although I probably would have a hard time proving it, unless I opened Pandora's Box completely and told the whole story of the book, our experiments with the rings and the huge stash of money I had found in the basement of the old mansion on the hill. With that in mind and in order not to incriminate myself in anyway I was determined not to divulge any information at all. I would just say the professor had been here, stayed a few days and had left rather suddenly, for some unknown reason. I would not be to far from the truth with that statement. Just then, my visitor came hobbling into my office and the moment I saw him I realized the few short weeks of my tranquility was about to end.

He was a short man and he drug his left foot ever so slightly. He steadied himself with an odd looking cane in one hand and in the other he held a black suitcase. He wore a long flowing black robe with ritual fringes. Around his neck hung a Star of David on a silver chain and on his head a very dusty black hat, not a western style one, but one that would have been fashionable in the Middle East. I could not see his face real well because the brim of the hat obscured it and he held his head down, as if looking at the floor. As he neared my desk, he did not stop in front of it as is customary, but walked around to my side of the desk and stood right beside me. As he did, I held out my hand to greet him and said, "How do you do, my name is, and before I could finish my sentence he interrupted me, looked up and said, "Yes I know, Zack Heikel."

He did not take my hand and at first I thought he might have not seen it. However, looking at my outstretched hand he made the strange comment that he never touches anyone. Not only did this sound bizarre, he also looked strange and somehow vaguely familiar but I could not place the face. Then I asked, "I'm sorry sir, you seem to know me but I can't quite place you. Where have we met?"

It was at that moment in his response that I knew my nightmare of the black night several weeks ago had returned to haunt me. He casually looked around my office and then said, "Why, we have met right here in this room."

This shocked me to the point where I almost gagged as I swallowed hard, but I kept my composure and said, "I don't quite understand, you say right here in this room? I don't ever remember seeing you here."

"Yes you did one night not too long ago. You saw me and I saw you through one of these." He held up his right hand and there on this index finger was a replica of,.... *MY RING*.

I was so startled I could barely get out my next expression, "Where did you get that?"

Acting as if I did not know what he meant and still trying to hide my knowledge of the rings.

"Oh, come now Zack, there is no reason to pretend you do not know what this represents. You know exactly what this ring is, what it means, and how it operates.

Becoming a little irritated I said, " So what if I do. Okay, if you know so much about me and say we met somehow through your ring, then tell me then how did you locate me?"

He paused for a moment, looked up at the wall over my desk and pointing with his finger said, "I found you because I saw that!"

Looking over my desk I saw how he had pin-pointed my location, it was a big seal of The State of Texas with bold type that read, State Bank Of Palomino, Texas. The guy knew what he was talking about. He had definitely seen me in his ring. Then it came to me, his face, it was the one the professor and I had seen in the red bubble that night.

Trying to be tough I said to the oddly dressed Jew, "Look old man, are you going to tell me who the hell you are and what you want from me or do I have to throw you bodily out of my office."

Setting his suitcase on my desk he said, "That would be a very big mistake for you to try. You are aware, I am sure, of the power I have right here on my finger."

He then took off his hat and I got a good look at his face. I was shocked at how just removing his hat changed his appearance. Because on the top of his forehead, held by bands was a small black box, about the size of a pack of cigarettes. His hair was strange and not normal because for a man his age it was all black and woven in tight ringlets. It fell down to well below his shoulders and must have been three feet long. The portion of his face not covered by the beard was wrinkled and scared and had ugly warts in several places on his cheeks. His nose was long and bent. He looked scary as hell and must have been at least eighty years old.

He smiled slightly though long pearly teeth and said, "Zack, my name is Rabbi Asher Levison and I have been looking for the ring or the messenger since it had last contacted me from somewhere in Michigan over forty years ago. I was beginning to think all the rings had been lost forever, rendering mine worthless. Then after all these years, one evening several weeks ago my master ring was activated for just a few seconds. That is when I saw you and that other person's image. I knew instantly that you, unlike I, had enough rings to form a circle and create a Xenon plasma."

"Hold it right there!" I said becoming irritated. "There is no way you could have been looking for me that long, I'm only thirty eight years old. What are you trying to pull over on me?"

The old man almost caused me to faint when he said, "The day you discovered those rings, Mr. Heikel, you became as one of us, a protector, even though you were not aware of it at the time. You were captivated and then obsessed with keeping the rings and protecting them at all costs, even using force if necessary. Then by discovering how to activate the circle of rings you took the place of the former person who had them in his possession. Now that you have discovered their secret powers, you will have to assume your duties."

Even though I was shaking like hell I said, "Well it's certainly true that when I discovered the rings I was very taken with them and eventually the thought of even killing a person to keep them enter my mind. Thank God, I never had to act on that thought, but you are right I was fascinated with them. Oh! And what's this, one of us, bullshit you're talking about? And what do you mean my duty?"

Opening his suitcase almost answered one of my questions by itself, because when I saw its contents I realized he was right, we did have something in common. Sitting there in velvet holders was four *SLAVE RINGS, ONE MASTER RING* with a beautiful emerald stone in its center and the word, "*JUDAH*" engraved below the gem.

In the other side of his case sitting by itself was, *A SILVER PLATED BOOK*. It was similar to the one in my possession although minus the wooden book that protected mine. These objects were our connection; we did share the same problems and evidently the same responsibility.

He then said to me, "You, like myself, are the protectors of the rings. Like it or not it is your destiny. The day years ago when you found the rings in that old abandoned vault, you became responsible for the safety of them. When you placed one of the rings on your finger a few months ago and survived the discharge, you were, unbeknownst to you at that time, possessed by the power of the ring. I know you are finding this very hard to believe, that they have that kind of power, but they do. Can't you see! It was all preordained, planned out very long ago. You were destined to find them. Now you must do your duty."

I felt my heart racing and blurted out, "I still don't understand. What do you mean, my duty?"

Tapping on his suitcase with his long fingernails, he said to me in a different tone of voice and almost as if he was speaking in old English, "Go get thee your rings and come back to me. I will show thee the beginning of your quest."

"The beginning of my quest," I muttered under my breath. "Somehow, I am going to wake up and find this is nothing but a dream," I went to the vault to retrieve the rings.

Returning with my briefcase that held the book and the five rings, I found that I had not been dreaming. The old strange visitor was still standing in the same place he had been when I had left the room. Handing him the brief-case, he took it and carefully emptied its contents onto the desk without touching the rings. Instantly he stated that there was no need for the German pistol because I was in no danger from him. I quickly said that the gun was not for my protection but was used as a key to un-lock the metal book inside the wooden one.

He smiled, picked up the metal book he had brought with him and showed me that the real key made eons ago for the lock was built right into its cover. It could also be used to safely handle the rings. He proceeded to slide out a long slender key from a groove in the binding of his book. It was in the same location which on my book was empty, its key evidentially having been lost sometime in the distance past. As he used the key to unlock his book he said that there were many mysteries he would solve for me much more sensational than the key.

Looking closely at his open book, I could see that the wording was the same as in mine. The professor had been right, the book was nothing more than an instruc-tion manual on how the rings were to be activated and to what purpose they could be used.

The Rabbi did not hesitate at all in his translations from the Hebrew into English. He understood the ancient language very well as if it was his native tongue and cautioned me strongly to never place a slave ring on my finger without first discharging it. I said I was all too familiar with what could happen if I did and then told him about what had happened to the professor during one of our experiments.

He said that this occurrence was not new to him. He was aware it had happened several times in the past but was surprised that the professor had not taken heed of the warnings issued by the book. He told me that the possibility of electrocution was built into the ring by the designer to prevent it from being used by someone who was a thief or not in the secret society. They would not know that its deadly power could mean instant death.

The spooky old guy asked me a very weird question when he said, "I am preparing to show you the beginning of the rest of your life and you must be ready to suffer the pain of being one of the chosen ones. You will be fascinated beyond your wildest dreams with the things you will see in the ring. Things that had been recorded in the distant past and so all consuming that nothing else of your life on earth will matter to you. Your life as you now know it will become uninteresting and irrelevant. You must pay close attention to what you see because once I have shown you the workings of the circle I will give my rings to you and leave your presence. After which you may not be able to contact me. Placing the rings and their secrets into the hands of someone young and strong like yourself and one that has enough slave rings to power the masters, will allow me to pass peacefully on into the hereafter, knowing the rings will someday be used to their full capabilities. Are you ready to accept your charge?"

Not giving a second thought about the real ramifications of what he had just said because I was so excited to hear what he had to say about the rings, I quickly said, "Yes I am ready!"

He said, "Alright then let us begin." Quickly he went about reading from the book. After a short time he did a little figuring on a piece of paper then stated that seven slave rings should provide enough power.

Of course I had no idea what he was referring to but heard myself say, "Okay."

Using the long book key, he lifted from the collection of rings scattered about the desk. He set a master with a green stone and seven slave rings upon the metal plate that also served as the cover for the book of instructions. Then he attached them together using their hooks and eyes until all were connected and in a circle. He explained that the plate was a type of high voltage insulator that enabled one to safely handle the slave rings without discharging them. At least seven would be needed to provide enough power to create a highly charged electrical field to form what he called a Xenon Plasma.

Instantly when the last ring was connected, we heard a low hum and then an eerie green glow began emitting from the emerald stone. He told me to turn off the room lights then he cautioned me that we should stand a good distance away from the rings as they gave off bursts of electro- magnetic energy pulses. Until the force field stabilized itself, the rays were dangerous to us because we lacked the proper safety clothing.

The precautionary measure he mentioned made me remember the strange illness I had suffered the day after the professor died. Now I understood what caused it. Being unaware of the danger, I had stood too close to the force field and the radiation from the high voltage caused my face to become redden, break out in sores and my red blood cell count to plummet.

Concentrating once again on the circle of rings, I saw the faint green glow grow darker and more intense. Every few seconds a slight flash would emit from the green haze, fly through the air and disappear into the darkness. After about an hour, a bubble began to form over the circle of rings. Rabbi Asher declared that it was now safe for us to approach the bubble.

Upon looking into the green haze he said, "Now you will experience something that only a very few humans have ever seen. The ring will display an image of an event that it recorded somewhere in time. Look deep into the eye of the ring and concentrate." Almost immediately, I could see a landscape, the same as one the professor and I had observed, only much sharper. Evidently, the extra rings gave the needed power boost to bring in the image crystal clear. Several minutes passed with no change to the image, so I commented to Asher that we had seen him in the haze almost immediately. Why was it taking so long for something else to materialize? He said we were looking for something much farther back in time and that it had to do with things related to the word, Judah, the word imprinted on the ring. I was somewhat taken aback when he said, "Somewhere in time," insinuating that the ring projected a form of visual time travel.

I stared into the green mist and scanned for something to materialize. Suddenly, over the rolling hills and meadows came movement and then coming into focus I saw them; a group of men on horseback, dressed in suits of armor, with flags waving atop long poles, galloping up a small hill toward a castle in the distance. As they neared the castle, another band of men appeared on the horizon and seemed to be chasing the first group. Soon the two groups met in a tremendous clash of arms that sent some of the pursuers sprawling to the ground covered in blood and the rest fleeing for their lives. My mind left my body as I was in such awe that I could not take my eyes off the scene.

Rabbi Asher had been right. I was seeing fascinating, un-believable things that would render this present world meaningless. I was completely mesmerized and vaguely remembered Professor Schweitzer reading something similar to me about a battle from the pages of the wooden book.

The furious battle ended with the first group of knights victorious and as the image of the group came closer, I could see the faces of the warriors as they removed their helmets. They were all strong young men and I noticed that one of them had long, beautiful flowing hair. Look-ing closer, I saw that he clutched in his hands a large body shield decorated with a family coat of arms, dis-playing a bold, blood red cross on a white background and the name, *PENDRAGON* prominently written in black across the top.

The horsemen rode on toward the castle, but stopped to water their horses well before the main gate. The knight holding the shield continued riding on and passing through dense woods soon arrived at the top of a knoll, where the castle was clearly visible. The tall watchtower of the castle loomed high in the air and cast its shad-ow on the hill as well as on the waters of a nearby lake. The longhaired rider dismounted his steed and carrying his shield, weaved downward through the undergrowth soon reaching a partially hidden cavern in the side of the knoll. Two iron gates blocked the cave's entrance, but as he moved a large triangular shaped stone, the gates swung open enabling him to enter. The knight's way was illuminated by a brilliant shaft of sunlight coming down through a narrow opening in the top of the hill. Reaching a certain spot, in the tunnel he encountered a large plaster plaque in the cave wall that seemed to be a tombstone covering the opening to a grave. Acting as if he had been there before, knowing what he was about to do, he simultaneously pushed on a name at the top as well as on another at the bottom of the headstone. Suddenly an opening appeared to one side of the tombstone. Taking a large leather sack from the hollow of his shield, he placed it into the opening. Touching the same places on the plaque again, the opening mysteriously closed. Squinting my eyes I was able to make out the inscription on the plaque he had pressed upon,

Here entombed at Glastonbury Abbey
Lies the Mortal Remains
His Royal Majesty King Arthur
Sovereign of all England
Son Of Uther Pendragon
Born Jewish to the tribe of Judah.

As far as I was concerned, there it was written in stone, King Arthur, one of the legendary figures of ages past was not only a real person, but in fact, one of the Knights Of Zion. Even more surprising, *JEWISH* by birth.

Now I was finally beginning to make the connection between the master ring Rabbi Asher had brought with him and the name Judah which was imprinted on the tombstone in the cave.

Breaking the silence in the room, Rabbi Asher said strangely, "Make thee a mental note of what thee views, you will soon need this vision."

Sliding the long key from out the side of the plate, he touched one end to a place on the cover, and then slid the other end of the key into the master rings center. The moment he touched it, the green bubble instantly vanished while still displaying moving images in its interior.

He amazingly had used the key to extinguish the plasma, which made a loud popping noise as it disappeared.

He then turned to me and very ceremoniously as if commissioning me with an obligation said, "This is your challenge. You must find the Abbey at Glastonbury, wherever it is and take into your possession the artifacts that were secretly hidden so long ago. They may be needed in this day and age for a coming event that is of unparalleled significance in all of mankind's history. Your mission is of the utmost importance. Do not fail or you will spend eternity looking for the pieces that will be so desperately needed by mankind."

As he finished speaking to me, he held out his hand and clasped my right hand in his. I felt a tremendous surge of energy pass into my body and something squeeze my finger.

Turning from me, he quickly walked out of the room. Almost as if he was fleeing and disappeared into the darkness. Switching on the lamp over my desk, I instantly saw that the master ring he previously hand on his hand had mysterious passed from his hand to my finger. Examining it closely, I saw embossed beneath its beautiful blue stone the engraved word, *LEVI.*

Somehow, with the transfer of the ring as well as the hasty ceremony that had just taken place and the charge Rabbi Asher had bestowed upon me, I had the distinct feeling of having just been inducted into the brotherhood of the Knights of Zion.

The ring hung heavily on my finger, almost as heavy as the challenge he had given me hung on my shoulders. It was as if all of mankind's future rested on me, and who knows maybe it did. However, where was Glastonbury Abbey and what could possibly be in that leather sack?

The first place I planned to look was in my old wooden book. The name of this Abbey seemed to ring a bell with me, so I went to my briefcase, took out the old journal, and began searching through the pages. It was difficult going because many of the words were in different languages, but about midway through the book, the name Arthur caught my eye and scanning down the page there it was, the name Glastonbury Abbey. It seemed to be described as being located somewhere in Southern England, but the dates were ancient; the place probably did not even exist today.

Leaving my office locked behind me I headed home all the while trying to figure out an explanation for Peggy Sue when she was sure to ask me about the ring on my finger.

I realized I would need a very good story because if I did travel to England, which I felt I must do, I would be gone a long while. I decided to tell her that the professor had told me of a treasure he knew was hidden in an old cathedral in England and he had given me all the details. He thought I could do the traveling for him, as he was getting so old and feeble. I was not sure she would go for the tale but I wanted to spare her the strange details of what I had witnessed tonight because there was no way she would ever believe them. I sure as hell was not going to tell her about the weird and spooky Rabbi Asher. However I was sure of one thing, come hell or high water, I was going to take that trip to Glastonbury Abbey.

When I arrived at the house and parked the car I took a few minutes and just sat there in the quiet. After several minutes, I happened to look toward the front door and there was Peggy Sue peering at me through the curtains she had pulled slightly open. We stared at each other for a few seconds then her hand came into view and she waved at me, oh so slowly. As I walked up the sidewalk to the door, she came running out, grabbed me and gave me a passionate kiss right on the lips. Then looking lovingly into my eyes said, "I was just admiring you sitting out there in your car. You know you are a really handsome guy, I love you."

Holding her close in my arms with the smell of her perfume sending my senses soaring, I realized how tough it was going to be leaving her alone when I went off chasing something that could turn out to be nothing but a dream.

Walking arm in arm into the house where the aroma coming from the kitchen meant only one thing, Peggy had made me my favorite dinner, chicken with raisins, mashed potatoes and green beans.

As I was washing my hands, preparing to eat the dinner she had slaved over all that afternoon just to make me happy, she noticed the ring on my finger. Immediately she popped the question; where had I gotten it?

"Oh that!" I said quickly and immediately let the lie I was going to tell her play out in my head. She was looking straight into my eyes and smiling through those ruby red lips, she stood waiting for me to answer. I thought, "What a woman I have here." There is no way in the world I could lie to her about something this important. I had to tell her the truth because honesty is always the best policy and anyway I owed it to her. Since we had been married, she had always been at my side in everything I had ever done and supported me unconditionally. She was a part of my soul and would sense that I was lying. I had to come clean with her. I was sure she would understand me, however, I did not know if she would believe me.

Telling her that if she would put the food back in the warming oven and sit beside me, I would tell her the entire story of how I got the ring. She looked at me strangely, put the food in the oven and sat down.

I went on for over an hour, explaining about the rabbi who had came to the office. About him showing me how the rings went together and then about the vision in the green haze and what the rabbi intended me to do. She sat there with her mouth agape, shaking her head from side to side.

When I stopped to get a glass of water, she put her arm around my shoulder and said, "Honey, if this is what you want me to believe, then I believe you. You must have a good reason to tell me this is how you got the ring. I know you have been feeling better these last few days but since you had your face burned and was ill for weeks your personality is not the same as it used to be. You seem so cold and distance from me and the kids, and not the least bit interested in anything I am doing. Do you think I should drive you up to Austin to the hospital and let them do some tests to determine if there is something wrong with you physically."

Not answering, I just sat there thinking, "This is just how I expected her to react. Who in their right mind would really believe such a fantastic flight of fancy. They would act just as Peggy Sue did, thinking I needed some help with my thought processes. Maybe they were all correct. Maybe I was going nuts, but I knew that the ring was real, it was on my finger and I also knew Rabbi Asher was real because Martha had seen him, talked to him and even escorted him into my office. The only way I could prove to Peggy as well as myself that everything was true, was to make that trip to England and see if there really was a treasure in that old cave. She would just have to bear with me and let me figure this mess out for myself."

I asked Peggy to serve the food and then we sat without saying a word to one another and ate. Somehow the food, which normally tasted so good, had suddenly lost its yummy.

After dinner, we both got our shower as it was almost midnight and went to bed. Peggy slid over on my side of the bed and into my arms. The room was completely silent except for the crickets outside our window, who were playing an insect serenade that lulled us to sleep.

The following morning as usual, we awoke in the very same position in which we had fallen asleep, in one another's arms. The warm sun beaming through the open window indicated that today was going to be bright and beautiful. However, I had a strange sense of doom lingering in the back of my head but something deep within my body was compelling me to get on a plane. Maybe it was that little voice inside of me that kept repeating the words the rabbi had spoken, "An event of unparalleled significance for mankind," these were powerful words to my ears. I was hooked on the thrill of discovering what this event might be, almost as bad as if I was addicted to opium. I knew I had to get on with it so I called American Airlines in San Antonio that very morning and booked a one-way flight to Heathrow Airport in London for the following day.

Early in the morning, followed by a teary eyed wife; I loaded my luggage into the trunk of the Ford. She had helped me pack a few of my things the night before, shirts, pants, socks and several changes of underwear. Peggy Sue had a feddish about packing for a trip regardless of how long it would be. She always insisted on taking an overabundance of under panties. It was either she was concerned about having an accident or going to the hospital with dirty undies, or maybe it was just the desire to keep her body clean, I was unsure of which. Making sure for the umpteenth time that I had enough cash, my credit cards and my passport, she finally gave me my goodbye kiss and I was off on my three and a half hour drive to the airport.

Arriving at San Antonio International and checking in, I looked over my flight itinerary and saw I would be making several stops on my way to New York for my connecting flight over the Atlantic. Even though San Antonio used the word, "International" in its airport name, conjuring up images of a vast complex, it was nothing of the kind. It was so small, remote and had such a short runway that we had to use a puddle jumper to get to the nearest true, international hub, Dallas. It stopped twice just to get there, confirming once again, I was indeed living on the fringe of civilization.

I finally boarded a large four-engine jet and settled into my seat for the three-hour jump up to New York. After a short layover, I flew another five hours on across the pond to London.

My seatmate on that leg of the flight was a rather young, nice looking woman who in passing me a drink from the stewardess noticed my ring and was admiring it. Taking my hand in hers and looking closely at the engraving she asked if I was Jewish. I said I was not and why did she ask? "Well" she said, "I saw your name on the ring and I just assumed that Judah was Jewish." Preferring not to continue with the subject, I nonchalantly and somewhat rudely said, while trying to dislodge my hand from hers, "Oh, that's just the name of a society I belong to." Sensing that I was not in the mood for conversation or for that matter anything else, she released my hand and returned to her novel. One only someone from New York would be reading. Its cover read, "12th & McGraw, Growing up Mobster." She must have assumed I was an old grouch and definitely not on the make because she never said another word to me the rest of the trip. However, even without conversation, I was not bored at all, because my mind was preoccupied planning what equipment, I would need and how I was going to go about finding a cave on a deserted hillside in a town that may not even exist.

Once during the flight, I looked down at my hand and the blue stone in the ring. It seemed as though I saw movement inside of it. I was sure it was just my imagination playing tricks on me but it did upset me a little. Another time I awoke from a brief nap and raised my window shade as the setting sun cast a golden ray into the cabin and hit the stone in the ring just right, immediately it reflected a blue flash of light across the passenger cabin and danced eerily on the ceiling. Somewhat apprehensive and remembering what the ring was capable of projecting, I imagined that an image might suddenly appear and scare the hell out of everyone on board, so I quickly placed my hand over the ring extinguishing the beam.

Not only had the ring and its meaning taken over my life and my dreams, it was now influencing my thoughts while awake. It had gotten so bad that I did not even want to converse with a beautiful young woman. I had become very serious and focused on where was Glastonbury and what was in that old grave. I wanted to find out, if only for my own sanity, if these things actually existed at all. If so, I would do what I had to do and then get back home to my family. So, when my plane touched down in London, I was eager to get on with the job at hand.

Gathering my luggage and exiting the terminal, I hailed a cab. A rather rough looking individual drove up in a noisy Mercedes diesel taxi. He looked as though he was a man of the streets and knew his way around so I thought I would ask him a few questions as I entered the cab.

"Where to, govner?" he said as he lowered the flag on his trip meter and pulled the car into first gear.

"Hold on a second," I said. "I need some information from you. Have you ever heard of the town of Glastonbury?"

"Why yes I have. Its about a six hour drive from here, but I am not permitted to go that far out of town. If you are a tourist I can fix you up with a good guide for a price because you will need one going out there, nothing but an old bunch of ruins."

"Oh no, I'm not here to see the sights and don't want you to take me there, I just needed to know where it was. Do you know of a nice hotel here in London? Preferably in a section of town near a hardware store and a car rental place?"

"Sure do Gov! It is a bit of a piece away but it's real nice. My cousin owns the place and I can get you a good rate, if that is where you want to go? What do you do? Study rocks or something?"

I was not about to tell the guy what I was up to so I just flat out lied and said, "Well that's right! You guessed it. I am a geologist. You win a cigar. Yea sure, take me to your cousin's place."

Laughing as he pulled away from the curb he replied, "Right you are, Gov. But I have to say no thanks for the smoke, the wife made me give them up, said they stunk up our apartment."

After about a forty-minute ride we pulled up in front of a large apartment style building that's sign read, "The Ralph Emerson Inn."

Reading the sign I commented, "You did not tell me your cousin was a famous writer."

The cabbie just shrugged his shoulders and said, "Huh? Naw! he is just your average bloke trying to make an honest living, like I am. That will be twenty Pound six Ginny for the fare."

Not having brought any British currency with me, I jammed a fifty into his hand and said, "Here I hope this covers it and thanks for the help."

Taking off his cap and bowing slightly he said, "Why that's mighty nice of you sir, if you ever need a driver again just call London Cab and ask for Mortimer."

Holding my breath to avoid inhaling any of the diesels smoke the cab made as it sped away, I quickly picked up my bags and hurried into the hotel office.

A pleasant looking gentleman greeted me at the counter and asked if he could help me.

"Yes you can! I need a room for at least a week and your cousin Mortimer said you might have one at a good rate."

Laughing he said, "Oh Mortimer, he's not really our cousin, he brings us customers all the time and we take care of him with a little something. I do have a nice suite on the second floor I could let you have for a week at one hundred and fifty pounds."

Nodding my head up and down I said, "That will be just fine. May I pay with my credit card?"

"Yes Sir, no problem. Please sign in and here is the key. Are you here on holidays or just sight seeing?"

Handing him my card and at the same time keeping up the charade I said, "No I'm a geologist here on a soil study. I was wondering if you could answer a few questions for me. I need to rent a truck or van and to know where a hardware store is located."

"You have come to the right neighborhood, the lorry rental agency is three avenues up this street and the what-not store is just behind them on the next corner."

Thanking him, I took the lift to the second floor and found my room. It was tidy, clean and had a nice view of a small park next door. Feeling a little bushed I lay down on the bed for a little shut-eye before going over to get the truck. When I awoke it was dark outside and looking at my watch, I found I had slept for several hours. Sure that everything was closed I undressed and crawled into bed.

The early morning traffic on the street in front of the building gave me a very rude awakening. I jumped out of bed feeling a little groggy so I took a long hot shower, then shaved and got dressed. Boy did I ever need a cup of coffee. I found one in the lobby on my way out to the auto agency.

The sun was bright and warm and the coffee really hit the spot as I sipped on it walking the mile or so to rent the truck. I had left most of my valuables including my passport, watch, most of my cash and the master ring, locked in a closet in the room for safekeeping.

A few personal essentials, credit card and a small amount of cash I took with me in a small duffel bag slung over my shoulder and it felt weightless as I hurried along. I was feeling comfortable and confident here in my new surroundings, everything had gone off without a hitch so far. I only hoped that my good luck would hold out, as I was sure I would need a bunch of it to complete my mission.

I managed to rent a fully fueled, four-wheel drive Land Rover with a rear seat, that made into a folding bed, just in case I had to have a place to sleep. The agency gave me a well-marked map with directions to Glastonbury because the roads turned to dirt when one got near to the old ruins of the Abbey.

My next stop was the hardware store, where I purchased a back pack, some boots, coveralls, a flashlight, gloves, two blankets, a shovel, a pick ax, a length of rope and a tool belt to hold everything, as well as a single, six foot piece of half inch steel rod.

As I was checking out at the counter I mentioned to the clerk that I was going camping. After adding up my purchases she said that I had forgotten something, "Oh!" I said "What?"

Laughing she said, "Well Sir, the umbrella!"

"Is it supposed to rain?" I said stupidly.

"Sir, this is England, where rains or mists can come up at any given moment. One must always be prepared.

Enough said I immediately picked up an umbrella and a raincoat.

Then it was on to the food store where I bought some snack food and soft drinks as well as several bottles of water and a few towels and some matches.

I felt I had everything I would need to go in search of the cave, so after a quick lunch I hit the road going south. One convenient thing was to reach the town of Glastonbury I only had to travel on two different roads. Getting to the old Abbey would be another thing. There were no roads leading directly to the ruins and one had to approach on foot. I figured I would get as close as I could with the Land Rover then walk the rest of the way. In addition, I was having one hell of a time with driving on the left side of the road and it was extra challenging on tight curves, which the road took several times in the hills as I neared the coast.

The scenery was spectacular, beautiful rolling deep emerald green hills with small lakes nestled in their valleys. Flowering trees and shrubs grew everywhere on the hillsides, making it real easy to understand how this island nation got the nickname, "Enchanted Emerald Isle."

The beauty quickly vanished as dark clouds rolled in off the ocean and it started to rain like crazy. Not taking any chances getting lost and it was getting late anyway, I pulled into the first motel and took a room for the night, vowing to get an early start the next morning. I took a shower, ate some snacks and went to bed.

My deep slumber was broken with someone pounded on my door yelling, "Check out time!" Looking at the clock radio it read twelve thirty in the afternoon. I must have had what they call jet lag. Something I had not experienced before, and anyway whatever it was made me tired as hell. I quickly dressed and vacated the room, not wanting to draw the wrath again of the loud mouth, cigar smoking, and bald headed man wearing the dirty tee shirt.

Back on the road it was not long, maybe an hour or so, when I saw a sign. It read Glastonbury and its arrow pointed left. Taking the turn and in another twenty minutes, I was in the heart of town.

It was not much of a place, a few old dilapidated buildings, a Pub with the unusual name on its sign of, The Knight's Arms." There were as well as some shack-like houses and a petrol pumping station, where some very savory looking men milled around, carelessly smoking cigarettes. Clearly, the town was not a place where one would want to spend the night. I was thankful my truck had that bed.

I saw a fairly decent looking person walking on the sidewalk, so I stopped and asked him if this road led out to the old Abbey.

Pointing with his finger the same way my vehicle was heading he said, "That's right old chap, just stay straight about ten kilometers, then take the first turn to the right on the old dirt road that leads to the abandoned town of Somerset. The old Abbey is off to the right a ways, you will see the tower, which is all there is left standing. Nothing much out there to see except a big pile of rocks, but if you are a geologist, it might be interesting. Good Luck!"

I had to chuckle to myself as I drove off, there's that job description again. I must have really looked the part but if it was working I was happy to use it as a cover for my real intention, which was to find and steal what could be, if true, an English national treasure.

I took a reading on my odometer and motored on. When I reached ten kilometers, I started looking for the road to the right. Suddenly there was a turn off, however it was more of a dirt path other than a road. Not wanting to be stuck out here in the boonies, I slipped the Land Rover down into four-wheel drive and turned onto the dirt pathway. Venturing along another mile or so, I saw in the distance and on top of one of those beautiful emerald hills, the crumbling watchtower of the ancient Abbey.

Seeing the old tower, my second thoughts of whether it was a bad idea of coming over to London vanished. I was relieved and whispered to myself, "Well at least the old church actually exists."

Now that I had my objective in sight, I only hoped I could drive over to it, as everything was densely overgrown. It might be near impossible to find that small knoll with the cave, if it existed. Excited that there well may be something to the vision in the rings, I was not about to stop in my quest to determine if anything else displayed was true. I continued driving slowly until my truck could go no further.

So placing the ignition key under the floor mat, I got out. Packing some things in my backpack and placing my tools in the belt, I threw the rope on one shoulder and on the other, slung the shovel, took the steel rod in my free hand and continued on foot.

The path grew smaller and smaller and soon I was working my way through heavy brush and soggy soil. The going was tough, so I stopped occasionally to drink water from my backpack and then struggling onward. I finally reached the top of a small hill where I had a clear view of the ruins. Just below from where they sat was a rather large lake. Looking for a better route and one that was easier to transverse, I spied a way along a ridge that led over and came up behind the tower.

Taking the ridge and trudging along, I eventually made it to the backside of the tower and climbed up to the top of the hill to the old ruins. What a spectacular view, one could see for miles in all directions. This was the perfect place to locate a castle. The lake was probably the source for the water used to fill the old mote that must have at one time surrounded the hilltop. Trying to orient myself in relationship to where I remembered the knoll would be, I stood with the watchtower at my back and looked out over the lake. I could see two large hills in the surrounding terrain and on the far side of the lake, there was a small island which fell into the approximate range from the Abbey, where the cave might be located.

Before taking the hike over to that site, I removed the heavy load I was carrying and sat down on a pile of rocks and rested. I made myself comfortable and soon begin daydreaming. I could visualize how beautiful this must have all been so long ago, knights in armor, damsels with long gowns and tassels on the top of high cone shaped hats, all parading gracefully around this once magnificent castle where flags flew from every tower and the strains of a string instrument, wafted through the courtyards, the muscled well groomed steeds with their beautiful saddles and bridles. It was easy to imagine how so many romance novels have been written about the middle ages and the gallant men with their fair ladies who had lived during those times.

Up in the clear blue sky, a large hawk caught my eye. It was gliding and making lazy circles on uplifting air currents. The bird suddenly hovered overhead and then silently swooped down to the ground in a power dive and grabbed a screeching rabbit with its talons. Soon the sounds coming from the rabbit stopped and the hawk began to tear at the animals flesh with his hooked beak.

The rule of the wild, death can come silently and swiftly. The same swift death could have been met by knights jousting or fighting hand to hand with long swords right here in this very place in by gone days. So it was with life back then, beautiful, romantic and serene one day, then the next, a cruel death in the afternoon sun at the hands of a superior fighter. If one survived that day, he may live long enough to die at the ripe old age of forty.

Now that the strength had returned to my legs, I was ready to attempt crossing over to the lake to see if I could somehow get out to that small island. Picking up my tools and venturing forth, I soon reached the far side of the lake. The little island was rather close to the shoreline, maybe fifty yards or so. My being in the middle of the wilderness, I removed my boots, socks, pants and underwear and placed them in my backpack to keep them dry. The water was clear and quite warm so I waded out to find that it was only a little more than waist deep.

Carefully negotiating the rocky lake bottom and steadying myself with the steel rod, I reached dry ground and the island, which appeared to be approximately eighty acres in size. Standing in the warm sun, I let my legs dry out a little, while surveying the knoll whose most prominent feature was a huge old Oak tree which sat right on top where several of its offspring saplings surrounded the big fellow. After a few minutes, I put my clothes back on, walked to the top, and from that vantage point could clearly see the watchtower on the next hill.

Remembering the vision in the green plasma over the rings, I positioned myself with the tower to my front with its image reflecting on the lake surface and the hillside at my back. The tower's shadow however did not strike the hill at all and appeared on the lake shoreline. I thought this might be because the tower was only half its original height and therefore the shadow it cast could be considerably off.

Setting down all my equipment, I started looking and probing with my metal rod for the entrance of the cave. Working for several hours I was thankful for the pair of gloves I was wearing because without them my hands would be a bloody mess. I must have touched or moved every bush and piece of vegetation on that hillside but found nothing resembling an opening to a cave. Taking a break from searching, I nibbled an a few snacks, drank some water then suddenly realized it was getting dark. Not wanting to try to make it back to the Land Rover before nightfall, I decided to bed down here on the hill-top. I had spent the whole day just getting to this point. A point where all I could prove was that there was an old Abbey. But no cave, no treasure, nothing at all, except a very quiet and surreal landscape, beside calm warm waters of a lake.

The only sound made was the wind rustling the leaves on the Oak and the song of a passing bird, calling its mate.

Flowers were in full bloom everywhere and my nostrils caught the exotic scent of sweet smelling honeysuckle mingled with wild roses.

Even though I was alone and in a remote part of rural England, I did not feel lonesome at all, but completely at peace. At that moment, it seemed perfectly plausible that a person could stay here, on this small hilltop, for the rest of their life and love it. In other words it was a place of utter tranquility.

Removing the raincoat from my pack and spreading it beside the tall Oak tree, I lay down, used the backpack for a pillow and covering myself with a blanket, closed my eyes, and cradled in arms of grass, in a miniature Garden Of Eden, nodded blissfully off to sleep.

I was awakened sometime in the middle of the night by the sounds of the mating call from an owl whose, "Who, Who" rang out clearly in the night air disturbing my sleep.

Opening my eyes, I saw the magnificent night sky filled with millions of dancing and twinkling stars. Its depth and majesty seemed to reach out into infinity. I imagined how awe-struck the people of the middle ages would have been when viewing this very same hemisphere with its impressive celestial display.

I was however, very intrigued by a group of stars which made up a small constellation directly overhead. Six very bright stars formed two perfect triangles, and strangely, they seemed to be slowly blinking in some form of sequence, alternating left then right. Having used a telescope many times, I was familiar with the heavens and attributed this unusual phenomenon to passing clouds or just the way their light waves were deflected by earth's atmosphere.

Just then, my attention was distracted from the Cosmos when I noticed movement directly in front of me. Looking closely, I saw a rack of huge antlers silhouetted against the starry background. Then slowly making his way past my makeshift bed walked a dripping wet, stately stag. As he did, he turned his head and looked directly at me. His dark eyes seemed to glisten in the starlight and his expression was as if to demonstrate his prowess and that this hilltop belonged to him. Pawing the dirt, he threw his head back, gave out a loud bellow, which seemed to echo off the surrounding hills and then sensing that he had duly impressed me, disappeared into the brush.

The sound of the lake waters gurgling on the shore and the wind in the trees seemed to be playing a lullaby, I was so comfortable that I fell back to sleep and did not stir again until early morning when a group of chattering Blue Jays arguing in the Oak startled me awake.

The first thing to come to mind when I rose to my feet at daybreak and saw a bright golden haze on the surrounding meadows was a song from the musical Oklahoma, "Oh what a beautiful morning." I could not help myself. My surroundings were so breathtaking that I broke out singing the tune at the top of my voice. I thought it sounded pretty good, but the Blue Jays must have thought they could do better. Just like a feathered choir they threw back their heads and all began chirping in unison which made me snicker.

Opening my backpack and taking out some bottled water, a package of beef jerky and a few crackers, I had breakfast sitting in the open fresh air and it tasted delicious. The birds, maybe never having seen a human before, were very curious and fluttered down unafraid from the tree unto my blanket. I gave one of them a cracker crumb, which turned out to be a bad idea because soon I was surrounded by a couple of dozen noisy Jays all wanting my precious crackers. When they got so bold as to start pecking my hand and then my head, I decided it was time to vacate the area and look elsewhere for the cave.

Rolling up my blanket and placing it in my pack along with the food, I picked up and put on all my equipment.

Grabbing the rod and shovel in hand and with the annoying birds in hot pursuit, I made a mad dash to get away from them. Just before the base of the big oak tree, the ground gave way under my feet and I was momentarily weightless. Suddenly I found myself falling through the air and down into a pitch black hole. Then just as sudden, landing on my back in three feet of water. Struggling to stand, coughing and spitting water out of my lungs and catching my breath, I looked around to see where I had landed.

I stood there in total darkness except for the single ray of sunshine coming down through the hole I had just made in the earth, which was about twenty feet over my head. Reaching into my backpack, I felt for and found my flashlight, its beam, when I turned it on revealed that I was in some type of subterranean chamber. Then it hit me, I had found the cave or something like it. The light beam illuminated a large ledge of dry ground so I made my way out of the water and onto the dry area.

Checking my tools, I found that they were still attached to my belt and thankfully, my backpack was intact. However I had lost my rod, shovel and for a moment thought also my rope, but found it in the lights beam, floating on the water. Retrieving it I sat down and pondered my predicament. After collecting my thoughts and taking the light again in my hand, I played its beam around and found that I was in an area about the size of a large auditorium with solid rock walls, twenty-foot ceilings and a few feet of water for a floor. There were three openings that ran back into the walls of the cave, one to my front was half full of water, the two smaller ones off to the side, seemed to be dry and above the reach of the water.

By the looks of things I knew I was in trouble. It seemed to me to be so ironic that one moment I was in a beautiful paradise-like setting and the next instantly cast down into the bowels of the hill and a nightmare. My primary thoughts of course were of survival and these thoughts told me I would need that shovel. Tying it to the rope, I might somehow throw it up through the hole in the cave roof and if lucky catch on the brush enabling me to climb up and out of my dungeon.

Reentering the water and searching where I had fallen, I located the shovel and rod. Finding them, I breathed a sigh of relief and felt my chances get better, however after several failed attempts I began to feel a sense of despair. Trying one last time, I swung the rope with the shovel tied to its end in a large circle over my head, cowboy style and then pitched it upward toward the opening, and just like that, it sailed right out into the blue sky. Pulling the rope slowly down toward me it suddenly grew tight in my hand so my theory was working.

However, planting my feet against the rock wall and holding the rope, I began my climb, upward. It was very difficult to climb up hand over hand and about midway up the shovel lost its grip on the vegetation, and I came crashing down into the water for another dunking. Immediately following me was the rope and then the shovel, which hit me in the head, causing a cut that bled profusely sending crimson red droplets into the clear water.

Rushing over to my dry place and the backpack I used one of my towels to stop the flow of blood, but man, did I ever have a headache.

It was becoming more apparent each moment that I was trapped in this cave and could possibly starve to death. It would be a horrible way to die and the thought was so ghastly that I quickly put it out of my head and tried to think positive, however, stuck in a deep pitch black hole, *THAT* was almost impossible. I was worried and began to pray to God to take care of my family and let my end come quickly and painlessly or show me a way out.

My fears turned to almost panic when night fell and I lost that ray of sunshine shining down the hole. The darkness was almost deafening it was so silent and black. Just to keep my sanity I had to turn the flashlight on occasionally to be sure I was not in a nightmare only to find in the light that I was.

When my circle of sunshine finally returned, after a night that I thought would never end, I tried endlessly throwing the rope and shovel unsuccessfully at the opening until I was totally exhausted. I thought of every way possible to get out of the hole but none seemed even remotely plausible. I was even down to the thought of breaking up some crackers then luring the Blue Jays down into the hole where I could catch a few of them, tie my rope around their legs and they would miraculously fly out and attach it to the big old Oak that was just twenty feet above my head. I realized I must have been hallucinating and all I was doing was grabbing at straws. I was stuck in this hellhole and was going to die here,......... I just knew it.

I took out some food from my pack, and found that the plastic wrap kept it from getting wet when I fell into the water. Starting to eat my jerky and crackers, the crumbs from them made me think about the fairytale of Hansel and Gretel that I told to my kids so often when they were infants. I could go exploring up these tunnels in the cave walls and drop crumbs along the way so I could at least find my way back here. It was a sound plan as long as the crackers held out as well as the batteries in the flashlight. Losing some of my precious commodity, the food, made me nervous, but I was getting desperate, I had to try something.

While I still had the sunlight streaming down the open hole above me as a homing beacon, I thought this just as good a time as any, so leaving all my belongings I took the flashlight, my shovel and the half consumed package of crackers, slid into the water and headed for one of the tunnels.

Climbing up into it's opening and shaking off, I dropped a few crumbs in a crack in the wall and played my lights beam up a narrow crawl space about six feet wide and about that tall. After only a few hundred feet and a couple of turns and tight places, where I had to crawl on my stomach, the passageway stopped abruptly ending in a wall of solid black rock. It was a dead end.

Retracing my steps and following the crumbs, I made it back to the big room where I had started. There was still a light coming down from above, so I felt I had time to try the other passageway. This one went upwards for a long way. I then stopped abruptly at a huge hole that fell away into empty space. Nothing was in front of me except a gapping hole where even my flashlights beam could not find its sides. Neither was there a sound emitted from the pit when I dropped a stone into its emptiness. There was no way around this obstacle, but it did offer me one thing, a way of instant death if it came to that.

That night as I sat in the darkness, saving my flashlight batteries, I thought about my wife and family and the good times we used to have up in Michigan. Sure the winters were rough but there was the ice skating on our lake, the steaming cups of hot cocoa that Peggy Sue would fix for us, and the weenie roasts we would have on those warm summer nights. The thoughts of these wonderful moments caused me to weep openly, imagining I might never see my family or those good times again.

I did not sleep that night reminiscing about my past life and when the sun returned to the tiny opening in the roof of the cave, I walked out into the water and let it shine on my face. Standing there in the warmth with my eyes closed, I suddenly felt something brush against my leg, startled and looking down I saw a small fish.

This was a surprise but welcome sign, he had to be getting in here somehow, possibly in an underground stream. I immediately found new hope, especially after I tasted the water and found it drinkable. The thought entered my head that I could drink the water, catch the occasional fish in the pond for food, and survive, for how long only God knew the answer to that question. I did however, not need to die at all, I could live out my life right here. Then I remembered about my previous thoughts of spending my life on the pleasant hilltop just above me. I did not know it then but I might be spending it *UNDER* the hill, in this hole.

That is when the last passageway came to mind. Maybe I did not really want to know what was at its end, because that way I would always have a bit of hope that it might be a way out, however if I explored it and found it also a dead end, that could be devastating.

Shaking my head for such a stupid thought, I said aloud, "You dope! It could be your pathway to freedom." Feverishly grabbing the light and the remaining crackers, I rushed across the water and waded into the opening of the last passageway.

Hurrying down its rather large opening and not more than thirty feet, the water got much deeper, up to my shoulders. Holding my flashlight over my head, I suddenly caught a glimpse of what looked like iron rods. Moving closer I saw I was right, they were iron rods, lots of them. I was looking at the top on an enormous iron gate.

Thinking in my head about the vision in the green plasma, these looked just like the ones the longhaired knight opened when he enter the cave, these had to be the same ones. Pushing against them was fruitless, not only were they nearly submerged, but I could see past them and there was nothing there but large boulders and deeper water. Even if I could somehow dig around them and swim underwater, I could not get past the rocks.

My mind swirled with two emotions, one with elation for I had confirmed that this was indeed the cave from my vision. The second left me heartbroken, because for a moment I thought I had found a way out of my dark domain. But no, I was still locked tightly in its death grip.

Making my way back to the dry space in the big room for some food, I ran my hand against the wall to steady myself in the darkness, when suddenly I touched something large and slimy that seemed to move slightly and for a split second I thought the wall was something alive. I quickly switched on my flashlight and the sight illuminated in its beam caused me to jump violently because covering the entire wall were huge, black and twisted tree roots, just dangling there, still moving from my touch and dripping with green slime. I mean big scary looking roots, some as big around as my leg, others thinner, white and covered with small seed like pods. This mass of vegetation was crawling down through cracks in the rocks from above and they extended from ceiling to floor. They had grown like the arms of a giant octopus, down the cave wall and out into the water as if a huge monster was feeding on the pool. They were obviously from the big old Oak tree overhead whose exterior branches were reaching up towards the heavens, however its black slimy roots were descending downwards, to where I was, toward Hades.

Stepping back away from the wall a few feet and playing the beam of my light on the giant roots, a thought occurred to me. If the hole I had fallen through represented the hole in the ceiling of the cave that lit the knight's way, were one and the same. The iron gates were to my left, which they were, then the cave wall directly in front of me covered with tree roots may be concealing the tombstone, the one with the secret space in it, the one with the animal skin bag containing what I was after.

With extreme caution, I approached the giant roots still expecting them at any second, to reach out and grab me by the throat. Moving my beam over them trying to see the cave wall or a sign of the tombstone, my light caught something behind the hanging vines that looked like a rather large hole in the wall. Pushing the icky roots to the side, I bravely wiggled into the opening.

Crawling on my stomach for about four feet with my flashlight glowing weakly in front of me, a large room came to light. Regaining my feet and scanning the room I could see the tree roots had extended all throughout its interior. They had made their way through the ceiling and in doing so broke up the plaster that now lay scattered all about, along with a foot of dirt which covered everything in the room.

Moving deeper into the room, I saw a large pedestal in its center covered with dirt. I began to scrape it away when I unearthed the visor of a rusted metal helmet, moving more dirt and pushing aside smaller roots that had grown completely around the pedestal I uncovered what used to be a complete suit of armor, but was now rusted very badly. Inside the armor lay a skeleton, which was woven throughout with the crawling roots, some even protruded out of the eye sockets. The encroaching roots had made a shambles of what was once a magnificent burial chamber. Beside the armor was a long rusted sword and then something shiny caught my eye in the weak flashlight beam. Looking closer, I saw beautiful precious stones on the handle of a silver dagger, whose leather sheath had long since disintegrated. Picking it up, I saw that it was intact, so I slid it into my belt.

Shining my feeble beam around the room, many ancient gold artifacts, drinking cups, old candleholders, crosses, remains of what could have been flags, as well as three other suits of rusted armor came into view. I assumed all along that I was in King Arthur's tomb. But until I saw the headstone on the cave wall and read its inscription, I still could not be positive. I needed to find that stone because beside it was the secret opening that contained the leather pouch which I was seeking.

Obviously if I was in the tomb I must have crawled right past the tombstone, which I was sure lay broken into pieces by the crush of the growing roots. I made my way back out to the opening, scanning the ground for any broken pieces, but found none. The stone appeared to have disintegrated. However, the bag or its contents had to be here somewhere. But where?

Taking a moment in the utter darkness to conserve what little life was left in the flashlight batteries. I played repeatedly, in my minds eye, the vision of the knight and what had he done the day he put the leather pouch into the wall. Then a light flashed in my head, he had not put them in the tomb, but into an area outside of the headstone behind some movable rocks.

Switching on the flashlight I fell to my stomach, shimmied out of the burial chamber, and slid into the water.

Searching the cave wall was difficult because of the roots, but I kept at it when suddenly some small rocks, set rather peculiarly in the cave face and arranged in the shape of a triangle caught my eye. They were right in front of me but the roots of the old Oak blocked my way. Not having an axe to cut thru them, I thought about the shovel.

I turned to get the tool I tripped on something lying underwater on the cave floor. Directing my light into the clear waters I saw several broken stones. Turning one over with my foot I detected a piece with an inscription on it, which read, Jewish to the Tribe. It was a piece of the tombstone that had covered the entrance to King Arthur's tomb. This clinched it for me! Everything in the vision had been true so far, but I still had to find the pouch.

Wading across to the dry ledge that held my equipment, I grabbed the shovel and began attacking the roots covering the triangle of stones. The shovel blade surprisingly cut through them quite easily. With each blow, water, sap and bark flew every which way and soon the cluster of rocks was exposed.

Nervously and with great anticipation, I pushed on the center stone, but nothing happened, which did not surprise me. After all, they had not moved in over nine hundred years. I knew this was going to be a challenge, but I had plenty of time. I wasn't going anywhere anytime soon, if ever. But I was determined, even with the knowledge that I would probably die with it, to see what had been hidden so long ago.

With my pain-wracked body, I waded once again over to my tools and got the six foot steel rod.

Placing the end of the rod into a small crack beside the top stone, I gave a mighty pull downward, and felt movement, tugging again the whole group of stones came loose from the wall and fell into the water at my feet. I took the flashlight I had been holding in my mouth, and leaning against the wall looked into the opening that was behind the rocks, there it was, *THE BAG*.

I reached in and grabbing it, pulled it toward me. It was much larger than I had imagined and the animal skin it was made of had become so hardened with age that it was almost like tin. When I thumped on it with my finger, it made a hollow sound.

I carried the heavy old leather sack reverently to my dry ledge where I could examine it closely. Setting it gently down on my outspread-sleeping blanket I sat across from it and just stared. Here in this bag was the article Rabbi Asher said would be needed at some time in the future and that the world's fate might hinge on it, something that powerful was sitting right here in front of me in this dusty, mildew covered cave. I could no longer hold my anxiety so picking the bag up I attempted to untie the golden rope, which held it closed, however over so long a time it had fused together. I tried to tear the bag but it had become hardened. I felt for the dagger I had taken from the tomb in my belt and using it; I pierced the bag and tore it open. What fell out and onto my blanket struck me like a thunderbolt. It was the most beautiful jewel encrusted golden bowl I had ever seen, and laying beside it, of all things and completely unexpected was, *A MASTER RING* as well as a *SILVER INSTRUCTION BOOK* just like the one I had back in Texas.

Not only did the master ring and book confirm that King Arthur was one of the Jewish knights, the golden vessel was nothing less than, the most beautiful thing I had ever seen. It had to be one of the holiest relics of antiquity and maybe even *THE GRAIL* itself.

The bowl, which was about 18 inches in diameter and stood approximately 10 inches high, was made of solid gold and had an assortment of 12 precious gems set evenly apart on its sides. One strange thing seemed to stand out to me, the bowl's base, it was not round, which is customary, but was in the shape of a square. Each side of the square was about 10 inches long and two of them had grooves that ran their length, a very unusual set-up for just the base of a vessel.

I could not take my eyes off its utter beauty and was afraid to go near it or touch its surface. I sat there watching the Sun's lone ray coming through the hole in the cave roof. It was drawn toward the bowl then bouncing off the jewels. Oh! My, the jewels, they sparkled unbelievably in the sunlight and sent multi-colored rays all around my prison room. It was the most magnificent display of color I had ever seen in my life.

I became so mesmerized that I did not realize that the sunlight was slowly fading and soon it disappeared from my patch of blue sky in the cave roof. I was now in total darkness, which did not bother me much anymore because I had gotten used to the black, silent, emptiness.

Now that I had solved the mystery of what was in the bag, I had no one to share it with, unless some kind of a miracle happened and I should be set free. I was doomed to die right here in this cave and the fate of the world would have to be saved by someone else, who at some time in the distant future might stumble upon this forgotten cave and find the golden treasure as well as my mummified body.

Suddenly, was so tired and bone weary I did not even have the strength to get to the food in my backpack and lay back on my blanket and fell asleep hungry.

A few times in my sleep, I dreamt of food and suddenly there before my eyes, bathed in a shimmering white light was, the golden bowl. I saw it filled with bread and fish that I ate. Then at another time, it was filled with apples, dates and grapes, which I also consumed. Even though I somehow knew I was asleep, I felt my stomach grow full and no longer desired food. I was completely satisfied.

I do not know exactly what woke me from my sleep, but it sounded like someone's teeth chattering. It was a sound I had not heard all the many days I had been here in the hole. I felt my eyelids with my fingertips to be sure my eyes were open and saw only darkness. Hoping my flashlight batteries still held a charge, I turned it on and before cascading its beam around the room I made sure that the Grail was still at my head.

Breaking the pitch-black emptiness with the light beam, I slowly moved it across the waters surface then onto the rear cave walls, Suddenly, two brilliant close-set yellow dots reflected the beam. I closed and re-opened my eyes to be sure I was not seeing something only in my head, but the dots were still there. The reflections came from one of the passageways across the water.

Picking up my shovel for protection, from what I did not know. I slid quietly into the water and turning off my light, moved silently across the pool and nearing the small opening, I switched it quickly on. That was when I saw two yellow eyes staring, unblinkingly directly at me. Concentrating hard in the weak light I could see they were in the head of a small animal with a large tail. The two of us stood there for a few minutes eyeballing one another. I was not sure what was about to happen but expected an attack at any second.

The animal was small, but if he was hungry enough he might attempt to take a bite out of me, but that would be his undoing because I had a weapon, the shovel.

Unexpectedly, instead of him attacking me he seemed to be quite docile. The creature turned and walked up the pathway a short distance, then stopped and again stared back in my direction and directly into my eyes. It was as if begging me to follow, and for some reason, I seemed compelled to do so.

I followed the animal, which I had determined to be a red fox, up the pathway that I had already explored and knew it led to a dead end at a rock wall. When I arrived at the wall the fox was nowhere in sight and I felt a little foolish, thinking I had been chasing a mirage.

As I turned to go back to my bedroll, I heard that funny noise again, like teeth chattering, just above my head. Looking up I saw the fox staring down at me.

He had been real all along and not a figment of my imagination. He was perched about fifteen feet overhead on a ledge about two feet wide. Turning away from me, he ran up the ledge and into a hole in the dirt then came back out again, and did his staring thing. He seemed to be so tame almost as if he was someone's pet.

I felt it necessary to climb the rock face and then crawl up the ledge to the hole, where I shined my flashlight into the opening, and there sat the fox in a den the size of any overturned bathtub.

Looking closely, I saw a pile of moving things, which turned out to be his female and five suckling puppies. However there was another amazing sight in the fox's burrow, a hole about two feet in diameter. What was unusual about it was there was *MOONLIGHT* streaming through it. Instantly the thought of escape from my underground dungeon surged in my head.

Feverously I began to enlarge the opening to the den with my shovel and when it was large enough I began to crawl in with the fox. He was not more than three feet in front of my face surrounded by his pups. If there ever was a time when I would accept a bite to the face it was now. I would gladly, just to get to the opening and the outside, but the fox sat there motionless and he was not the least bit threatening. I was so surprised by the actions and timidity of this animal that for a fleeting moment he seemed to remind me of a small pet dog I once had as a child. Not only did he seem tame but he also had a strange expression on his snout resembling a smile.

Wiggling the rest of my body into the den and pushing the shovel in front of me, I began stabbing at the earth where the starlight was coming through, showering the two cowering canines at my elbow with dirt, but seemingly unafraid, they stood fast.

Suddenly with one last mighty push, the dirt gave way and my shovel broke open the side of the fox's den. Before I could get my body through the opening to the outside, the fox scurried past me and out of the den as if leading me to freedom.

Trembling with excitement I pulled myself upwards and in an instant I was out and onto the starry hilltop. I just sat there exhausted and let the fragrant night breeze fill my lungs with fresh sweet air.

Then the euphoria of freedom hit me and the feeling was overwhelming. I jumped to my feet and with my arms outstretched toward the stars, I shouted at the top of my voice, "*HALLELUIAH*, I'm free!"

All thanks to a furry little creature that must have been heaven sent.

I stood there looking at the starry heavens and said a prayer of thanks to the Lord God Almighty for sending that small creature to save my life. I was convinced this had to be the only explanation for my new-found freedom. He had finally answered my nightly prayers.

Then I remembered the quest that Rabbi Asher had given me, the one to find the object that was going to be of utmost importance to all of mankind. I knew instantly what it was, it was the golden bowl and I had found it. God had sent me falling down through that hole in the cave roof and into the underworld. He had lead me to find the tomb of Arthur and the Grail. I really believe he then sent the fox to lead me back into this world. Like the Rabbi had advised me, everything that was happening to me was preordained ages ago, and was now coming true.

Just then a jolt of fear shot through my brain, the bowl was still in the cave.

Shaking nervously with terror, I fell to my knees and prayed, "My God! Please give me courage because I have to go *BACK DOWN IN THERE*. Back down into the darkness, back down into my prison."

Waiting until sunrise I gathered all my courage and with my trusted lifesaver, my flashlight in my bloody hand, ignoring my elbows, which also ached and bled, I plunged headfirst down into the fox's den and the darkness.

Surprisingly, the batteries seemed to have new life and were full of power because my light shown brightly and lit the way down through the passageway to the pool of water which I waded across to my sleeping place.

My bedroll, backpack and all my tools were just sitting there and I looked at them as if for the first time and with a completely different perspective. Not as my treasured lifesavers which they all had been but merely as just ordinary everyday items which I no longer needed for my survival. Even looking at my remaining food, which I had measured out so carefully all those lonely days and nights, took on a different meaning, almost one of contempt. Instead of my devouring it ravenously, I just threw it to the side, it somehow looked rotten and sickening, anyway I seemed to be completely full and did not desire food at all.

I rolled the golden bowl, the master ring and instruction book in one of my blankets and placed it inside my backpack along with the jewel-studded dagger. I was ready to go, but strangely took the time to once again scan the underground room that had held me captive for so many days. Now knowing my way out, it seemed as though I was leaving a darkened movie theatre just after seeing a spooky film and realizing it was not real at all, just a movie, and I need no longer be afraid.

With the utmost confidence, I turned and in a brief few seconds, traveled a route I could not previously find even after exhaustive searching. Now ironically its existence came to me so easily. It lead me up the passageway to the opening in the foxes den and then out into the sunlight. I would begin once again the life I thought I had lost, but one that would be changed forever.

Wading across the warm waters of the lake and up the adjoining hill, I stopped to take one last look at the island hilltop. Looking back I saw a lone sentinel standing at its crest. It was my friend the reddish fox with his tail whipping in the air as if to say good-bye. I turned my back to him and started the long trek to my waiting Land Rover.

When I arrived at my vehicle, I was astonished at how effortlessly my hike had been. I felt as though I had just awakened from a long restful sleep and was full of vim and vigor. Looking down at my feet I saw that they were no longer injured nor were my elbows. There was not a hint of the cuts or bruises I had received during my escape from the cave, they seemed to have miraculously vanished. Feeling my head where the shovel had hit me, I found that the gash had also disappeared. I wondered if I had just dreamed I ate from the Grail or if I actually did partake of the divine nourishment and its healing powers. Something like this had to have taken place, because cuts and bruises do not just vanish so quickly and my newfound energy was amazing.

Finding the ignition key where I hid it and placing it into the starter slot, I crossed my fingers for good luck hoping that the Rover would spring to life. Instantly the engine turned over then revved to full power. I was on my way back to the hotel in London, leaving behind the gravesite of Arthur to be discovered by some other explorer in the future.

On my long drive back to London, I was not the least bit hungry or fatigued and took only water from the bottles that were on the seat of the truck.

Arriving at my hotel and taking only my backpack, I entered the lobby and approached the desk to ask for my room key. The desk clerk looked at me as if in amazement and asked if I was all right.

"Why yes, I feel fine," I said. Although I knew I must have looked a mess, standing there in my dirty, torn clothes with a mud caked pack on my back and not having showered or shaved for weeks. Not only did I look a sight but must have smelled to high heaven, after all I had spend the better part of a week stuck in a hole in the ground.

Handing me my room key, the man said nothing and just stared at me bug eyed. When I got to my room the thought of a nice hot shower was utmost in my mind. I dropped my backpack and hurried into the bathroom.

Glancing into the full-length mirror, I saw a man that I did not immediately recognize as myself. He was skinny and wore filthy, mud covered, tattered and torn clothing. His hair and beard were long, matted and filled with twigs and small pieces of leaves.

There was dirt in the corners of his eyes, around the mouth and in his ears as well as covering every other part of exposed skin on his body. Looking deep into the man's eyes that appeared in the mirror and asking who he was, I was startled to realize that it was indeed me.

Removing the pieces of clothing that just barely clung there, I let them fall to the floor. Turning the shower on as hot as a person could stand it and stepping in, I stood there letting the water cascade down my body and wash away every particle of soil from the cave.

The scent of the soap in my nostrils and the feel of the washcloth on my face made me want to shout for joy. Then I suddenly remembered the last time I sang out, it was on the hilltop and the thought of the birds pecking me for doing so, and then my plunge into the darkness. It was as if I had experienced a terrible nightmare, but I knew deep down inside it was real. A happier thought came to mind, the Grail. I had found it and it was mine, but what was I to do with it? I would just have to wait and see what Rabbi Asher said would be revealed to me as time went on and God worked his way. Therefore, waiting and resting were the order of the day and then all the next day. When no answer came to me from out of the blue, I began to think of home and my family.

Someone slipped a note under my door. It was from the front desk and stated that because I had paid a week in advance for the rooms they had not rented them out for the second or third week and had just left the room closed, assuming that I would be returning. The note caused me to realize that I must have been in the cave for far longer than I had thought.

Not wanting to keep the room any longer because I was anxious to be homeward bound, I picked up the telephone, called the airport and contacted American Airlines about a flight home to Texas and managed to book a ticket for early the next day. It was costly but I was suddenly in a hurry.

I spent the remainder of the day, paying my room bill, returning the Land Rover and throwing out all the clothes and boots, I had worn while in the hole. I retrieved my valuables from the suite's closet where I had hidden them, and packed them into just one suitcase. I also washed and brushed my backpack so it would be presentable for me to carry onto the plane, then rolling each in a clean hotel towel, I placed the bowl, ring, dagger and book in the pack, and anxiously waited for the next day.

I did not sleep much that night, because I was dreaming of home and Peggy Sue, so as soon as the sun was up, I called The London Cab Company and asked if Mortimer was on duty and if so, I needed a ride to Heathrow. The dispatcher said that yes he was working and would be over to pick me up in about forty minutes.

When the cab arrived, driven by Mortimer and as I was about to climb into the back seat, I asked him in a joking way if he got a kickback on trips to the airport the same as he got bringing them to the hotel. He became very sarcastic with me and asked what I meant by that crack.

I could see that he was serious and very irritated by the off-handed remark so I said, "Mortimer, don't you remember me? The geologist that you dropped off here a couple of weeks ago?"

"Yea I do, but you ain't him," he said with a nasty frown on his face.

Smiling so he might understand I was just kidding I said, "Sure I am, don't you remember I told you that you had won a cigar guessing my profession and you said the wife would not let you smoke in your apartment. That it stunk up the place?"

Turning and looking into the back seat he said, "Right you are governor, what with the beard and all. Well blimey! It is you. What happened? You look completely different."

"Well Mortimer, you might say I was out of this world for a while. Now I'm back and plan to really enjoy myself, no more worrying about tomorrow. You know in the good book it tells us that if you are saved and believe in Christ our Lord there is no need to worry. It's all right there in John,14 verse 27, and the beard, it makes me look a little like a holy man,. Doesn't it?"

Boy, I thought to myself, after quoting the bible passage, that is unusual for me, I do not think I have ever done anything that spontaneously spiritual before. I guess I was a changed man, in more ways than just my looks.

Mortimer gunned the diesel and we were off in a cloud of fumes to the airport. Arriving there, I paid him the fare and slipped him an extra twenty. He tipped his hat as usual then told me to take care of myself and get something to eat because I looked a little thin. Although his parting statement rang true, strange as it seemed I was not thinking of food at all.

Presenting my passport at the gate to the customs officer, he questioned me extensively about my photo not resembling my face. I explained that I had gotten lost while on a field trip and had lost weight and my hair and beard had grown out. He was so interested in my changed appearance that he neglected to ask if I had anything to claim. Instead, after he was convinced that I was who I said I was, he let me pass. Relieved that he had believed me, I then checked my suitcase in and getting a claim check proceeded to the ramp to board my aircraft. However, when I passed through security, the guards said that they would like to make a spot check of the contents of my backpack.

"Oh! My Lord," I thought, what are they going to say and do when they see the bowl and other items? How stupid of me to have them right here on my person, I should have put them into the suitcase that went into the baggage compartment and not subject to inspection.

I had no alternative I had to comply. So calmly I set down my pack and opened it. When the young guard unrolled one of the towels and saw the golden bowl, he asked what it was and had I claimed it at customs.

As if a small voice was in my head telling me just what to say, so it sounded believable, I opened my mouth and out came an excuse that stunned even me. "Well you see officer, these are old religious relics that I found and they do not exceed the value which I am permitted by your government to take home with me."

"Oh, so they are not worth six hundred pounds, then it is alright for you to board your aircraft, and have a nice flight."

As I boarded the plane, I thought I had not lied to the officer at all. I really had found them and as for price, there wasn't one that a person could put on any of these items, they were all *PRICELESS*. For some reason, I do not remember being so concerned about lying. I used to just do it and thought nothing of it. Not sinning had somehow become important to me.

My flight back to the States was uneventful, my seatmate and I slept almost the whole trip. We woke only to eat the meals prepared for us by the steward, however after only a few bites I was satisfied. I surmised that my stomach had shrunk from going almost without food during those lost weeks of mine.

The best part of my return trip I found to be on the small propeller driven airplane from Dallas down to San Antonio. The flight was slow and flew rather low, giving me plenty of time to admire the beautiful green farmland it passed over and I let my body just drink in the warmth of the brilliant late afternoon sunshine which filled the cabin of the small plane. It was so amazing to me that here I was flying through the air, full of life and in a far different place than I had been just a few days earlier, down in that pitch-black cavern and my close brush with death.

Picking up my suitcase from the lone baggage turntable, I walked out to the parking lot and was happy to see my Ford, because it was the means of transportation I needed to make it the rest of the way home to my family and my sweetheart, Peggy Sue.

On the long drive down to Palomino, I thought about all the things I wanted to say to her. How much I missed her and the kids. The despair I felt when I thought I might never see them again. I promised myself that I would tell her the whole story, there was no need trying to hide the treasures I had found. Somehow, I felt they would become the main focus of our lives. Surely of *MY* life.

I was so thrilled as I drove nearer the house, that when I pulled into the driveway I could hardy contain my excitement of seeing my Peggy. It was the same thrill I had when I first saw her on the night we met. I looked down at my sweaty hands, they were trembling and I felt just like a nervous kid going on his first date.

As I got out of the car I looked up, here came Peggy rushing towards me. Suddenly she was in my arms, and we kiss. Her sweet tender kiss, the smell of her hair, the touch of her skin, the look in her eye, told me she loved me. Suddenly she pulled away from me and said in hurried speech, "Honey, why the beard and long hair? And you have lost so much weight. What has happened to you? Almost five weeks is too a long time not to hear from you and I thought that something bad might have happened. Have you been sick?"

Looking into her deep green eyes I said, "No, nothing is wrong with me, I'm just fine. I know I've lost weight but I must admit I have never felt so fit and so alive, enough about me, what about you and the kids? Is everything alright?"

"Yes darling, we are all doing well, except I missed you terribly and so did the kids. Please don't ever leave us again for that long a time."

Just then my children came running out screaming, "Daddy, Daddy," and threw themselves on me almost knocking me to the pavement. They certainly were glad to see their dad, but I think I was much more ecstatic seeing them because I had come within a hairs breath of never seeing them or Peggy Sue again.

Peggy, putting her arm around my shoulder said, "Come on into the kitchen and I'll make us some coffee, then you can tell me the whole story of your trip."

Taking my suitcase and backpack from the trunk of the Ford, I followed Peggy Sue and the kids into the house. I plunked my baggage down on the kitchen floor and slumped in a chair, all the while not taking my eyes off Peggy. She seemed more beautiful and radiant than ever. I could not help myself and started to weep with joy. Suddenly, her arms were around me and I felt her tender touch again. I muttered quietly, "Peggy it's so good to be home. I love you."

Giving me a cup of coffee and stroking my hair she said, "Here, drink this and then tell me everything that happened, just start at the beginning."

Taking a few sips from the hot brew, made just the way I like it, I began telling her the long torturous tale of what had happened and what I had found.

I must have went on and on for what seemed like hours, about where the book had led me as well as what Rabbi Asher had predicted I would find. Peggy Sue spoke up as if seeking something tangible that could prove my story was true. "Zack this is awfully hard to believe, I can't wait any longer. Show me the golden bowl you said you found. You do have it with you,.......... don't you?"

Reaching to the floor and picking up my backpack I said, "Why yes I do, it's right here in my pack." Pulling out the towel that held the artifacts, I unwrapped the bowl and sat it on the table.

A very surprised Peggy Sue appeared to be holding her breath and her eyes widened as big as saucers. She swallowed hard then said, "My God, you really did find something! Zack, it's beautiful, look at how it gleams and all those jewels. It must be worth a fortune. It is real? Isn't it?"

"Sure it is Honey! Not only is it real but so valuable that it is almost beyond human comprehension. Not so much for its jewels and gold content, but for it's mysterious powers. You see it is capable of miraculous healings. Something I think I can actually prove.

Peggy Sue interjects with a puzzled look on her face, "You mean it can cure serious human ailments miraculously? Like heart attacks or cancer? Things like that? It all would be so wonderful, but for heaven sakes how can you prove it?"

"Well I'm not exactly sure, but I think just eating something from it works wonders. Remember my telling you how I got hurt in the cave? Look! Here is my proof. My head where the shovel hit me and my hands and elbows, not a trace of any injury, and the energy I have without eating much food is also unbelievable. Another thing, look here at my crooked finger that was broken playing football. See it is perfectly straight again.

I must have actually eaten from it instead of just dreaming that I did and its powers cured my injuries. There is no other explanation.

You see Honey, I know this may be hard to fathom, but this vessel, is what knights and crusader, have spent centuries searching for, the actual cup that Christ drank from at the last supper. Peggy, this golden bowl sitting on our kitchen table so unpretentiously, I think is none other than, *THE HOLY GRAIL*."

Giving me the third degree she asked, "Zack, how do you know there is a real holy grail? I thought that was just a myth"

She had asked a good question. I thought for a moment then said, "I don't, not for sure. You know it does not have a sign on it that says, HOLY GRAIL. But it did come from a grave who's tombstone read King Arthur and then there was the story that Professor Schweitzer read to me from the black book. He seemed to think it plausible that the grave might hold the grail. But you are right, I can not be 100% sure."

"Wow! This is unbelievably awesome! Even if it is not the real Grail, you had better keep it in a safe place, like the bank vault. My God! What in the world are you going to do with it?"

Peggy Sue had strangely just asked the question which answer I have been waiting for, ever since I first found the Grail.

Nodding my head I said, "You are absolutely right I plan on placing it under the tightest security I can devise. As for what am I going to do with it, I don't have a clue, but something tells me it's too important to mankind than for it sit in a bank vault and collect dust. If the good Lord led me to find it, then there must be a reason, and he may well provide the answer. I only hope it is soon."

Hearing the children racing down the stairs from their bedrooms, I quickly picked up the bowl and rolled it back up in the towel and stuffed it into the backpack. Their eyes and mental capabilities were much too young to contemplate something so mystifying as the grail.

As they kissed me and took seats around the table, each wanting to tell me what had been happening to them at school, so one by one they went through the last several weeks of school activities.

After all four kids had explained every last detail, and we had drunk the entire sauce pan of hot cocoa that Peggy Sue had made, I grabbed Peggy around the waist as she passed by and pulled her down onto my lap and asked, "Now what has the cook been up to all the while I was away?"

Laughing as I tickled her she stuttered, "Why she has been busy slaving away, keeping house, cooking and taking care of her vagabond husband's kids. There is though, somewhat of a surprise that needs to be brought to the husband's attention. His oldest daughter has been getting visits from his friend Wes's youngest son, Josiah."

Kim piped up, "Oh No! Mom you promised not to tell dad until Josiah asks to take me to my prom."

Initially, I was surprised when my daughter said "her prom," then it hit me, time had slipped by so quickly I had not realized, she was almost sixteen. Only one year younger than the age her mother was when I married her. Choking back a tear, I said jokingly, "Well I was wondering when someone was going to come along and take her off our hands. She is getting kind of expensive to keep and has outgrown all her clothes and eats like a pig.

Anyway, Josiah is a nice kid, but what's he doing down here? I thought he was living up in San Antonio with his brother."

It was Kim's turn to be funny, "Dad, don't be so square, we are not getting married you know, we only went to church together a few times. I think he only asked me just to show off the new car his dad bought him for helping out on the ranch. Anyway, he may be too young for me, he's only nineteen."

Chuckling I said, "Well its alright with me if you go out with him. Anyway if he gets out of line with you, I know for sure his dad will give him a busted lip. So Josiah's got a new car, big deal. Why is he back to living on the ranch? Has Wes bought some more cattle or has there been a boom in calving out at their place?"

Kim brushing her hair back said, "No Dad! Now that they have struck oil again, Mr. Johnson has him working full time with the oil crews showing them around their spread and helping out wherever he is needed. He's even been over here several times this past week helping the survey teams lay out a road back to the oil well they discovered by our old windmill."

"I don't get it. What do you mean over here? I said puzzled.

That's when Peggy Sue jumped into the conversation saying, "Zack, there is something I need to discuss with you. If you remember several weeks ago, you told me to go ahead and talk to the oil companies. Well, I did and the same company working at Wes's ranch, Mobil, drilled a test well out back down near the river and hit what they called, pay dirt. They tested the well and it is flowing at the rate of three hundred and fifty barrels a day. With you, not being around I told them to set-up the tank farm up on the hill by the old tumbled down windmill. I hope you will go along with the decisions I've already made. But I will need your assistance with telling them where to drill the next well. They say there are several sites that look promising. Honey……., Honey…., are you listening?"

I was listening all right, but just sat there for a moment in silence thinking that not to long ago I was concerned with being able to spend all of the millions I had found in the secret room in the old mansion. In addition, I had succeeded in spending most of it through giving those bank loans. Now it looked like we were going to be richer than ever. On the bright side, I suddenly realized that Peggy Sue had become a pretty good business women and quite capable of taking care of our assets. Then I heard Peggy Sue again, "Zack, are you with us?"

"Sure Peggy, I hear you and I think its just wonderful. Sounds like you have done a great job. Since you have been working with the oil companies, why don't you continue to do so until I can at least get my feet back on the ground? Boy! A lot of things have happened around here in just a couple of months."

Peggy Sue said with a smile, "Well you are right, it seems that there may have been. However, the thing that pleases me the most is your way of instilling confidence in me, and thanks for doing it again this time. I was very nervous making those decisions, but they just had to be made and I'm glad you agree with me. I was so worried about that. Maybe tomorrow after a good nights sleep we can saddle up two of our ponies and take a nice leisurely ride out and look at the well."

"That will be just fine," I said, "But it has to be very early because I should get over to the bank and check things out there and put, you know what in the vault."

"Okay, that will be great. But there's no work tomorrow, it's Sunday. And no need to worry about the bank, I have been going over to help Martha every now and then and Wes has been real good at overseeing things. Oh Yea! Speaking of Wes, there were two men here at the house just last week asking to see you and I told them that you were out of town. Then when one of them flashed some kind of a badge and asked me if I was sure you were out of town, I calmly shut the door and told them, through the glass, to go in to town and talk to your business partner, Wes Johnson. I don't know if they did but what I said got rid of them. There is one thing for sure, I know you will be pleasantly surprised at how well your office staff has done in your absence."

On hearing her positive report, I felt very relaxed and relived that things had run real well here at home while I was off in a foreign country trapped underground, lost, desperate and hungry. As for the men, I thought that there is always someone looking for me and I was just too happy to be at home to be worrying about who they might be, so their inquiry made no difference to me whatsoever.

Just then, the scent of Peggy Sue's pot roast hit my olfactory nerves in my nose and made my mouth water, I was suddenly famished, and said, "Hey girl! What does a guy have to do around here to get a good meal?"

"Well you could start with kissing the cook, then sit back and see what happens," Peggy said as she kissed me hard on the lips then headed to the stove and brought back food to feed her man. I thought, "Man! Life is good," then proceeded to eat all the food in sight.

Of course eating that much food and being so relaxed, I felt drowsy, so I lay down on the living room sofa. Peggy Sue came over and took off my shoes and began to massage my feet. The next thing I remember was waking up in the night still on the sofa and covered by a blanket put there by my love. I just rolled over and slept like a baby.

The dawn arrived bright, golden and beautiful, making this Sunday morning seem special. It was the dawn of the first day of my new life and I felt filled with joy and wanted to be with my woman, so I snuck upstairs so as not to wake the kids and slid into bed with sweet smelling Peggy. Surprisingly, she was awake just lying there looking out the window.

Playfully I said to her as if mimicking an old rock and roll song, "Hello…….. Baaby" and grabbed her around the waist, pulled her tight to my stomach and said in my sexiest voice, "Is anything going to happen this morning?"

"Yes it is!" she said emphatically, "You are going down stairs and make ME a pot of coffee."

Laughing I said, "What do you mean, make *YOU* some coffee. *YOU* are in charge of cooking around here so *YOU* should go down and make the coffee and then bring ME up a cup."

"Well actually! No, you should do it, and besides, it states in the Bible that the man should do the coffee," Peggy Sue said with confidence.

"In the Bible? That's a good one! You have just got to show me that!"

Peggy slid out of bed and ran laughingly across the room and got the Bible from her dresser, then returned and jumped back into the bed. She then opened the good book to the New Testament and running her finger over the top of the pages said, "See its right here in bold black and white, "*HEBREWS*."

At that, we both began laughing so hard and so loud we woke the kids and ended any chance that I may have had to be amorous ….. so I continued laughing all the way downstairs to, you guessed it,……..*MAKE COFFEE*.

After a hearty breakfast and the kiddies were off to Sunday school, we went out to the barn, to saddle a couple of horses.

When we entered, the horses were standing so still in their stalls they looked like statues. Then coming to life they turned, looked our way and whinnied. The smell of the new cut alfalfa hay gave the air a sweet aroma and the scent of the horse's tack and leather saddles were a horse lover's nasal symphony. Peggy Sue picked her favorite Palomino mare and I my faithful chestnut gelding. Throwing them some of the alfalfa, we cleaned their hoofs with a pick while they happily munched. After brushing then, we put on saddle blankets and then the saddles. When we slipped the bridle and bit into their mouths they knew what was coming next, a leisurely stroll out over the hills and trails then possibly a stop at the first apple tree. They snorted and pawed the dirt with their front hoofs indicating that they were ready to go. Taking the reins, we eagerly lifted ourselves into the saddles and were off on our ride to look over the well site.

It was a wonderful morning. The sun was just starting its daily trip across the heavens, occasionally hiding behind a passing fluffy white cloud. There was a soft warm breeze coming across the meadows and every now and then, we would see a rabbit scampering to its hole. There were Meadow Larks everywhere and they sang out cheerfully. After a couple of hours riding and with the old windmill in sight, Peggy Sue decided to pick up the pace and took off at a gallop while urging me to follow. Even with a head start, her mare was no speed match for my sixteen hands high, very long striding gelding and I was almost instantly on the mare's rump. I could see Peggy's long shiny auburn hair flowing in the breeze, her buttocks and breasts' moving up and down in syncopation with each stride the horse took, and the sight was unbelievably exciting. So exciting that when we reached the windswept hilltop where the windmill once sat and dismounted, I took her in my arms and kissed her hard on those smiling red lips. This time there was nothing to stop us from making love. No kids, no telephones, not even the noisy Larks. So tearing off all our clothes and taking our saddle blankets we lay down in the grass on the sun drenched hillside and made mad, passionate love,............*TWICE*.

After our romantic interlude, we lay there on our backs, buck naked in the warm sunshine and watched the clouds parade across a baby blue sky. We talked and talked about our life together and expressed our deep love for one another and vowed never to part. Suddenly, Peggy Sue jumped up from the blanket, threw on my shirt, as if someone could see her nude in the middle of over a thousand acres, and announced that she had a surprise for me. Walking over to her grazing mare, she retrieved her saddlebags, returned and opening them, laid out my lunch. Ever the homemaker and thinking ahead, she had quickly gathered left over cold chicken legs from the fridge, had buttered some French bread and filled a thermos full with the coffee she had kidded me into brewing. She had thought of everything and I lay there in amazement thinking that someone like her could love a guy like me, but that's the way it was and at that precise moment in time, I considered myself the luckiest man on earth.

Finishing my lunch, I refused Peggy's requests for some help picking up the dirty dishes and cups because I was so at peace with the world, and in such a state of bliss, that I just would not move. However, when she begun getting dressed and said we should get on over to look at the well because it looked like it might rain, I took the hint and put on my clothes, then helped her clean up. One last kiss and then we remounted our ponies and cantered the few miles to where the well had been drilled.

As soon as we got within a hundred yards of the well, I could detect the rotten egg smell of oil, which was floating on the drilling mud held in a small dirt dam. Two oil stained dark green holding tanks sat on a freshly made bed of sand, one filled and the other taking on more oil which flowed under pressure from the wellhead. I could see and smell why so many ranchers hated to let companies drill for oil on their land. Once a well came in, the pump jacks, looking like huge black praying mantis seemed so out of place on the horizon, mixed in with the beauty of the landscape and the roving cattle. But the lure of almost unbelievable wealth went a long way to subdue this ill feeling.

With the sight of the well on my property and the prospects of more to come, it was apparent that we too had succumbed to the lust for money. Even though I had enough of it, I found it to be very fickle and I was trying my hardest to get rid of most of it. I had always felt that, over and above a persons daily needs, with a little set aside for a rainy day, anything more was like a burden around ones neck. More or less, anyone who found they had too much money always tried to get some of it and then came the struggle of trying to keep from going broke. What a hell of a viscous cycle.

Peggy Sue pointed out dark clouds forming on the horizon so we skedaddeled back to the barn just in time to avoid getting wet from a deluge of water that fell from the sky which all but ended the perfect day I would remember forever.

The next day it was back to reality and when I entered my bank, I realized just how special the day before had been because the place seemed to be in such pandemonium. Typewriters clacking, telephones ringing off their hooks, people chattering back and forth, and Martha with all kinds of problems and her questions about my appearance. Oh how I longed for that windy hilltop, not the one that I had fallen into and almost died. No! I wanted no part of that one. I meant the one with my Peggy Sue yesterday, when the birds sang love songs to us.

I asked Martha to come into my office so we could discus in private the many issues she had faced while I was away. First, in order to quell her anxiety about my health, I explained to her that my new shaggy look came from having been lost for several days in the wilds of England and that I was not ill or on the verge of passing away. She seemed satisfied and relieved that I was going to be in the upright position for some time to come, then proceeded for over an hour to give me her report. Listening intently,

I then determined the solution to most of the bank problems was as usual, lack of cash. Asking her to return to the outer office I said I would soon bring her the needed money. Slipping out the side door of my office to the trunk of my Ford, I picked up my backpack and moved un-noticed back into the bank and the vault. Finding an empty footlocker, I placed the pack, which contained the mystic vessel, the ring, book as well as the dagger, in the container, then stacked several empty lockers on top of it, making the area look as inconspicuous as possible.

Finding another locker or trunk which still contained currency was not as easy as a few years before. Out of the original six large steamer trunks and fourteen footlockers, all full and containing well over four million dollars, I found only two trunks and six footlockers which still held cash. Judging by the empty lockers it was apparent that I had loaned out or spent over half of the fortune I had found in the old mansion.

From one of the cash laden lockers, I took the necessary amount of money Martha needed in order to fund the loan applications she had piled on her desk. On my walk to her office, a pleasing thought crossed my mind. Even though I only had a little over two million dollars cash remaining in the lockers, it was not as if I had lost or thrown away the other two million. Most of it was safely invested in interest bearing loans made to good hard working people who were using the funds to secure the future of our small town. I was thrilled to think that the cash horde I had found, and had become such a burden to me, had somehow through my bank, become the means for making hundreds of poor people productive citizens. In doing so they were living happy, fruitful and productive lives. Who says money is the root of all evil? In this case, money had done some good, and to some, it was a blessing.

Martha was gracious as usual when she took the greenbacks from my hand and complemented me on my generosity.

With the temporary problem of a cash shortage out of the way, I walked back to my office with a feeling of pride brimming over inside of me. The telephone on my desk was ringing loudly, so picking it up I heard Wes on the other end of the line say, "Well howdy pardner! I heard y'all were back in town. When y'all get in?"

"Hey Wes! I've been home since Saturday afternoon. How are you doing?"

"Mighty fine, If I says so myself. If things get any better it might be illegal. I thought I would come and fetch y'all and take ya ta lunch. I got a heap of things to tell ya. If yer ready to put on the feed bucket I'll come git ya. We can eat and I can bring ya up to speed on what's been a happin."

Looking at my office clock and surprised at the time I said, "Is it lunch hour already? By God it is! Sure old buddy come on over and we will get some lunch."

It seemed as if I had just hung up the telephone receiver when Wes came bounding into my office. Giving me a big hug, he shook my hand and then plunked down into a chair. Looking at me strangely he said, "Hey cowpoke y'all sure yer Zack Heikel? My friend and business pardner? Cause y'all looks like a skinny bum just off a banana boat."

I was happy to see Wes and tickled to hear his colorful expressions, but unhappy that my appearance had changed so much that he had to comment on it. I said in my defense, "Yea! It's me alright, but I sure hope I don't have to give an explanation about my looks to everyone I meet in the next few days. Maybe I should make a little recording about them and then just play it whenever someone asks.
On second thought, why don't we just have Martha go get our lunch and bring it back here. It sure would save me a lot of time on explanations."

Wes chuckled slightly and said, "Ya knows y'all could be right, If we go over to da cantina everyone will be a wonderin who is the long haired lunatic I have comin ta eat with me. Y'all be doin so much talking we aint got time to down our vittles."

Getting Martha on my intercom, I asked if she could have someone go to the diner and bring Wes and myself two specials to eat here in my office. She answered that she would do so right away.

Turning to my friend, I asked what had been going on in his life the last few months. However, he insisted that I first tell him what had happened to me because looking at my changed face, it must have been something drastic.

I knew there was no way I could come clean with Wes. He would never believe a word I would say so I had to stretch the truth. I told him that I had become separated from my hunting party and become lost in the wilderness for over three weeks. With my only food being an occasional berry and just water from streams were the reason I had lost a lot of weight and my hair and whiskers had grown out.

With a puzzled look on his face Wes said, "I did not know y'all went off ahuntin and I didn't think England was that big whereas ya could get lost over thar fur three weeks without someone aseein ya."

Answering his questions I said, "Wes, England is a big country and it is quite easy to get lost and I proved it could happen. But that's all ancient history now, and I'm tired of talking about me. What has been going on here in the real world? I hear that your son, Josiah is back living at home with you. Any truth to that."

"Why yes it's all true. Ma boy is back up at da house, which sure makes me and the misses happy. There is just no way I kin get by without him now that we's got so much activity with dem oil companies adrillin everywhere. It don't pain me none either, that thar bank account is sure a risin fast. Hey! I bet Y'all was surprised about the well they all found on yer spread? Both of usins is goin ta be millionaires."

Just then, our lunch arrived from the diner across the street, being carried by none other than our sheriff, Billy Flynn Barrett, who, after setting it down on my desk said hello to Wes and then said to me, "Well, welcome home stranger. I was over eatin and when I was fixin to leave saw these here lunches sittin there with a note a sayin they was fur y'alls so I thought I'd bring'um ta ya. I need to talk at ya anyways. Say, what the hell happin to yer face?"

I thought, "Oh no! Here we go again. I better get a shave and haircut and put a stop to all these questions." But before I could say a word Wes spoke up, saving me the trouble and said, "Zack here, got himself lost whilest on a huntin trip over thar in England, didn't eat nothing but grubs and water fur a coupla of weeks."

Now the sheriff throws in his two cents making fun of me by saying, "I didn't know y'all was a hunter, and why in the dickens would y'all be agoin that fur aways. We gots some of the best shootin in da world right cheer in Palomino. Why I even seen a bob cat yestidy."

Taking a bite out of my tuna fish sandwich I asked, "What was it you needed to talk with me about sheriff?"

"Oh yea, remember the burglar dat got burned ta bits?" Billy Flynn commented in the form of a question.

Rather sarcastically, I said, "Now sheriff, how in the world could I have forgotten about that. Sure, I remember. What about it?"

Taking his hat off and scratching the top of his head he said, "Well there wuz a couple of agents of some kind, been at ma office askin questions about his demise and wantin to talk to ya. They wants me ta call um when I next sees ya. They's all from somewheres up north."

Just then, Wes chimed in again, "Thems the same two pokes in black suits that's been out to yer place. Peggy Sue sent'em down ta talk ta me. Asked me some mighty strange questions about the professor and ast if I sawd any unusual finger rings. I had no eye dee what they was asayin."

The sheriff commented that if I had time to see the men, he would telephone the hotel room where they were staying, tell them I was back in town, and ask them to come right over.

I said with a mouthful of sandwich, "Sure why not. Get them over here and let's see what this is all about."

They must have been most anxious to meet with me because ten minutes could not have passed before Martha escorted them into my office.

After saying hello to the sheriff and Wes, one of my visitors asked my two friends if they would please excuse themselves because he and his partner wanted to meet with me in private. When Wes and Billy Flynn were leaving the office one of the men walked over and closed the door behind my two parting compardaes.The other stranger took a seat in front of my desk and said that he would like to ask me a few questions about Professor Schweitzer.

Rather unhappy at the way they seemed to take over my office I said abruptly, "Just a minute here, who in the hell are you two jokers?"

The guy seated in front of me said as if surprised, "Oh! We thought that the sheriff told you we are investigating the disappearance of Professor Schweitzer."

"No" I said, "He just told me that you wanted to see me and said nothing about anyone disappearing. Do you men have names and maybe some credentials?"

The seated fellow took to his feet as if coming to attention and the man at the door said striding toward my desk, "Yes sir we do, I am Gabe Simeons and this here is agent Jed Cohen. Here is our identification."

Taking from their outstretched hands and looking at the ID and badges, I was surprised to see that they were both from the CIA. Handing them back to the agents I asked, "What does the CIA have to do with a missing person? I would think this is responsibility the police would assume."

"No sir not in this case." Agent Cohen said, "You see Sir, the professor was working on some very classified government projects as well as one for NASA and when he turned up missing it became a federal case."

"Okay," I said, "I understand that, but a federal case usually gets the FBI involved, not the Central Intelligent Agency. What gives here?"

"Yes Sir, you are right and normally that is the case, but this is a very unusual situation. Due to the very sensitive and secret material Professor Schweitzer was working on, his disappearance could affect national security. That is how we became involved."

"Alright, now I have the picture. Now what's this about Professor Schweitzer missing, missing from what? Where?"

"Mr. Heikel, there is no need to jockey back and forth with us on this, so why don't you just come clean and let's cut right to the chase. We know for sure he came down here over six months ago and never returned to Michigan. We know this because a certain letter was turned over to us by one of his colleagues; it was sent from you inquiring about diagrams in a rare old book you had found. We know he communicated with you and then took a plane down to San Antonio and we know that he was here in Palomino. Now please make it easy on yourself and tell us everything you know."

I sat there silent for a few minutes looking at my two visitors and thought, "My God so many strange things had happened over the last several months to me and some right here in this office. I had the overwhelming sinking feeling another one of those event was about to take place. They seemed to know a hell of a lot more about the disappearance than they were telling me, so I had the weird impression it was just a matter of time before I was placed under arrested for suspicion of murder.

"Alright," I said "I'll talk, but keep my family and friends out of this, they know absolutely nothing about what happened."

"Okay we will, if we can. But what happened. Tell us."

"Yes, the professor was here! He was helping me to decipher an old Hebrew text I had discovered in an ancient manuscript. He was here for about a week when he got a call from someone up in Michigan saying he was needed back at the university. I took him to the airport that very evening. The last time I saw him he was boarding his aircraft."

"Now there you go again, trying to put us on a wild goose chase. There was no call from the university and there was no trip to the airport. He never left Palomino. Did he?"

"As far as I can remember he did," I said nervously.

"Sir we have every indication pointing to you as being involved in his disappearance. We do not think, in fact we know, he did not leave this office."

"What do you mean you know he did not leave this office? How do you know he was even in this very room? Tell me that, why don't you?"

Agent Cohen, sliding to the edge of his chair and looking directly into my eyes said, "Mr. Heikel, we know just about everything that took place here in this room. You see we intercepted the image projected by your circle of rings. We just don't know what happened to the professor. You can rest assured that we will understand and believe everything you will say and nothing you could describe will amaze us. Go ahead and divulge to us the burden we know you have been carrying for so long."

He had come right out with it so I was the one amazed that they knew about the rings. Taking a second to get my head screwed back on, I then said, "You know about the rings and what they can project? Then you must know about the book of instructions."

"Yes Sir! As I said, we know about everything, except the whereabouts of the professor or his body."

I realized I was dealing with people that probably knew more about the rings and their capability than I did, so without any further deception on my part I asked them to follow me into the bank vault. I took them to where the footlockers lay and pointed out the one with the yellow check mark on its side, then asked them to carry it back into my office, which they did. I closed and locked my door behind us as we entered. I wanted to keep my arrest as private and quite as possible.

Agent Simeons was the first to speak and asked, "Now that we have this locker in here, do you mind telling us what's in it."

Trembling with fear I said, "Why the professor's body!"

"Are you sure, it seems awfully light to be holding the remains of a two hundred and fifty pound man."

"Yes I'm sure and its light because there is just ashes left of him."

Agent Simeons, opening the locker saw the plastic bags and looking in one of them said, "Ashes, nothing but ashes. It will be next to impossible to identify anyone from these. Why don't you just tell us how this happened?"

"Okay I will but you have to promise me that you are capable of understanding what I am about to tell you. I don't want to end up in a straight jacket."

"Mr Heikel, rest assured we will understand. We know about Rabbi Asher if that will help satisfy you."

If they knew about Rabbi Asher, they were definitely in the know about the rings and how dangerous they could be. So I went on and told them about how the professor died during an experiment that ghastly night when a lightning bolt struck nearby just as the professor placed

one of the capacitor rings on his finger and the result-
ing electrical surge that swept through his body and how
grotesque his death had been. I explained to them it was
an accident and how I tried to stop him from putting on
the ring but could not do so in time. The ring discharged
into his body and he was incinerated. I paused for a moment to catch my breath and surprisingly Agent Cohen
walked to my side of the desk, put his arm around my
shoulder, and told me to take it easy. He understood just
how I felt because he had gone through a similar experience watching one of his co-workers die in exactly the
same manner.

Somewhat confused, but relieved that someone else was
experimenting with the rings and therefore could understand and believe all the strange phenomena surrounding
them, caused me to completely relax and totally drop my
guard. Now that I was at their mercy, so to speak, I wondered if they would be carting me off in handcuffs out
through the lobby of the bank, or just out the side door
thereby saving me from total humiliation.

I had resigned myself to going to jail and asked Agent
Cohen if he was placing me under arrest. His answer
shocked and surprised me but confirmed what I had
thought earlier, that they knew everything there was to
know about the rings. I still however, held out hope that
they did not know anything about the four million bucks

I had found in the mansion. Not wanting to blow this thing wide open about the found money, because I felt I must be guilty of some type of Federal offense in that regard. I vowed silently to myself not to utter a word about that subject.

Cohen took from his pocket a notepad and pencil and then told me, "No! I do not think we need to do that just yet. However, a lot will depend on how much more you want to tell us and if you are willing to co-operate completely. We know that Rabbi Asher gave you his ring and two others and that you men managed to put together enough rings to have a viewing. Now! Just what did you see and did you act on any of the rabbi's suggestions?"

Faintheartedly I said, "I am willing to co-operate with you men, if only for my own satisfaction and to keep my sanity. I have got to find out just what this whole mystery of the rings is all about. I have come close to death twice because of them and they have just about scrambled my life. It's apparent to me that the CIA has all the answers. But first, before I tell my story, you have got to tell me how you knew about Rabbi Asher?"

Now it was Agent Gabe Simeons doing the talking, "Zack, if you are straight with us we will be straight with you. The agency has known about Rabbi Asher for years and thought at one time that he may have died, but when we saw him in the ring generated plasma we recognized him immediately. You see Zack we in the CIA have been monitoring the ring transmissions at Langley Air Force Base for decades but in the last several years, they had all but stopped. You first became known to us and that you had a master, as well as enough capacitors rings to start a cycle, when you and the professor fired them up the night he was killed, but the transmission was so short and weak we could not get a fix on exactly where it originated. We tracked you down when the professor came up missing. Now if you keep talking, we will keep talking and the things we reveal to you will be breathtaking. So go on now with what you saw in the force field the night with the rabbi, and then what you did, if anything, about your vision."

I could understand why these guys were CIA agents. They were forceful and assertive and knew just how far in front of me to dangle that carrot. So wanting more answers to the bizarre story of the rings and the red plasma, I continued my tale and began to speak, "Well, after the night the professor died, I all but gave up on solving the riddle of the book and rings I had found in the old mansion up in Michigan. Anyway, the professor was the only one who could decipher the ancient Hebrew writings and that left me completely helpless. So I just threw the rings into a briefcase and locked them in my vault here at the bank. Then one day, out of the blue, this strange old guy, Rabbi Asher came strolling into my office with a suitcase containing enough rings to complete a circuit and had the knowledge of how everything went together. Saying that he had seen me in that short transmission the professor and I had put together and because I now possessed one of the rings, I was now as one of them. One of them meaning, I guess, The Knights of Zion. I hope you men do know about that organization, don't you?"

"Yes! We do Zack! The CIA has been keenly interested in it for years. It is a very ancient and secret order of Jewish men. I don't want to get to deeply involved in a conversation about that subject just now, but basically," ………….. he paused shortly then continued, "Now let me explain something to you here. First, I don't have all the answers, but there are guys up at Langley that do and we may eventually have to take you up there. But this much I do know, The United States Government has known about the Knighthood of Zion for hundreds of years. They first became aware of the existence of the knighthood when during an exploratory dig in some old tombs in the Sinai Peninsula in 1836, they unearthed a hand cut stone box containing several very unusual rings and a most unusual metal plated book. The book, which outlined what the mission of the knighthood was and how the organization was structured, also mentioned a communications system using the earth's magnetic field in connection with atmospheric static electricity somehow inter-connected with the rings. This is something the agency is still researching even after all these years.

Of course because of the advanced technological knowledge contained in just the plated book, and such information being unheard of at the time and well above and beyond the knowledge of the worlds brightest scholars and top scientists, everything was kept totally secret. They spent several years decoding the Hebrew Texts and collected from all over the world, whenever they were found, enough rings to form a circle. They finally succeeded in gathering at least seven, created the first force field plasma in 1888, and were amazed at the visions they could project. They determined through decoding that there were 12 master rings and 144 slave or capacitor rings which were used to power the masters. Extensive testing has been done over the years, and much information and many scientific advances have been made, but there is still so much to be learned and just what the main intention of the rings truly are has yet to be revealed, and until the CIA has all of them assembled in one place, the experiments cannot go forth. So you see Zack it is imperative for you to divulge all the knowledge you have about the rings and where any can be located. Believe you me, your government will be most gratified and grateful. It could be very rewarding for you if you can help. Now tell us how many rings you have in your possession and then get back to what you saw in the flux."

Talk about being flabbergasted, I was. This was almost too much information hitting me all at one time. However, what the professor had deduced from the Hebrew Texts had been right on, so that was not much of a surprise. What was a surprise, and becoming more apparent to me, was the rings were just a small part, although a fascinating one, of something much larger than their being able to project an image of past events of ancient history. I was beginning to see a much grander picture, something on a worldwide scale, an event of some extra ordinary huge magnitude.

The more these guys talked, the more I was convinced they were describing something very radical and of biblical proportions. Extremely inquisitive to learn more details from them, I talked some more, "I was wondering when you were going to ask me how many rings I have. Well I have seven, two masters and five slaves. One thing is for sure, you, the CIA or the US Government are welcome to all of them. I just want to get rid of them. They have been nothing but grief for me since the day I found the first one. The grief turned to being almost deadly for me when I went over to England to investigate a vision the rabbi and I saw in the plasma. It was a vision of the middle ages and of knights in a very desperate struggle, then after the battle, we saw them hide something in a leather pouch in a cave next to a tombstone. I went over hoping to locate that cave and the pouch."

Before I could utter another word, Agent Cohen spoke up abruptly and said, " Well Zack did you fall into anything of importance?"

"Man you hit the nail right on the head. That's exactly just what happened I actually fell *INTO* an opening in the roof of a cave in the wilderness and spent over three weeks trapped inside. If it were not for my following a small red fox up one of the tunnels and escaping through his burrow, I probably would have died there from starvation."

Wide-eyed and intensely interested the agent exclaimed, "The tomb, Zack. Did you find the tomb?"

Wanting to please them and interested in getting this secret information off my chest, I continued with my confession, "Yes I found the tomb and I hope you both will believe this one. It was the tomb of the fabled King Arthur."

With a blank look on his face Cohen said, "What makes you think it's his grave?" Surprised that he was so unimpressed, I said, "By the writings on the headstone, which read, "Here lies the remains of his royal majesty King Arthur."

Cohen still expressionless said, "That might be interesting to some people but actually we do not care whose tomb it was. We have investigated, over the years, many discoveries of ancient tombs, some rather famous others not, and a few that were downright frauds. But in most cases, we found they contained nothing of sustenance or interest to us. Therefore, it is not very exciting who was interned in the grave. However, what may have been in the grave is another matter. Something in the leather pouch might be of the utmost importance to us, we would be most interested in that thing. Did you locate the sack?"

"Yes I did!" I said emphatically.

"Well man out with it, where is it?"

"Hey! Take it easy. It's safe! Its right here in the bank's vault, with the rings."

"All right then. Let's go get them! And I mean everything. The sack, the rings, the books, anything you have. We want it all."

The three of us scampered out to the vault and I gathered the contents of the safety deposit box containing my old briefcase and the old wooden bound book. Carefully selecting the footlocker with the backpack and retrieving it, I put everything in a large empty box, so as to conceal the articles from any prying eyes in the banks outer business office. Then carrying the box, we retreated once again into the sanctity of my personal office.

The two agents could hardly wait until I closed and locked my office door. They then went directly to my backpack, opened it and removed the towels in which I had rolled the artifacts. When their eyes fell upon the unrolled content of the towels, I thought they were going to die right there from an overdose of excitement. Holding the heavy golden bowl in his hand, Agent Simeons turned to Cohen and jubilantly said, "My God Jedidiah, look at the square base and the gems. This is it! I think it's the *GRAIL*. After all these years of searching, now we have it. They are going to be unbelievable ecstatic with this back at Langley."

Turning to me he said, "Zack you do not have any conception what this golden vessel means to the human race. What you have found could be the most important discovery of all time!"

Perplexed by his statement I said, "Don't you think you may be overstating this discovery a little? I can think of several very impressive finds in the past. Why, I have had that bowl sitting on my kitchen table, carried it around on my back and I even ate some food out of it one night when I was stuck down in that cave. So its not all that impressive to me other than it might be worth a fortune because of its age and all those jewels inlaid in its sides," I said nonchalantly.

The frown that swept across Agent Cohen forehead gave his face a very serious look and the tone of his voice told me the question he asked deeply troubled him, "Zack, did you say you ate from this vessel?"

"Sure!" I said. "It was a trying time the day I found it. I was totally exhausted and fell asleep with it at my head, and sometime during my sleep I dreamed about food. Suddenly, I woke abruptly to see it sitting there filled with bread and fruit, so because I was hungry as hell I ate most of it. I must say that since that time I don't think I have ever felt so good and so many of my health problems just seemed to vanish. I don't seem to require a lot of food after that night, I just don't seem to need much anymore."

Quietly rolling up the grail once again in the towel and replacing it in the backpack with the other articles, the agent said in the most earnest way, "Zack, I'm afraid that you and the relics will have to come up to Langley with us immediately."

Shocked I said, "Hey wait a minute you said that if I told you everything I knew and gave you all of the artifacts that you would not arrest me. Now you say you are going to do it. I don't understand. How long will you be keeping me?"

"Zack, we can arrest you if need be or do whatever we feel is necessary to take you with us, but I'm afraid your stay............ will be permanent. You have acquired too many secrets about the rings to be living among the general populace. Now by your own admittance partaken of the food of the grail and touched the divine. Even though you may not be aware of it as yet, partaking of the food from the grail makes you a very special person. You now will have to dedicate the rest of your life to a much higher calling. Believe me Zack when I say a higher calling, I mean of the utmost *HIGHEST*."

I felt as if I was about to throw up the moment I heard the word, permanent, and said almost as if begging; "Please don't take me away from my family. I have kids and a wife I love dearly. I do not know if I can even live without her. Look, the CIA doesn't have to worry about me. I won't say or divulge anything about what we have discussed here today or what I found. You can trust me to keep still."

"Zack I'm afraid it's not a matter of trust. You have crossed over and entered something much more profound than one petty life and it would be impossible for us to describe what you have gotten yourself into. You must see it for yourself. You know Zack, we both also have a family just like you do, but they think we were killed in an aircraft accident. We understand what you are going through because we had to make the same decision and that it took a lot of courage to gave up that life to be part of an earth shaking event like none other ever in the history of mankind,......... but we did. Now, you too are going to be a part of it and unfortunately, like it or not, you *WILL* be joining the project. Unlike us, you have no choice.

Eventually, after a little while, you will get used to the idea and realize that you made the right decision, especially after you see the scope and impact of the project and how it will ultimately affect all of mankind. Now you must decide what you are going to tell your wife and kids. We could arrange for a cover story of an accident, if you like, that usually lets them down the easiest."

Enraged that they thought that they could dictate to me how I would spend the rest of my life I said, "Listen you two bastards, I've had it with this bullshit. This is a free country you know or maybe the CIA doesn't see it that way, but it is. And another thing, I have never let my family down in my life and I don't intend to start now. Anyway I could never leave them just like that," as I snapped my fingers loudly.

Proceeding with my dressing down of these interlopers, I said angrily, "Not only are you two bastards, but you are liars as well. You said that if I co-operated with the CIA and gave you everything I had in regards to the rings and the grail, which by the way I risked my very life to find, our government would be most pleased and gratified and I would be rewarded. Well if taking me away from my family, then lying to them about my death is my reward, then there is no way in hell I will believe anything you two might promise. Now get the hell out of my office and take those damned things with you!" I shouted at the top of my voice while pointing to the box containing the artifacts.

Cohen, the larger of the two men, moved closer to me and said almost in a whisper, "It's unfortunate that you are taking it this way, but as I said you have no choice."

Looking down at his clinched fist, I saw he held a large caliber silver handgun with its barrel pointed directly at my belt buckle.

"Zack, I had hoped you would understand our position and the gravity of the opportunity we are offering you to serve mankind. But I can see that even if we explained to you the sanctions we could take against you and your family, it's apparent by your demeanor that you are adamant about not coming with us. Now I will give you one last opportunity to say farewell to your family and if you don't take it, we will be forced to handcuff you and take you bodily, if necessary, up to Langley. I think you will believe me this time, and you know I am dead serious.

You do believe me now,.............don't you?" he said looking at me menacingly as I felt the nudge of the pistol in my stomach.

I suddenly realized this guy might just eliminate me as a problem by pulling the trigger, as I am sure he must have done many times before to anyone that did not go quietly. After all, they had everything they wanted and did not really need me. So I decided to co-operate because I knew I was out of options. Furthermore, I was very inquisitive about the project Cohen had mentioned. I was sure it involved the rings and the grail but to what extent I could only guess. But I must admit I was intrigued. However the thought of never seeing my family again was beginning to soak in and it was a frightful thought. One I had to cope with somehow. I needed time to think and asked Cohen if I could be alone for a few moments. He said I could have fifteen minutes, but he would be just outside the office door and Simeons would be at the side exit. He did not want any tricks out of me.

As soon as I was alone I realized that my situation was much too intense for me to work out myself. I needed some help. I remembered how I had prayed when I was trapped in the underground tomb and how God had sent the small animal to help me escape. Then Cohen's words reverberated in my mind saying that the divine had touched me. I thought there might be something to that after all. Ever since, I found the gold bowl and eaten from it, I had become a completely different man mentally and physically. So, with that in mind, I lowered my head and began to pray, "Dear Lord, wherever you are, please hear my prayer. Give me the strength to do the thing you have laid before me. Fill my brain with the wisdom to select the right words that will exit my mouth, and enter my loved ones ears so they will accept my leaving with enthusiasm and hope of my swift return. When I don't, watch over them, and fill their lives with happiness and success. Amen"

I sat there for a while and used several pieces of tissue to dry the tears that cascaded from my eyes. Then the tears stopped abruptly and I felt much better. I had the sense that a huge weight had been lifted from my shoulders and everything was going to be all right. I was sure my family would be in the Lords hands and would be well cared for, how I knew it, I was not sure, I just did. Nevertheless, to be extra sure they would have every advantage, I had to get some assurances from the CIA that Peggy Sue and the kids would get government assistance in any way they needed.

Just then, the two agents re-entered my office and Cohen asked if I had figured out what to say to my wife. I told him I was not sure what I would say, but I would think of something. However, I had a question for him. Now that I would be out of my families lives, who would take care of them if they needed some assistance? Cohen said he understood my concerns but assured me they would be provided anything they needed as a safety net and would not want for anything and made the remark, "The agency takes care of its own."

Somewhat relieved there was a plan for families of those involved in clandestine activities, I told Cohen I was ready to go with them. I asked him if we could delay our departure an hour or so until I saw my kids. Cohen said a flat, "No" to that. It would not be possible, as we had to leave immediately. We had delayed to long already, and there was only time to see my wife. He added that I seemed to be in better spirits and asked what had changed my attitude so quickly. All I said was, "I prayed."

Cohen smiled and said, "You know prayer always helps and I was sure it would in this case, especially with you. I was about to suggest prayer earlier to you, and that maybe you should "say your prayers" but having showed you the gun, I did not want you to be alarmed that I was about to shoot you. Zack, I am sorry I had to threaten you with the firearm, but you must accompany us up to Langley and you were resisting. You know we do have our orders."

"Alright" I said, "Lets get on with it. I'm ready to go, but first I need to have a few words with my bank manager."

Summoning Martha into my office I informed her I would be leaving again, and that she should take all her orders from my wife Peggy Sue. Winking to her I said, "Any money that the bank may need from our "Special Fund" (meaning the remaining cash stashed in the foot-lockers), you should have Peggy Sue get it for you. I told her how much I admired her for her dedication to her job and I hoped she would help Peggy Sue as much as she had assisted me." Saying she would co-operate any-way she could with my wife. We shook hands and said good-bye.

As we exited the bank, I started toward my Ford out of habit but Cohen and Simeons grabbed me under the arm-pits and lifted me slightly off my feet, "Sorry Zack, you won't be needing your car where you're going. You are coming with us," Cohen said as they pushed me into the back seat of their black suburban.

As we sped toward my home, several opening lines went through my head that I might use when I attempted to tell my precious that I was leaving her again. However, each line I stumbled with rang hollow and meaningless. I was afraid I would not be able to speak at all and might break down crying, giving away the whole fable that I was just going up to Langley Field for only a few days, not for the rest of my life.

When we pulled up in front of the house, my rehearsing had done absolutely no good at all, because when Peggy Sue came out to greet us, all I could do was hold her close to me. I stood there holding her in a tight embrace when she suddenly said with a happy note in her voice, "Are you here with your friends to eat or just to visit?"

Even the mention of food at a time like this gave me the feeling that I might want to puke, but I managed to say with the best look I could put on my face, "No Honey, I have just stopped for a second to pick up a few things. You see, I have to take a fast flight up to Langley Air Base with these two gentlemen. I'll only be gone a couple of days."

"Oh no Zack, you have only been home a few days from your overseas trip and now you have to leave again. That is not fair to me, and what about the kids? What do I say to them?" My sweetheart said disappointedly.

"I know it's not fair to anyone especially the kids, but I am sure you will think up some unique answer that will have them laughing. But Honey, you must understand I am not going of my own accord. I have no choice, I have got to go. Isn't that right Mr. Cohen?" I said motioning towards agent Cohen.

"That's right Madam, and we don't intend to keep him too long." He said lying through his teeth.

As usual, she accompanied me up to our bedroom where she filled my suitcase with a few changes of clothing and my toilet articles. I studied her intently and it was all I could do to keep from breaking down. She was her usual beautiful self, smiling and helping me in any way she could. I reached out, grabbed her and kissed her warmly then gave her a few brief instructions about the bank, left her my office and car keys and told her to take care of herself and the kids. Grabbing my suitcase and closing it, Peggy commented that she was not through packing it yet. Little did she know that I had to leave at that precise moment because I could not take the hurt I was feeling in my heart and felt as if I was going to die right there! I knew to stay and not go with these men meant certain death anyway. They would shoot me where I stood and possibly even kill Peggy for good measure. I turned my back to her, so she could not see the tears streaming down my cheeks and ran to the door, shouting at the top of my lungs, "Peggy no matter what happens, I will always love you,………… always. Goodbye." ……..My throat closing tightly in a lump around the end of my sentence.

As we drove away, I took one last look back over my shoulder only to see her smiling face and waving hand high in the air. I cried openly when I made out the expression on her lips, "Goodbye My Darling."

I cried for so long and so hard I was not even aware that it had gotten dark and we had been driving for two hours. As we passed through a heavy wire gate and entered a large complex, I asked the agents where we were.

Agent Simeons replied that we were at an airbase in Beeville. We drove onto the base and to some barracks where I was given a shave and a brush hair cut. I was then moved to a small hospital where after having me remove all my clothing, they subjected me to a complete physical examination, which included passing my body through three of the strangest looking machines I had ever seen. One was very noisy and made my hair stand on end.

Several vials of my blood were drawn for a complete blood profile work-up. My eyes were of intense interest to them and were studied through lens that made the doctor's eyes appear monstrous in front of my face. I was told to read over and over an eye chart at the far end of a darkened room.

After more prodding, listening to my heart and running on a treadmill, they pronounced me fit. They then gave me a Navy flight officer's uniform without any insignias, and told me to put it on. When I requested my old clothes, I was informed they had been thrown away along with my suitcase. Surprised, I asked what had become of my watch, wedding band, driver license, credit cards and the cash I had in my pants pockets. A smart aleck airman said with a smirk, "Oh! You will not be needing any of those things where you're going. Don't worry about them, you'll get an ID card that will cover everything when you get up to Langley." Not only did he give me the impression I might be going to prison, but I definitely was to have a new identity and nothing to do with my old life. It was if I was going to be re-born as a completely new person or some other unknown alternative.

Agents Simeons and Cohen asked if I was hungry and said that they were going over to the mess hall to eat and thought I might like to join them for a bite. Cohen said I should eat some food because we were leaving that night for the flight up to Langley and might not have the opportunity to eat again until late the next day. I thought they were asking just as a friendly gesture be-cause I was sure they were not going to let me out of their sight anyway, so I accompanied them and ate as much as I could without getting sick to the stomach. It was still churning from the emotional upset of leaving my family and knowing that I would never see them again.

Just as we finished our dinner and were leaving the mess hall, I heard the high pitched whine of jet engines. Then suddenly out of the darkness came a small twin-engine military aircraft that landed not three hundred yards from where we were standing. Agent Cohen spoke up and said, "Well, there is our ride to Langley."

When the three of us boarded the jet, I had the strange feeling of being in limbo and not sure whether I was just having a very bad nightmare or this was really happening to me. I had walked onto a plane heading for an unknown destination, without any luggage, no identification, no cash, nothing. It was the most overwhelming feeling of an impending doom I have ever had in my thirty-seven years of life.

Fearing some kind of panic attack and thinking an aspirin might help relax me, I asked agent Cohen if there were any on board the plane. He asked if I had a headache and I replied that I just felt a little nervous. I saw him go to the galley area and remove from his pocket an envelope containing a white powder, he poured a small amount into a glass and then filled it with coke.

When he handed it to me to drink, I asked what it was and he said it was his personal headache remedy. At this point in time I could have cared less about what he had put in the coke and drank it down in a couple of swallows.

I heard the plane engines reve to a high pitch, then suddenly I felt the surge of their power pushing against my back, and almost instantly, we were airborne and climbing rapidly into the night sky. The pilot turned off every light in the aircraft and the only thing visible was the moon, dodging in and out between passing black masses of clouds as the ship hurdled through the air at several hundred miles per hour carrying me into an uncertain future. About twenty minutes after takeoff and my having downed the drink, I felt very comfortable and slipped off into a deep dreamless sleep.

It seemed only a few minutes later when I felt someone shaking me by the shoulder. Opening my groggy eyes I saw agent Cohen looking down at me as he said, "Wake up Zack you slept the whole trip. We have arrived at Langley Airbase in Virginia.

Yawning, I looked out the aircraft window and saw that it was still the middle of the night and just then, a black sedan screeched to a stop alongside the ship. Cohen shouted, "Lets go."

Hurriedly the three of us piled into the sedan, and were driven to a nearby barracks where we found beds waiting for us. It wasn't long before I was catching up on the remainder of some much needed shut-eye.

The following morning I could hardly believe my ears when I heard the sound of a bugle blowing revelry. Looking at a clock on the barracks wall, I saw that it was 5 am. Quickly I jumped into my coveralls and stood by my bunk, waiting for something to happen. Amazingly, I fantasized that I had made the jump from banker and family man to the military all in just one day. Then I heard the sound of voices coming from the other end of the building, looking down a long hallway I saw agents Cohen and Simeons talking. Seeing me standing there agent Simeons came my way while Cohen left by a side door. "Where's he going so early in the morning?" I asked inquisitively.

"Oh! He is taking the artifacts to the CIA lab for analysis. That's where we are supposed to go right after chow, for your debriefing." was stated Simeons.

"My debriefing?" I said. "This sounds more like the Army every minute."

"Well maybe not your debriefing, more like your orientation." Simeons said correcting himself.

After a breakfast of chipped beef on toast, fruit and the worst tasting coffee I have ever drank, we drove over to a vast complex of mysterious, windowless buildings in a remote section of the sprawling airbase.

On our drive to my…. ah! Debriefing or whatever they were going to do with me, we drove past rows and rows of the most radical looking fighter aircraft, I had ever seen as well as what seemed like hundreds of other planes. Aircraft were taking off and flying precariously low over the road on which we were driving so when they kicked in their afterburners and thundered to gain altitude the sound was almost deafening.

Impressed by the size of the installation I asked Agent Simeons how large the base was. He rattled off statistics as if he had been asked the same question numerous times before and sounding like a travel agent said, "This complex is situated on 3200 acres and over 10,000 people work here. Although some say that number of workers is actually much larger for those working in secret operations. It is so large it's fairly easy to get lost if you don't pay close attention to where you are going. As you have probably noticed, there are no addresses on any of the buildings.

Just then, almost as if on cue, Simeons pulled into the parking lot of a white building with a heavy wire fence around it. Parking the car and shutting off the ignition he said, "This is it. This is where you will be working for a while. We exited the auto and went to the door of the nameless white building. Agent Simeons showed his identification and badge to the guard and he permitted us to enter a glass-sealed walkway, where he then swiped his ID card in a slot and another door hissed open. Stepping in I knew instantly this was some kind of secret operation, because the security was very tight. Even though the two well-armed guards we approached seemed to know

Agent Simeons quite well, they still put him through a very rigorous search, and then turning their attentions to me, searched me thoroughly, and took my fingerprints.

Agent Simeons walking away from me and up a long hallway said over his shoulder that security would escort me to the laboratory area. After passing through a scanning device of some kind, I was driven a distance by one of the guards in an electric golf-cart-like transport and then we stopped in front of a set of glass doors. The guard punched a code into a locking device and one of the glass lab doors slid open. He told me that I was expected and that someone would call him, when I had finished getting my ID card, to take me to my next interview.

As I entered the sanitary-looking, brightly lit, white room, I saw along one wall a bank of refrigerator-size high-speed computers which hummed loudly and had little red and green lights blinking off and on. A buxom female, dressed in a crisp Air Force medical officer's uniform with gold bars on the shoulders was bending over a bench, that held, test tubes, petrie dishes, beakers and other sorts of lab equipment. She was peering through a microscope at a glass slide containing a black substance.

I saw a solitary desk with an empty chair in front of it. Figuring it was for a guest, I took the seat. The woman, hearing the chair squeak as I pulled it away from the desk turned, and with a very military like style, walked over to the desk, sat down and fingered the computer in front of her. After in-putting some data, she then raised her head and greeted me, "Good morning Mr. Heikel and welcome to Langley. My name is Lieutenant Hoff but since you are not in the military, you may call me Carole."

"Well thank you Carole, that's a relief to know!" I said

"Oh! I like to be called by my first name." She said bubbly.

"No, not so much your name, it's the part you said about me not being in the military that's a relief. I'll tell you what would be even nicer, now that I'm not surrounded by my keepers. Could you please tell me just exactly what I am IN?"

"Mr. Heikel this area is where the CIA operates special projects and my job is to insert your microchip, get you set up in the computer and issue an ID card. Now if you would not mind placing your left hand, palm up on the arm of the chair."

She spoke with such authority that I followed her orders and thought nothing of it,...... that is until she picked up a syringe and filled it with the black liquid from the slide and approached me with it in her hand.

"Whoa there Carole, I hope that is not for me."

"Yes Sir it is!" She said as she grabbed my wrist with her free hand.

"Stop right there! You are not injecting me with that under any circumstances." I said emphatically.

Her grip was strong and she held my wrist tightly, peering down at me she said, "Mr. Heikel! Believe me there are numerous methods I could use to inject you and none would be to your liking. Please understand this is something very important to you for your personal safety and protection. It will be painless and the syringe contains only a small microchip, which is encoded with all your personal history. We can also use the implant as a means to immediately identify you. The microchip as well as your ID card will be the only identification you will have from now on. In addition, the chip allows us to track your position using GPS so in the event you are ever lost or injured while off post and taken to a hospital, we can retrieve you immediately and bring you back here for treatment. You see in the program you are entering we must know your whereabouts at all times. Now are we going to do this the easy way or do I need to call for some help?"

I knew it was hopeless to resist, all she had to do was push a button and two goons would come in and hold me down and then she would do her thing anyway. So I took the easy way and told her, "Carole if you say this shot is for my protection and safety, and it won't hurt, go ahead and do it."

As the needle penetrated my skin and I saw the black liquid disappear into my veins, she whispered, "This is not a shot per say, I am just placing the micro-chip that is no larger than the end of a pencil lead under your skin. There, see! That did not hurt one bit, did it?"

Looking down at the palm of my left hand, I saw a small half inch black line just under the skin. She had been right it did not hurt me a bit, not physically that is, but mentally I was filled with apathy, knowing I had taken one more step into the helpless unknown.

Returning to her computer terminal and imputing more data, she then turned to me and said, "Now you are activated. From this day forward only a number will identify you. Anything you may need, and I mean anything, just use the card you will get in just a second, to pay for whatever you need, and might I add, within reason. The accounting office will take care of the charges. I should also mention that use of your first name in conversations is still permitted. Now if you would kindly look into that eyepiece in front of you, we can record your iris for additional identification.

I have entered your chip information and old identity and cross referenced it with your new number."

I heard the computer chatter and then spit out a totally black, seemingly blank credit card.

Looking at it from my chair I said, "You sure that thing will work? It looks blank from here."

"Don't worry sir, it is embedded with a microchip holding all your pertinent information. Be careful with it, it is very valuable."

Hearing her tell me about the chip in my card, I said sarcastically, "Seems like everything around here has a microchip in it, including me."

Looking into her computer, Carole said as she raised her eyebrows, "No, not everything or everybody, only people who are in protective custody. Oh, My! You are one of the special ones assigned to Project Enigma. They have designated you number 017."

"017? If I was that important you would think they would have at least made me 007 like James Bond," I said still trying to be sarcastic.

Not seeming to have the slightest clue to what I was talking about, the lieutenant said sincerely, "Oh no Sir, 007 is someone else's number. I know her personally, her name is Hillary"

"Okay you have straightened me up on that, now about Project Enigma. What in the world is that?" I said straight-faced.

"Well Sir, I have no idea. All I do is assign numbers. Now I would say the person who could tell you about that project is," She paused and gazed into her computer screen then finished her sentence, "Is Doctor Gabe Weinberg! He will be your main contact and almost all of your time will be spent with him or his subordinates."

"That's interesting! When am I supposed to meet this genius?" I said in a demeaning voice.

"As a matter of fact, I am to take you to his office as soon as I am finished with your processing, possibly another five minutes or so."

Carole radioed the guard station for transportation. Soon we where traveling in the golf cart up a deserted street and eventually approached another much larger building.

Telling the guard to wait for her, Carole instructed me to try my new card on the door security system. So, taking her suggestion, I swiped my card and it worked, activating a touch screen that flashed the notation, "Place left hand where indicated and touch nose against screen and look unblinkingly at red dot." Following the instructions I then heard a loud click and the door rolled open and a computerized voice said, "Welcome 017 to the science lab. You may proceed to office 600 on the sixth floor."

Looking back at Carole she waved and said, "This is a far as I am permitted to go. It was nice to meet you Sir. I hope you have a happy day."

I waved back to her and pushed the elevator up button. When it stopped at the sixth floor and the doors opened, there before me was two glass doors with a very impressive title painted across them, "Chief Astrophysicist," was spelled out in bold letters.Passing through them, I encountered an older looking secretary, wearing a long white lab coat, who just smiled and announced into her inter-com that 017 had arrived. I heard a muffled voice say, "Please show him in."

Following the woman into the room I had a strong sense of deja vu because looking at the man standing beside a humungous desk was someone who resembled my old friend, Professor Schweitzer, same mane of snow white hair, thick eyebrows, and droopy mustache, except this man was much taller than my old friend and considerably younger and in a lot better shape. He had to top out at six four or six five and was as thin as a pencil. He held out a long bony hand and said, "How do you do Zack? It is a real honor to meet you. I am Physicist Gabe Weinberg."

Taking his hand, I shook it and said curiously, "I'm doing alright, but I've done a lot better, however right now I'm a little confused. Lieutenant Hoff, the medical officer who gave me my ID card said you were a doctor and the sign on the door read Astrophysicist and you just used Physicist as your title. Help me out here, how do I address you? Which one is it?"

Laughingly Gabe said, "Well I guess it's all of the above. I have a doctorate in Astronomy and Archeology and masters in ancient scripts. So I would say all those titles fit me rather nicely."

Impressed I said, "I bet you can even read and speak Hebrew."

"Oh Yes, fluently."

"So did a friend of mine. He's dead now. Professor Otto Schweitzer was his name. By the way you did not happen to know him, did you?" I questioned

Surprisingly Gabe answered, "Yes! I once had the pleasure of working with him for a few weeks at NASA. We were involved in a study of Electro- Magnetism and how it might be applied for propulsion in flight or levitation."

I hesitated for a moment and thought carefully about what to say next, because I did not want to comment further on HOW I knew the professor. I tried to redirect the conversation and said, "One of your titles is Astrophysicist, does that have anything to do with the stars or space travel? Just exactly what do you do?" Silently in the back of my head I was trying to figure out where this guy fit into my nightmare.

Gabe seemed to be quite proud when he said, "Yes both of those ideologies and several others, but my favorite is ancient artifacts. Like the ones you found over there in England."

Surprised I said, "Oh! So you know about those, do you?"

"Yes Zack! I know about those and about the rings. Fact is, I have been studying them and their capabilities for years. I inherited this project from my predecessor who ran it for over forty years and died not knowing how all these pieces fit together. Fortunately, now that we have the gold bowl and ring you recovered along the rings that were already in your possession, we can go forward with our experiments. These had been at a dead end for some years because we lacked these very important components. Zack, because of your very impressive finds and the experiences you went through, you will be an intricate part of these tests."

Surprised again I said, "How am I so special?"

His voice now sounding very serious, "You are very important in the scheme of things, mainly for your experiences. Specifically, you are the only person that we know of that has survived a full discharge from one of the slave rings. Most of all, if that gold bowl checks out to be what I think it is, you could have come in touch with something of a divine nature. Would you mind explaining to me a little about dreaming of eating from the bowl and how you felt afterwards?"

Before I answered, I remembered one of the CIA men saying when they abducted me that I may have been touched by the Devine and I wondered what in the world that statement meant. If just re-telling stories that I have told several times before is how I am going to be used, then they are just going to pick my brain then probably discard me somewhere in a Looney ward for the delusional. So to play my part to the fullest and make myself as important to them as possible, I went on to outline the whole story of finding the bowl, eating from it and how all of my injuries and afflictions had vanished. Strangely, I felt I had been reborn into a new and much younger man.

Gabe then asked to see my finger where it had been burned by the slave ring. After seeing that no visible scar remained, possibly proving to him that the bowl really did wipe away any old injuries of mine, he seemed to be satisfied. Then he asked if I had any mental or lasting effects from the electrical jolt I received from the ring. I told him that after a few weeks of convalescence I felt perfectly fine.

When I asked if he could answer a few questions from the extremely long list that I had about the rings and their meaning, he interrupted me in mid-sentence and said, "All that will be revealed to you in good time. It will be much easier for you to understand when you observe things with your own eyes (seems as if I have heard that one before.) Now let's go over to the metallurgists and see if they have dated that gold cup you unearthed."

Following Gabe out of the office we passed through several doorways that opened automatically when he waved his hand in front of a small light source in each wall. Then, as we passed through, the doors would quickly close tightly behind me. Afraid I might be hit by one of those sliders, I mentioned my concern to Gabe. His reply was, "Don't worry! You are safe! The computer that operates the doors knows exactly where you are, it's the microchip you know."

Having demonstrated to myself that my hand could at least close doors, Gabe and I soon arrived at the metallurgists' lab where the golden bowl was being tested to determine its age.

"Good afternoon men!" Gabe said loudly to a group of men standing at a workbench looking at the gold vessel which was turning slowly in a glass enclosed machine of some kind.

"How close are you in determining an age for the cup?" was his next question.

One of the young guys with a brush haircut and wearing the customary white lab coat spoke right up, "We are getting the results right now boss."

"Oh good," and in the same breath Gabe said, "And shake hands here with Zack Zero Seventeen. Zack is the man that unearthed the bowl you are examining. Zack, this is 044, but you can call him Sol if you like." I shook hands with the guy and hearing me referred to by number for the first time gave me the feeling that I had been transmuted into something ninety percent man and with that chip in my hand, ten percent robot. However, when Gabe referred to Sol as 044, I was pleased to hear that someone, with a number, other than me, was actually hard at work within the project.

044 or Sol, to use his human name said to Gabe, "Looks like its going to come in between twelve to thirteen thousand years old. Give or take a few hundred."

Gabe says with a big grin on his face, "Boy that's exciting! Hits the time frame just about right, doesn't it?"

"Sure does! Just the date we're looking for." Sol says shaking Gabe's hand in congratulations.

Gabe asked another question that seemed rather pertinent, "Did the gemologist look at the stones yet?"

"Yes Sir! Sure did! She finished her analysis about an hour ago and left the report with me. The report indicated the gems are all the real McCoy. The mountings holding the stones are all worked in pure gold, then set in such a way that they all fit flush with the gold ring around the top of the bowl. Now here was a surprise to her, directly behind each gem, is an opening. The size of the hole is exactly ten millimeters round. Gabe, she even speculated that with this kind of arrangement, the artist who constructed the vessel seemed to have made it in this fashion for a specific function. The only idea she offered, just as an example, was the design could have been for ceremonial purposes. For instance, if a candle were lit in the center of the bowl its light rays passing through the gemstones would give off an unusual display of colors.

Another thing that amazed her about the jewels was their size and purity. She had never seen or even thought something that big and flawless existed. Also puzzling to her was how the craftsman took his time in cutting them, because each of the gems is precisely the same weight and size, 200 carats."

Gabe, pushing his glasses back on his nose, said, "Did she find anything else unusual?"

Sol pointing at the revolving vessel inside the machine said, "No, she did not, but our group here is unsure why the base was crafted in the form of a square, and those two grooves on either side of the base has us baffled."

Gabe, nodding his head in a yes gesture said, "I think these test results have all but confirmed what I felt would be consistent with the bowl, and pretty much validate its authenticity. When is your group going to take a look at the rings that 017 has just brought in?"

Sol spoke up, "Already have, Boss. It was a simple identification. They are all authentic. We sent them over to the depository, for safe keeping."

Referring to the huge gems in the side of the bowl I said in amazement, "I don't think I have ever heard of gem stones that large. Man, those would be worth a king's ransom on the open market."

Sol speaking with authority said, "You are right 017 they would be of unheard value and there are 12 of them, ruby, emerald, sapphire and several others. At exactly 200 carats each, not only are they perfect, they would also be priceless."

Gabe said rather mysteriously, "One thing you can be certain of Zack, they will never be available on the open market. Where they are going, only a very few select individuals will ever see their beauty again."

For some strange reason I heard the men speaking but the only words that stood out in the conversation were, individual, beauty and Emerald green which was the same color as my wife's eyes. All these adjectives were synonymous with Peggy Sue and made me long for her. I could just picture how gorgeous she would look with that Emerald hanging around her neck. It had been two days since I had left her weeping in the middle of the road as I sped off with the two CIA officers. I was sure she would have expected to have heard from me by now. So, without even thinking that it would be a big deal, I asked Gabe if I could make a telephone call. When he asked to whom, I said my wife. He said he would have his secretary call agent Cohen and ask him to join us for dinner. He could speak to me at that time about making the call. Having some paper work to do, he asked if I would not mind making myself comfortable and we would go to dinner in about twenty minutes.

While Gabe sat at a desk and worked on a computer screen, I briefly was thumbing through a magazine when I noticed a small vacant outer office and sitting on a desk was a phone. I slipped into the office and quietly closed the door behind me. Picking up the receiver and hearing a dial tone, I anxiously dialed my home phone number in Texas. After four or five rings a voice came on the line and said, "No out-going calls are authorized from this type of secure installation." Very discouraged because I had expected to hear Peggy Sue melodious voice at any second, I slammed down the receiver right in the middle of it replaying its recorded message for the second time.

Looking around the room I realized I was not in prison but I may as well have been, I could do nothing of my own free will. I was trapped and I finally acknowledged it to myself and wondered if I would ever be able to get off this base again, now that I was in its clutches.

Just then, I heard Gabe's voice, "I bet you are hungry? You didn't have lunch did you? Shall we go over to the cafeteria and have dinner?"

Somewhat sarcastic because I was so disappointed I said, "Now that you mention it I did not eat lunch, I was too busy getting pumped full of microchips and being examined. Those guys put me through every test they could think of and those machines, man I never heard or seen anything like them. Why I even had my eyes photographed. You know Gabe, the only thing they missed recording was the length of my genitalia and I expect they will do that tomorrow."

Gabe got a kick out of my comments, but I was not trying to be funny, I was serious.

Laughingly he said, "No that will not happen tomorrow, you will be spending the day with me and that kind of examination is out of my area of expertise."

Straight faced I said, "Sure you might think it is funny but it's apparent to me that I am stuck here on this post. At least you can go somewhere and get your Johnson worked on by some pretty young thing."

All the expression of amusement left his face and he said with a frown, "What makes you think I can leave!" He held up his left hand and showed me his palm and just the same as mine and Sol's, there appeared the small black line containing the microchip just beneath the skin's surface. He too had been implanted with a homing device, which was at that very moment recording our presences as we walked into the cafeteria to have dinner. He was trapped and could not leave, just the way I was………….. or was he?

Curious I asked, " Gabe, were you Shanghaied into this project the same way I was or did you come on board voluntarily?"

"Zack, I was born an orphan. The people who raised me spent a ton of money to send me off to the best university. However, even before I graduated they both died of old age and there was nothing left to continue my studies. When I was offered a position in a far out program set in motion by the dean of my college, I took the job, mainly to finish up my schooling. After I graduated with honors, I never even left my desk at college and stayed with the program because it was beginning to prove out to be extremely fascinating and not pointed at something fictional at all. I was still young and without anyone, so it did not take long before this place became my home. I certainly did not know much about the outside world so when this project, became a national security program and was given almost unlimited funds for research, I chose to become a permanent part of it for the rest of my life. Zack, if things work out like I think they will, you will realize that you too are part of something historic and have made the right choice by giving the rest of your life to this project. What you will experience and where you will go, no human has ever gone before. Now until I can do some calculations and a few more experiments that is all I can divulge to you at this time. In a few days, I will introduce you to Doctor David Ben-Gurrie, the Project Administrator and he can give you an overview of what we are trying to accomplish."

"Hey fellows wait up!" I heard someone shout loudly from behind us. It was Agent Cohen calling as he hurried to catch up as we neared the serving line at the cafeteria. As we were selecting our food and putting it on trays, he seemed awfully friendly, even patting me and Gabe on our backs and attempted to tell us a joke, like a regular guy. But the joke's punch line made absolutely no sense to either one of us whatsoever. That did not stop him from laughing hysterically.

Taking our trays with the food over to a secluded area of the mess hall we sat down at a table and begin to eat. I made the comment after taking a few bites that it sure did not taste the way my wife Peggy Sue cooked.

Cohen piped up, "Oh! You know old buddy, now that you mentioned her we have to talk. I heard you tried to telephone her today, Zack that will not be possible for you to do. You know what our deal was no contact whatsoever, period! The two of us need to work closely on a cover story about your supposed demise that you are comfortable with and one your family will accept as true.

I think that after these last two days you should be convinced that you are just like us! Here permanently and should act accordingly."

I wanted to tell him to you know what, but held my tongue, because after all he was right. I was so intrigued with what was about to happen to me and even though I loved my wife and family dearly, I was finally willing to forgo my life with them to be part of something earth shaking. What, I did not know exactly. But with the intelligence of the manpower deployed here and the amount of money being spent, it had to be something unbelievable. Perhaps even some kind of time travel.

I stopped eating and said to Cohen, "If you promise not call me "old buddy again" because I am definitely not your buddy, I will listen to what you have in mind."

Speaking in a low voice and sounding a little rejected Cohen mumbled, "Alright if that's the way you want it. I was just trying to be friendly. Zack, I still think the cover story of the helicopter crash is the best scenario, because there will be an explosion and everyone's body aboard will be reduced to cinders. We will run a fake story in a local newspaper about the chopper crash and all those aboard that were killed. Your name will be on that list. A couple of tough looking marines will deliver your ashes in an urn along with your wedding band, which I retrieved from your personal belongings when we were in Beeville. When your family receives these, they will accept the fact that you are not coming back.

I can arrange a semi-annual report sent to you updating their lives and how they are fairing. Not to worry about them, Zack, they will be well cared for if need be. They will never know they are being observed and we can intervene covertly to correct any problem that might come up."

I thought for a while and sadly said, "Alright go ahead and run the story, but I'm telling you one thing, and Gabe is my witness, if anything bad should befall my family because of your mishandling of this charade, I'm not holding the CIA responsible but you, personally, because you are the one who is making all these promises. Is that perfectly understood?"

Looking like I had just slapped him hard in the face Cohen said, "Zack, you do not have to threaten me and I do understand your concern. I told you before not to worry. Everything is under control. I have handled cover stories like this in the past with no problems whatsoever. You have my personal guarantee."

Angrily I said to Cohen, and not so much for what he had outlined but because I realized the fake story was putting the finishing touches on my past life as a husband and father and it bothered me. "And I will take it! Guarantee or not, Cohen don't you ever forget my threat, I mean it."

Disgusted I threw down my fork and said to Gabe, "That's it I'm out of here! How in the hell do I get back over to the barracks?" I'm done for the night and I know I can't just call a cab."

Gabe, taking a bite of food and then pulling a small radio from his belt pushed a few buttons, then spoke into it and asked someone on the other end of the line where I was to spend the night. Pausing to listen a few moments then replacing the phone-like device back on his belt he said as he stood up, "Zack it seems as though the powers that be want you to stay here in this section for the next few days. So you will be staying with us executives in the apartment complex at the far end of this building. I think you will be pleased with the accommodations they are really first class. Come on I'll take you to your rooms, which by the way are only a few doors from mine."

We both turned from the table and walked away without saying a word to Agent Cohen, who seemed to be in a heated argument with the green beans on his plate.

Because we had left the tight security of the laboratory area and could move freely without an escort, we walked back to the apartments. Upon entering my rooms, I saw what Gabe was talking about, they were first class all the way even including a fully stocked bar and refrigerator. In the bathroom were pajamas and a heavy bathrobe all laid out with the towels. I found hanging in the clothes closet several pairs of clean and pressed flight uniforms. Surprisingly all were my size.

Taking a nice relaxing hot shower, I put on the pajamas and slid between the sheets hoping for a good nights rest. That was not to be because as soon as I closed my eyes I thought of Peggy. Fitfully I dozed off but her memory haunted my sleep and lingered like a recurring song. There was no way I could ever kill her off in my mind. She would always be there like a song that would not die. The melody left me feeling so lonely that I cried myself to sleep, but I still dreamed in vain for peace, because in my heart her memory will always remain. She will be forever with me, wherever I went, or whatever I did, she will always be there.

Eventually unable to sleep at all, I just lay there in the blackness of night looking at the ceiling until a beautiful early morning sunrise lit up the room and rescued me from the torments of that restless and sad night.

Just as I was about to get out of bed, the telephone on my nightstand rang. It was Gabe asking me to go to breakfast with him. When I said sure after a wash up and shave he said he'd knock on my door in fifteen minutes and we could walk over together to the cafeteria. I cleaned up and just as I was putting on my fresh uniform, I heard a knock at my door. Opening it, I saw Gabe standing there smiling and asking how I slept. I told him I had a bad night but I would get used to sleeping alone. I'd have to learn to deal with my night demons. Maybe I would feel better after a good breakfast. On our walk to eat, I inquired about the days work and Gabe said that we would be meeting right after our meal with the project administrator, Doctor David Ben-Gurrie.

I asked Gabe what kind of a man the doctor was and how I should address him.

He explained, in no uncertain terms, that I should absolutely address him as Doctor Ben-Gurrie because he was a no nonsense kind of guy and a real stickler for detail.

He went on to say that Ben-Gurrie was an old timer, maybe eighty-five, and being a very devote Jew he practiced all the old customs. He had been head of Project Enigma for over fifty years, so he had seen everything and everyone that had come and gone in recent memory. Even though he was well advanced in age, he was very quick in his thinking and the word, genius still applied to him in every sense of the word. He was one of the foremost scientists in the world on lasers and their applications as well any other known uses of electromagnetic energy. He also was very well versed in Gabe's field, ancient artifacts.

Gabe warned me that I should treat him with the utmost respect.

I thought to myself as Gabe described the administrator, "Boy this is just what I need first thing in the morning, and after the night I just had, someone who thinks he is a legend, if only in his own mind."

I don't remember finishing my breakfast I was so preoccupied wondering if I would hit it off okay with Doctor Ben-Gurrie or if I would end up in the stockade or whatever they call their jail, here in wonderland. In my present depressed mental state, I certainly did not want to piss-off the old coot by saying something stupid. I vowed to myself to keep my mouth shut and speak only when spoken to.

I heard Gabe call security for an escort to drive us over to the lab's main office and the meeting with Mr. Wonder Brain.

After passing through the customary security checks and hissing sliding doors, we finally enter the administrator office.

Expecting to have a secretary announce us to the doctor via her inter-com, I was surprised to see an older man standing next to the secretary waiting for us. It was Doctor Ben-Gurrie himself and he greeted us warmly, first by saying hello to Gabe and then shaking my hand vigorously. He totally surprised me when he said to me with a broad smile on his old, wrinkled face, "So this is the man we all should be thankful to for saving our jobs by finding the grail. How do you do Zack. I'm very honored to meet you. Please come into my office. Oh! Zack this is Justine Bain my secretary, who you will be talking to quite a bit."

Saying hello to the secretary as I passed her on the way to his office, I took a seat in front of the doctor's desk, I could not figure out for the life of me, how he was so honored to meet ME?

So skipping the usual pleasantries I proceeded to ask him the question I was asking myself "Sir if you don't mind telling me, why are you so honored to meet me, I was under the impression that I should be the one honored to meet you?"

The old guy chuckled and said, "So I see that Gabe has been up to his old tricks telling someone how great I am. Well I may be great but you are very unusual. Very blessed."

Shocked by what the old guy was saying I asked again, "I'm sorry Sir and don't mean to seem impertinent but I don't understand the, "blessed" part of your sentence. What exactly does that imply?"

"Well I can see right off that you are a young man who does not mince words and comes right to the point. I had hoped to explain to you our main mission here at Langley. A mission that we have been pursuing for decades, but when I saw these blood test results, I felt it important to act on the possibilities we have before us in this area. Before getting into any specifics about the main mission, and in order to answer your question of why I feel you are "blessed," look at these."

Handing me several sheets of paper with columns of numbers on them he continued his explanation, "First, I want you to take a look at that lab report done on your blood samples taken a few days ago at our hospital in Beeville."

Taking the paper from Doctor Ben-Gurrie and studying the rows of numbers, which made no sense to me whatsoever I finally said, "I'm sorry Sir! They mean nothing to me. What are they?"

"I can understand that, they are meant for doctors to read. You see those numbers and formulas are your blood profile. Would you mind turning to the last page and read the summary at the bottom of the page for me?"

Turning to the last page of the report I could hardly believe what I was reading pertained to me. Just then, I heard Doctor Ben-Gurrie say, "Out loud please."

So I began to read aloud, "It is in my professional opinion that this individual known as Zack Heikel, has an immune system like no other I have ever studied in all my 37 years of practice. He probably is immune to all known diseases because his hemoglobin is so saturated with interferon that no foreign matter or bacterium could possibly enter his blood stream and survive. They would be attacked and neutralized immediately. The Erythrocytes, (Red Cells) seem to have a very strong, unknown mechanism to fight infection. Furthermore, all his organs are in perfect order and seem to have some type of regenerative powers, making them almost immortal. The Leukocytes (White Cells) in the blood are very unusual in their ability to carry off and dispose of, through the kidneys, any damaged muscle tissue or cells of uncontrolled growth (meaning cancer cells).

His eyesight is also very extra ordinary. A person with good eyes are said to have 20/20 vision. A few people, about 1 in 100, have what is called excellent at 20/15 however Mister Heikel's is 20/10, a range we have never recorded before.

If there ever were a perfect living specimen of mankind, it would be him.

Signed, Head of Forensics, Doctor Lorraine Hassler."

Flabbergasted I just sat there speechless and after a few minutes heard Doctor Ben-Gurrie say, "Now do you understand why I said you were so unusual. I attribute your fantastic physical condition due to your contact with the grail, which we can now refer to as The Holy Grail. Our dating techniques as well as it's square base dimensions precisely match what we were hoping they would, proving that it is exactly what it is. Zack, somehow through the grail you have been exposed to the Holy Spirit of God.

Just to be extra sure, we have had several other persons spend the night with the grail trying to duplicate your condition but none have experienced the phenomena that you have. I guess the good lord only selects just a very few he wants to convey this special gift onto. Zack, I think God finds you a very righteous man."

All the while the doctor was speaking, my mind was somewhere else thinking, "So this is what I got out of the nightmare in the cave, a night with the grail when it gave me the fruit of life and made me into something out of the ordinary. However, what the doctor just revealed to me certainly would explain my newfound vigor and the disappearance of my old injuries. I was certain there must be more to my mission than just having special blood there had to be another purpose for it. Could it be the earth-shaking event that Rabbi Asher spoke of so enthusiastically? That was yet to take place? The event that would benefit mankind for all eternity and he said I was somehow going to be a part of it? The answer to my personal thoughts I was sure would be found right here in this covert CIA program."

Doctor Ben-Gurrie spoke up and came right to the point, "Zack as you can see by that report, your blood is unlike anything we have ever seen. We were hoping that we might take several liters and infuse it into people that have fatal afflictions, and we ascertain if it might help them in some beneficial way. We might even synthesize it for mass utilization if tests were successful. Would you be willing to participate in such a program?"

"If you are sure that my blood can do all those things, then absolutely, I am enthusiastic about helping those that are ill."

Pausing a moment to collect my thoughts I continued saying, "If this means that I am going to be a living factory that produces a super blood that might rid the world of diseases, I'm all for it. When do you want to start?"

"Today if possible. Are you up to it, Zack?"

"Sure, just don't take too much and kill the goose that lays the blessed blood." I said laughingly, although deep down inside I was scared because I hated medical procedures. I was not worried about death, if the theory worked, I would happily give my life for such a discovery. Even though this could be a wonderful gift from God and put an end to a lot of suffering, I was sure that this was not the main event which was to come. The rings and the grail had to somehow figure into that final revelation.

Doctor Ben-Gurrie smiled and said, "Wonderful! I was hoping that yes would be your answer so I had a staff of nurses standing by just up the hall. If you will go with Gabe to the clinic, we can get started right away. Everyday someone dies of a disease that this blood may have saved, so time is of the essence. Gabe if you will please show Zack the way. Maybe the three of us could have dinner tonight and discuss Project Enigma at length say around six o'clock?"

Gabe and I shook hands with the doctor and said we would see him at six for dinner. The two of us proceeded down the hall to the clinic for the blood letting,....... mine.

Three very friendly nurses met us at the door of the clinic and it was no time at all before they had me prostrate on a table and a needle placed in my vein. Connected to the needle was a clear tube that extended down into a plastic bag. One of the nurses placed a small rubber ball in my hand and told me to squeeze. I began pumping the ball in my fist and my thought-to-be precious blood flowed in spurts into the plastic container, which hung beneath the table. The bag pulsed, as if alive, each time the crimson miracle fluid squirted into it.

I lay there letting my lifeblood trickle away, listening to Gabe tell a few corny jokes to the nurses over coffee. After what I thought was an hour one of the nurses walked over to the table where I lay and unplugged the tubing that carried my blood to the bag and placed a cap on the now full bag. I was relieved that the ordeal was over. When she plugged the tubing into another empty bag and more blood began to exit my body I said in a startled voice, "Hey Gabe! They're draining me dry. How much can I give before I run out?"

The nurse who was in a heavy conversation with Gabe walked over to my bedside and said nonchalantly while still sipping coffee, "Not to worry Sir! We are only going to take two units from you today. You will feel a little weak but we will give you some orange juice with a few vitamins in it and you will be perfectly fine in about an hour."

I tried to relax and stared at the clock on the clinic wall, which seemed to move in slow motion but eventually, I filled the second bag. The needle and tubing were removed from my arm and I felt as if nothing had been removed from my bloodstream,,...........that is until I tried to sit up when my head started to spin as if I had just gotten off a merry-go-round. The talkative nurse quickly grabbed me and had me to lie flat on my back for another hour. Drinking the orange juice did make me feel much better and before long, Gabe and I were making our way to the apartments to get ready for dinner at six with Doctor Ben-Gurrie.

Arriving at my room, I went to the refrigerator and poured myself a big tall glass of cold milk. Taking it into the living room to drink, I plunked down in front of the television and turned on the news. The TV news-caster's voice droned on and on like a boring broken record. I was only paying attention to how good the milk tasted, when suddenly a news flash appeared on the screen.

Another newsman speaking with alarm was standing in front of a smoldering wreckage, of some kind, explaining that a Bell Ranger helicopter with three people on board had went down in a wooded area of Southern Virginia. After clipping some high tension power lines it crashed and burned. All aboard the aircraft have been lost. He stated that more details would be withheld until the next of kin could be notified.

Instantly I recognized the blueprint of Agent Cohen's staged cover story. He had not wasted any time in pro-ceeding with the charade of my death. I took a sip of the milk and suddenly it tasted sour. I knew I was going to throw-up and made it to the toilet just in time. I was now officially a dead man and felt like one too.

I turned on the shower as hot as I could stand it and jumped in to clean myself up. Looking up I saw how heavy and sturdy the pipe holding the showerhead was and I envisioned that, just for a second, how easy it would be for me to hang myself from it. Even though I was feeling destitute, I quickly put the thought out of my head realizing that my death might deprive someone of a fresh start in life if my blood proved to be what they said it was.

After I had shaved and put on a nice clean uniform and got my head right, a thought occurred to me, that the average guy would probably have had a heart attack by now experiencing all the trauma I had. I just seemed to be letting this bizarre new lifestyle I was now living, roll off my back with ease and wondered when the next episode would strike. I did not have to wait long because another one was about to hit me right between the eyes at dinner.

I arrived at the cafeteria right at six and entering saw Gabe and Doctor Ben-Gurrie already seated at a table with a third person wearing a black hat whose back was turned to me.

Approaching the table, I greeted and shook hands with Gabe and then Doctor Ben-Gurrie who shook my hand hard, as usual. While turning to the stranger seated at the table he said, "I do believe you two know one another."

Looking down I received another shock to my system when my eyes gazed into the wrinkled face of none other than……….. *RABBI ASHER*. Taking a deep breath and swallowing hard, I managed to blurt out, "My God! Are you a part of this thing too?

Rabbi Asher speaking in his usual mystical way, returned my question in a twisted form when he said, "I can assure you that HE is definitely a part of all this. How are you Zack?" He held out his hand to me.

Not taking his outstretched hand because I was still in a state of shock at seeing the old man I said, "Well, Rabbi Asher as a matter of fact I am not doing well at all. Since I last saw you several months ago, I have been through some trying times. Ever since I went looking for and found that gold bowl we saw in the green vapor that night in my office, my life has changed for the worse. I am still waiting hopefully for that earthshaking day you said would be coming because I sure could use some good news. Why I just learned from a TV report that I have been killed in a helicopter crash, so you see Rabbi, you are talking to a dead man."

The Rabbi patting me on the back and still talking in riddles said, "Zack I know how you must feel and how confused you must be, but believe me that blessed day is very near. I have been working closely with Doctor Ben-Gurrie for several years and now that we have all the pieces, we will be putting them together in the next few weeks. Hopefully the end of a very, very long journey is at hand."

"That's right Zack!" Doctor Ben-Gurrie piped up. We can proceed with our experiments in the Enigma Project. Thanks to your fabulous find of the grail and the additional rings.

I know I told you this morning that I would explain the project at length to you but it is so complicated that it would be much better for all of us if we just waited until we can simultaneously view with our own eyes how this trial run works out. Zack I want you to go into training at our gym and get as fit as you possibly can over the next several days, and of course you will be giving blood regularly. When we are ready and things are all in alignment in about three weeks, we can then get back together and see what happens. I would like to leave everything hanging just the way they are until further notice. Now let's not talk shop and have a nice dinner."

I thought to myself, "Yea, right! How can I eat now that I am without a good portion of my blood? That coupled with the shock of seeing Rabbi Asher jump up out of nowhere. Not to mention, I did not have the slightest inkling, just what the hell these guys were talking about. On second thought, as shocked as I was to see the Rabbi again, I was not all that surprised he would be part of this operation because nothing is impossible in a world where the impossible is possible and the unthinkable is thinkable………….. Bon Appetit."

The next several days were a whirlwind of activities for me. Working out in the gym I encountered several of the men I first met at the Lab, Sol was one of them. He and I became quite friendly, occasionally Gabe would show up and do a few laps around the track. Other times I spent with doctors doing stress tests on my body and then there were the frequent trips to the clinic for blood letting, as often as my system could handle the loss.

Early one morning, about two weeks after my dinner with Doctor Ben-Gurrie, his secretary Justine called my apartment and said that he would like to see me in his office as soon as possible. Eager to hear what was up, I hurried dressing and skipping breakfast, went straight to the doctor's office. She ushered me to where Doctor Ben-Gurrie was already hard at work over stacks of papers. Looking up at me over his glasses he said, "Well good morning Zack! Take a seat. Would you like a cup of coffee?"

Unaware of the reason for my hasty summons and needing something to settle my jittery stomach I responded, "Sure do! Cream and sugar please."

"Justine, would you mind getting 017 a cup?"

Taking the hot beverage from her and taking a sip, I asked as I swallowed, "I got here as quick as I could. What's the urgency?"

"Zack, things are coming together much faster than I had thought they would. A couple of things. First, fantastic news, the test results of several inoculations of gravely ill patients with only a few drops of your blood have shown remarkable improvement. Why God would use your body as the vessel to carry this lifesaving treatment to mankind, I could only guess about. But it works wonderfully. Blessing be to God Almighty.

Also, more good news. Our scientists believe they have succeeded in isolating several enzymes from your blood samples and may be able to duplicate them in the lab, and achieve some of the same results. So you might not have to be a walking pincushion any longer.

Secondly, the conditions are fast approaching when we can conduct our first experiment on Project Enigma utilizing all the recently gathered components. Zack, You and I, Gabe, as well as Rabbi Asher and a team that has been working on this project for a long time, will be leaving for the Middle East day after tomorrow. I know this is short notice but it's the moment we all have been waiting for to hopefully have many of our questions answered by these tests."

Excited and happy that it was good news and not something I had done wrong I said, "This is just great! What do I need to do to get ready?"

The doctor chuckled a little and said, "Well, while the rest of us are getting our overseas shots for contagious diseases, which you can naturally forgo, you can just be taking it easy and conserving your strength. You never can tell, what you may be doing over there could be strenuous. Gabe will be in touch with all the departing details. I guess that will be all until I see you then." Looking down he quickly returned to his paper work

Rising to my feet, I said goodbye. At the same time, a statement echoed across my mind that I had heard many times in the recent past. No need for me to ask what we would be doing in the Middle East because I already knew the answer would be, "Just wait until you see it with your own eyes."

I did as the doctor told me and just lay around and relaxed in my apartment for the remainder of the day. That evening I received a phone call from Gabe with instructions about the trip and that he would meet me at 0500 in the aircraft hanger, directly behind our building, the day of departure.

When I awoke the morning we were to leave, it was dark and a cold drizzling rain was falling. Having a feeling of uncertainty and loneliness, I dressed and hurried out to the hanger where my spirits brightened because it was a bee-hive of activity. Men were hurry-scurrying everywhere, loading all sorts of vehicles and scientific equipment into the hold of an enormous C 5A Starlifter Cargo plane.

Sol, Gabe and several other men from the Lab were already in line getting breakfast, which had been hastily prepared by the cooks right there in the hanger. Motioning me over to them, they made me feel good by slapping me on the back and including me in the exciting talk about the flight across the Atlantic. Gabe explained to the group that we were to land and wait in Saudi Arabia until our captain could get clearance to over-fly the country of Jordan from its government. Having accomplished that, we were to proceed on and then land at a secret military airbase in Israel where project personal only, would be ferried up into the mountains, at the Southern end of the Sinai Peninsula by helicopter, with our equipment arriving later.

The trip across the Atlantic was very quiet and uneventful. The aircraft was so huge and lumbering, it was almost as if it were an airborne office building. Flying at forty thousand feet, we seemed at times to barely be moving in relationship to the ground.

After several hours in this flying behemoth, we finally landed in Saudi Arabia. Shortly thereafter, our flying building took off again, escorted this time by three

Israeli fighter planes. Within an hour we sat down at an unknown military airbase.

Before we set out on the final leg of our journey, we had a brief period to freshen up and get something to eat. After we loaded our gear, climbed aboard three Israeli heavy-lift choppers, and just at dusk, lifted off towards the mountains.

As we flew south, it grew darker and soon a moonless night fell on the desert we were passing over. After a while and when our aircraft engines suddenly began to strain in an effort to gain altitude someone asked Gabe if we were maneuvering to avoid some unstable air. He answered us that no, we were approaching the mountains. Gabe thought it might be more comfortable and easier to breathe if everyone, although not entirely necessary, donned the oxygen masks that were dangling from the ceiling of the aircraft. The inquisitive person asked what mountain in this area could be high enough that oxygen would be required, Gabe again answered, "At almost eight thousand feet above sea level, the summit of Mount Sinai, where we should be landing shortly.

Then, far off in the distance we could see a faint glow of lights. As we drew nearer we saw that the entire mountaintop was bathed in brilliant floodlights as a huge complex of military style tents loomed below us. We landed in a swirl of dust as the chopper blades stirred the sandy surface of the mountain.

Wearing our parkas because of the cold night air, we exited the aircraft and saw standing there in full desert uniforms, heavily armed and wearing goggles to protect their eyes, two Israeli soldiers. They shouted over the sound of the engines for us to follow them. Doing so, they took us to one of the main tents where Doctor Ben-Gurrie was already gathering everyone for an orientation.

As we took chairs in the small crowd, he started out by saying, "Welcome all, to the holy mountain of Sinai where God passed down to Moses, The Ten Commandments and where we are but a stones throw, geographically speaking, from the pyramids in Cairo, Egypt.

Before preceding any further, I would like to introduce to those who do not know them, the men seated here with me. Here on my right is Astrophysicist Gabe Weinberg and on my left is archeologist and rabbi, Asher Levison, to his left, Sol Zero Forty-Four, our carbon-14 dating expert.

As you may have noticed, I am having my helpers pass out Bibles to everyone. No,…..we will not be having a prayer session at this time. You will be using them later for reference to passages which will make it easier for you to understand just what you are viewing.

Now all of you in attendance have been a part of Project Enigma or connected to it by some special circumstance for some time and have an idea what we are about to attempt. However, I am sure there are a few of you that are asking yourself just why am I on an extremely chilly, high mountain top, in the middle of a foreign country at this particular time. Well, I could try to answer those questions for you but even if I had the time and used thousands of words, they would still not be enough to explain what you are about to see. As the old saying goes, "Seeing is worth a thousand words" well, in this case that statement could not be more accurate. So, I will save my voice and let your eyes tell you the story.

Now, before we adjourn to the test site, a few ground rules. First, under no circumstances do you touch any of the experiments, as it could be deadly. Second, do not look directly into any of the high intensity light sources, unless you have eye protection. Third, stand at least fifty feet away from any ongoing tests. Fourth, low voices must be observed at all times. Lastly, please keep an open mind on what you are viewing, even if it is beyond your comprehension. And of course there will be no smoking.

Now, if everyone would please follow the military personal, they will escort us to the test area."

I fell in line behind Gabe and Sol along with nine other men, and two women scientists, followed the Israeli soldiers, for about a mile.

Our military style single-file column stopped when we came to a brightly lit structure that resembled a large roped off compound. Except, in place of ropes, were walls made of heavy linen blankets that were draped over thick brass rods.

Doctor Ben-Gurrie announced in a soft voice, "This is the first place you will need your bible. Please turn to Exodus 27 and start at verse nine."

Opening my book and turning to Exodus, I began to read. Verse 9 was a description of a cloth fence surrounding a holy site called the Tabernacle. It was described as being 150 feet long, 75 feet wide and 71/2 feet high with a gate of blue and scarlet colored linen, in the East end 30 feet wide. Looking up from the holy word, that was exactly what I saw before my eyes. Someone had gone through a tremendous amount of trouble to duplicate the setting spelled out in this chapter of the bible.

Our small group was ushered through the colored cloth gate and into a large open area where there stood several other exhibits. Doctor Ben-Gurrie muttered softly only the chapter and verse to read next, which were all of chapters 25 and 26 in Exodus.

It took me about twenty minutes to read these two chapters but after I had, everything was coming into focus. This whole complex we were standing in was an exact replicate of the Holy Tabernacle described in the bible.

At the far end of the courtyard stood another structure, which I recognized from my reading in Exodus to be the Holy of Holies. Doctor Ben-Gurrie and Rabbi Asher were putting on strange uniforms and I asked Gabe, who was standing beside me what they were wearing. He whispered, "Its all explained in chapter 28. Read the whole thing carefully and I guarantee it will make a lot of sense if applied to some of your questions about the rings."

He was right! The reading of this chapter shed a lot of light on the meaning of the master rings and their particular precious stones. The chapter explained there were twelve of these stones, topaz, sardius, carbuncle, emerald, sapphire, diamond, ligure, agate, amethyst, beryl, onyx and jasper, all set in gold. Each stone represented one of the twelve tribes of Israel, as did each ring with its stone and the engraved tribe's name. They also were the same type of stones that surrounded the top of the Holy Grail and adorned the garments that Rabbi Asher and Doctor Ben-Gurrie were wearing. Also mentioned in this chapter were the words, Urim and Thummim the same two words that occupied the first page of the silver plated book of instructions on how to operate the rings.

Glancing at Rabbi Asher and the strange breastplate he wore I was shocked to see, embossed across its front in gold letters were the identical words, Urim & Thummim. In the same chapter, a small black box was said to have been placed upon Aaron's forehead and it perfectly described the one that was on Rabbi Asher's head when I first met him in my office.

Turning once again to Gabe I whispered, "You know Gabe, just this one chapter explained several of the mysteries that have haunted me for years."

Smiling Gabe said, "Zack, I know this book of the bible intimately and the mysteries in Exodus have frustrated me also ever since I first started working on Project Enigma. Back at Langley, we have been studying this chapter for years trying to make sense out of it. We are sure there is so much more to be discovered and these experiments may very well provide the answers. For instance go to chapter 31 for information on who the artists were that manufactured the silver plated book, the master and slave rings, as well as the Holy Grail itself, with the instructions on how to do so coming directly from God."

There it all was in chapter 31. Two men, Bezaleel and Aholiad were the artisans that crafted these objects and as Gabe had said, on the direct command from God using advanced technology that is still unknown to all of mankind.

Flabbergasted I said to Gabe, "No wonder we could not understand where the technology came from or who designed the rings. I remember Professor Schweitzer saying that the information contained in the silver book was light years ahead of our own. Now I can see why, it came from the Heavens.

As we watched the rabbi and Doctor Ben-Gurrie adding more paraphernalia to their uniforms I again turned to Gabe for an answer of why all the equipment and said how I thought that Rabbi Asher was too old for this much exertion.

He quietly explained, "The rabbi may be old but he would never pass up a chance to participate in a ceremony that his forefathers performed eons ago. Remember his last name is Levison, which indicates that he is of the family of Levi whose sole purpose in the bible was to act as priests and protectors of the holy sites as well as their sacred vessels. I again ask you to look to your bible and read Exodus, chapter 28 for a complete description of the special garments they had to wear when attending the altar and their duties. Or chapter 32, which outlined how the Levites became mercenaries for God.

Also Zack, to solve another major mystery for you that I'm sure you have been wrestling with every since you found the books was, exactly what was, the Knighthood of Zion. Basically, the knighthood was an offshoot from the Levi priests. These priests, as well as all their descendants, including their off spring, had positions and authority in the church that were set in a perpetual statute and ordained by HIM forever.

Chapter 28, verse 30 and 43 of Exodus, we feel may have set the stage for later day kings to grant knighthoods. Some kings, in an effort to mimic the almighty and impress their subjects, may have possibly taken their lead from these biblical chapters and granted knighthoods. As in the case of England, whose royal family is thought by some to be direct descendants from God, occasionally the reigning king will bestow the honor of, "Knight of the Realm" on a deserving citizen.

At sometime in the ancient past these sons of Levi evolved into an order calling themselves, The Knights of Zion.

You may also be surprised to learn that Rabbi Asher Levison is in fact a direct descendent of those knights and the last surviving member of that order, except for maybe yourself," Gabe said ending his mini-lecture with a strange statement.

"Now wait a minute Gabe! I don't know what makes you think that about me. What are you basing that assumption on?"

Well according to what you told us about how you obtained Rabbi Asher's master ring was similar to a knighting. Especially how his ring seemed to mysteriously appear on your finger and he said at that time, you were now like him, a protector of the rings. That whole scene sounds like a ceremony to me. After all, remember the rabbi is a priest of the Levi family and may have, in reality ordained you a knight.

Taking a few minutes to unscramble the thoughts he put into my head, I turned to the bible chapters he mentioned and read them and at the same time, thinking about that night in my office when I received the ring. I guess it was a kind of ceremony, however, I did not consider myself a knight, but he and others might think of me as such.

I then spoke aloud to Gabe, "Sure, I figured the rabbi must have been involved with the knights because he had the ring and he knew everything about them. You may also be right about my being a knight because I did have a master ring. In fact, I had several of them as well as a book of instructions. I think I may qualify as a member on those facts, however, I am not Jewish, which is a must to be in the order."

"That's right Zack, but your encounter with the Grail and how it transformed you plus the fact that sometimes the hand of God may favor certain persons with unusual powers as well as other mystical phenomena. Outwardly, you may not feel any different, but spiritually you are. You may not consider yourself akin to the Levi knighthood, but I think way down deep inside you must be thinking that you are somehow connected and definitely special. If you do not, then you must be in denial. You just finished reading Exodus 28 and 32, so those two chapters should have helped your reasoning."

"Sure I read them, but all they did was confuse the issue for me and I certainly do not fully understand the purpose of all the special garments and armor these guys had to wear. However, chapter 32 verse 27 sounds to me as if the Levities were nothing but a bunch of killers. I certainly can't associate myself with that, but it does help me understand how their future generations had such a lust for killing.

This particular chapter also clears up another lingering question I had about the judge that owned the old mansion I purchased up in Michigan and how he came to kill so easily. He was also a Levison, like the rabbi and a member of the Knighthood of Zion as well."

Gabe enthusiastically said, "Yes he was, and we knew about him too for years. He was in contact with other members of the knighthood using the rings, including

Rabbi Asher who all the while was working for us. Zack you are just beginning to comprehend the huge and complicated scope of this whole project, and as we kept telling you, just wait and see. There is still so much more to be revealed that I only hope it does not, as they say, blow your mind. Its that earthshaking. Speaking of earthshaking, what the doc and rabbi are about to do could be something that big.

Look! They are going into the main tent, which in the bible was described as, "The Tabernacle." I see they are motioning us to follow them inside the tent. Come on let's go, but quietly."

When we stepped inside The Tabernacle, I was amazed at the beauty of the surroundings. Drapes of purple, blue and scarlet linen suspended on rope made of heavy spun gold. Brass fittings gleamed everywhere. Animal skins dyed red hung from the walls. Directly in front of us was an altar where a solid gold, six branched candlestick sat, brightly shining in the spotlights that illuminated the interior of the Tabernacle.

I again asked Gabe to explain what we were seeing and he reiterated, "Go back and re-read chapter 28 which explains all the stations you see before us."

Just as I began to read, I saw Rabbi Asher and Doctor Ben-Gurrie strolling towards the far end of the large tent where another structure stood. Its walls adorned by beautiful drapes and hand woven tapestries. As they walked, the special made pant legs of their garments produced a clicking sound as they rubbed together. Their attire, from the helmet on their heads to the breastplate on their chest and the heavy padded gloves they worn on their hands made them appear as if they were about to engage in a medieval battle with forces unknown.

They approached the structure's entrance and disappeared behind the drapes into what is described in the bible as, The Most Holy Place or The Holy of Holies, this was where only priests clothed in the protective suits may enter.

We stood there for several minutes in suspense. Suddenly, the men slid the purple drapes on the side of the tent open. Majestically standing there in the center of the tent was a large container covered in solid gold plate with two, winged figurines perched on either side of its top facing one another. The high intensity spotlights coming through the now open roof of the tent bounced off the metal and almost blinded us by its brilliance.

My having already read Chapter 25 of Exodus I had a pretty good idea what was standing before me but could hardly believe my own eyes. Yet there it stood in all its glory. Fascinated I whispered, "Gabe am I seeing what I think I am seeing?"

Almost as if hypnotized by the sight of the chest he said slowly but distinctly, "Absolutely!............ Your eyes are not deceiving you. It is the Holy Ark of the Covenant. The exact one built to specifications dictated directly from God to Moses here on Mt Sinai eons ago and described in Exodus, chapter 25, and I might add, right here on this very spot on the mountaintop. I know it is hard to comprehend but it's the real thing."

Everyone stood there reverently, in awe and waited anxiously for the next ritual the men would perform. Doctor Ben-Gurrie walked over to a long bank of high-speed mainframe computers that lined the back wall of the tent, adjusted a few dials, and made sure they were recording everything that was to transpire here tonight. Rabbi Asher all the while had opened a large, black metal box and removed from its protective packaging,................ *THE HOLY GRAIL.*

He ceremoniously carried The Grail high over his head to the Ark of the Covenant and slowly slid its square base into two gold tracks on top of the Ark that matched its width perfectly and was centered directly between the two gold cherubim, who were exquisitely detailed in chapter 37, verse 7, 8, and 9 of Exodus.

He turned and walking away from the Ark headed in our direction and approached Gabe. I heard him ask while they both looked down at a note that the rabbi held in his hand, "I would like to confirm once again if these are the correct azimuth and inclination settings?"

Looking at his watch Gabe said, "Yes, those settings plus our location of 28 degrees latitude and 34 degrees longitude will put everything precisely in alignment in another ten minutes."

Rabbi Asher then returned to the side of the Ark and began slowly turning it.

This completely had me baffled so I asked, "Gabe just what was that all about?"

Pointing straight up and directly overhead into the black night sky he said "Look up there. Can you see those six stars that are shaped like two side-by-side triangles? And that very bright one,….. there to the left?"

"Yes I can." I said confused. "What about them?"

"Well those make up the Triangulum Constellation and sitting to the left of them is Sirius, the brightest star in the heavens as seen from Earth. Rabbi Asher will use the calculations I gave him to orient the Ark and point it straight at that constellation using Sirius as a reference point."

"My God Gabe, is the Ark a telescope or observation platform of some kind?"

"No Zack, we hope something much, much more than that. Just be patient and keep watching. We are not sure what will happen either, but we are just following the instructions outlined in the book on how the rings operate to locate the Shvill Afar or for the lack of a better word, pathway."

Before I could ask my next question of what does the rings have to do with the ark, it was answered when I saw Rabbi Asher open another padded black box and withdraw a drawer containing,.... of all things, the Master Rings, all twelve of them. He again very cautiously approached the Ark and examined twelve sockets that ringed the top of the Ark. I remembered reading about those sockets in chapter 26 verses, 19, 24 and 25 of Exodus. Each socket he observed had a name embossed under it and as if calling off a holy roll-call he spoke each name in a loud voice, "Reuben, Simeon, Levi, Judah, Issachar, Zebulun, Gad, Asher, Dan, Naphtali, Joseph and Benjamin." Continuing his description of the sockets and pointing to the bottom portion of THE ARK with his finger said, "Also there are smaller sockets scattered all around the bottom of the Ark and designed to hold all 144 slave rings."

Instantly upon hearing the roll call of names, I remembered from the Bible verses that they represented the *TWELVE TRIBES OF ISRAEL*. The rabbi, removing one of the twelve master rings from the drawer, pushed it into the socket *IN THE ARK OF THE COVENANT* whose name matched the one on the ring. When nothing disastrous happened he continued installing the other eleven.

After plugging in all twelve master rings into their corresponding sockets Rabbi Asher, with the aid of Doctor Ben-Gurri, took several more drawers of the smaller slave rings from the box and began to very cautiously fill the empty sockets that lined the bottom of the ark with the 144 slave rings.

With only a few slave rings left to install, Rabbi Asher stopped and turned to the crowd and said, "For safety's sake would everyone please back away from the tent about fifty feet and put on your protective eyeglasses. We are not sure what will happen when we push in the last capacitor."

Doing as the rabbi had requested and slipping on our glasses, the small crowd moved back, a safe distance and held our collective breaths. Rabbi Asher hesitated momentarily, adjusted his garments and his gloves, picked up the last slave ring and taking a deep breath, he shoved it deep into the socket, thereby completing the electrical circuit.

The moment the ring made contact with the bottom of the socket a tremendous bolt of electricity zapped across the top of the ark between the outstretched wings of the two cherubim and began to bounce back and forth. Each time the bolt of extremely high voltage returned, it made another huge snapping noise. Then suddenly we heard another enormously loud thunderclap from a dark cloud that had quickly formed overhead and lightning shot across the sky directly over the ark. From the main shaft of lightning, small finger-like streams of electricity touched down to the ark and were sucked into it. It was as if the ark had plugged into and was using the atmosphere of the whole planet Earth as an enormous perpetual static electric generating machine to power the slave rings.

Then without warning, the ark seemed to ignite from the inside and a pulsating shaft of faint yellow light began to streak skyward from the bowl of the HOLY GRAIL. After a few moments, the intermittent flashing beam turned to solid bursts of what resembled flaming red fireballs of lightning and these were sent streaming upwards as if being shot from a huge canon and reached far out into the night sky then disappeared into deep space. It seemed that the Ark was bombarding space with a flashing giant beacon, and sending electrical projectiles directly toward the Triangulum Constellation.

A loud eerie hum was also heard and just barely audible above the crescendo of the crashing beams of huge electric sparks reciprocating back and forth between the cherubim. The sound was deafening to everyone that is except Doctor Ben-Gurrie and the rabbi, who went about their business of observing. Undaunted, because evidently their protective helmets saved them from going deaf, just as the good lord had planned.

The interior light from the ark seemed to grow brighter. Then all of a sudden and simultaneously all the precious gem stones in the ark as well as those in the holy grail were ablaze in light and dazzling streams of multi-colored beams were sent cascading in all directions around the entire mountaintop. Along with the occasional blast of fiery cannonballs of electricity sent towards the heavens from the grail, it was the most spectacular display of every color in the light spectrum I had ever seen. Greens, blues, reds, yellows, and all the colors in-between, the sight was so absolutely awesome that everyone, including myself, stood there dumbfounded gazing at the spectacular light show!

It seemed like we had been watching for hours, gathering in the beautiful sights when our legs begin to ache so we sat down in the dirt to rest a while. Looking around at the other observers, I was startled to see that everyone's hair, that is…. those that had some, was standing on end. We were just close enough to the high voltage electricity to be included in its static field, which caused the laughable condition.

We sat there for quite some time unable to comprehend what was taking place in front of us. I thought it an opportune time to have Gabe enlighten me on a few things he may have been withholding from me, so I engaged him in whispered conversation, "Gabe, I was hoping you might clear up some loose ends for me, seeing that you seem to have all the answers. I think I have figured out one of them already, about the triangles on the side of the master rings. They represented those constellations up there. Isn't that right? But I still don't see where the star Sirius fits into all this."

"You're right about the triangles Zack. They do represented other things as well to kings and high priests in the distance past. For instance, they were very important to the ancients, in building the pyramids in Egypt, Mexico, Palenque and though-out South America, all these structures were built in the shape of triangles. This triangular shape also was the basics for what was known as "The Mayan Code of Sacred Geometry and was used to design most things in that ancient culture long before the use of mathematics. The swastika used by the Nazi government was an ancient design of a series of triangles and of course there is the Star of David, which is two triangles overlaid on top of one another, or even the word Zion is composed of two stacked triangles laying on their side, hence the insignia on the front of your books. Triangles are displayed prominently on many of today's items of importance, for instance on the face of the dollar bill.

Even the Freemasons are very interested in the triangular constellation and uses triangles as well as tee-squares to adorn their garments and finger rings. I'm also intrigued by the mystery that surrounds the secret Masonic Order, and have studied its history for many years. Mainly because of their connection with mystic numbers and secret codes. Many of the men who framed the American Constitution and the Great Seal of America were Masons, including George Washington. One popular theory has it that these men hid a secret message in the Great Seal, alleging a new world order in the Latin phrase, "Annuit Coeptis" over the unfinished pyramid and "Novus Ordor Seclorum" under it. Other Masonic hidden codes are in the seal. For instance, there are thirty-three feathers on the eagle's wing in the seal, which denotes the highest order that one can attain in Masonry and the Mason's contend that the eye above the pyramid is God looking out for mankind.

Even though experts have debunked many of these theories and contend the hidden message on the seal are actually hidden meanings which only pertain to the thirteen original colonies and have nothing to do with any type of new world order or secret Masonic symbols.

There are many theories about the origins of the mysterious Masons. In the most popular version, the fraternity looks back at two historical moments in particular. One is the building of King Solomon's Temple, which

Masons say was completed in the tenth century B.C. by stonemasons. The second dates to medieval times, when a group known as the Knights Templar, or poor Knights of Christ, were sent to protect Crusaders on their way to Jerusalem. Legend had it that the knights were actually on a different mission, having learned that a secret holy treasure may have been buried by Freemason when they build Solomon's Temple, which then lay in ruins having been destroyed about 600 years before Christ. Some historians are skeptical about the possibility of treasure at the holy site, but you and I know for sure, holy relics were dug up at many religious places around the world. Who is to say that they did not find something? The Knights Templar certainly have been associated in legend over hundred of years to many holy relics, even the Ark of the Covenant.

You know we in Project Enigma have speculated for a long time about the meaning of the two triangles on the sides of the rings. Some in the CIA have suggested that God actually left this insignia purposely as a guide and reminder to look heavenly towards the triangular constellation and the star Sirius. Supposedly that is the angle in the sky from which mankind's connection to the almighty would come.

However, personally, I think the three sides of the triangle on the rings signify the Holy Trinity, The Father, Son and Holy Ghost.

You asked about the star Sirius, well it could be used just as a reference point, but I think its somehow much more relevant than that. The early Egyptians thought Sirius was of the utmost importance, so much so that they oriented all of the pyramids on the Gaza plateau in exact alignment with the stars trek across the sky. Sirius was also considered by the ancient people to be one of their gods, it was spoken about in their prayers, and its image adorned many temple walls. Furthermore, almost all of the pharaohs linked their lineage and destiny to the star, which they held sacred and associated it with a divine power or being."

Impressed with his explanation I said, "Well I'll be darned! I never associated triangles with so many important structures in history. They certainly seem to fit someone grand plan, and are too well intertwined in society to be just a mere co-incidence.

Okay! I'm beginning to understand the triangles, but Gabe you have got to tell me how the CIA came in possession of the Ark of the Covenant. Archeologists and theologians have been searching for its whereabouts for centuries. Where was it found?"

"Well Zack, that is a long and complicated story. Basically the government had thought that it existed for many years before it was finally found. The first clue to finding the Ark was a brief reference to it in one of the metal book of instructions found along with a slave ring in an Egyptian tomb in 1836. Over time, more rings turned up, and through various experiments, the first plasma was formed and the unbelievable power the rings contained was revealed. Our government even back then knew this was something we had to have for our national security.

Then the big break came quite unexpectedly. During World War 2 the Nazis, found a slave ring and book in Bavaria in an old monastery. They hoped to use the ancient artifact's power for their military so they feverously searched the world for more rings. In looking for the rings, they got on the track of other ancient artifacts that they hoped might be used to make weapons of war if they could be found. They had archeological teams the world over digging and searching. They looked for the Grail, the Ark, and even Longino's Spear that was said to have pierced Christ's side as he hung on the cross, and which caused many at that time; to believe gave it special mystical powers.

The Nazis even searched for the remains of Atlantis, hoping to find some type of fantastic weapon from biblical times that might make their armies invincible. Anyway, they got lucky in an ancient mausoleum of a biblical king after they had occupied Ethiopia and unearthed The Ark from where it had been hidden sometime in the tenth century. They were doing extensive testing on it when we captured it at the end of the war. The forerunner of the CIA, the OSS, brought it to the United States and ever since, we have been searching for all the components. Now we have them, but until recently did not know what they would do when all assembled, but I think we are about to find out."

Several hours had passed when suddenly we turned our attention back to the pandemonium that was unfolding before us because a significant change was taking place. The fiery bursts of outgoing canon fire had subsided and in their place, a spike of incoming pale green light, beamed its way down from deep space and was focusing on the center of the Holy Grail atop the Ark of the Covenant and creating a quivering green plasma.

As the Sapphire green laser beam intensified and passed through the earth's atmosphere, its temperature must have been extremely high because it created a long streak of white steam as it vaporized any water in its path, thereby creating the most unbelievable vapor trail ever seen by anyone on earth.

The multi-colored light display emanating from the gem-stones on the Ark and Grail grew extremely brilliant and pulsated in a strange rhythm.

The stream of high voltage electricity bouncing back and forth between the two cherubim slowed and then ceased.

Without the crack of the huge sparks, the only noise that remained was the low deep hum coming from the ark.

Suddenly and quite unexpectedly, Rabbi Asher appeared to stagger and clutch his chest as if suffering a seizure of some sort and as he began to fall, he inadvertently put out his hand to steady himself and touched the ark. Instantly on doing so, he dropped to one knee and grabbed his throat as he fell to the ground and rolled onto his back. Doctor Ben-Gurrie, seeing his elderly co-worker in distress, rushed to render assistance. The rabbi was gasping for air so Doctor Ben removed one of his protective gloves in an effort to clear the rabbi's throat.

The moment he did this, we heard a loud zap and saw a jolt of blue flame spark from the side of the ark and surround his bare hand. Screaming in pain and hit so hard by the lightning bolt, the doctor fell on top of the rabbi and immediately both bodies were engulfed in a rolling ball of angry sparks and blue flame. The horrible scene happening right in front of everyone's eyes was exactly what had happened to my friend Professor Schweitzer and was a tragic example of how deadly the ark was.

We all stood there in shock and were completely helpless as we watched the two fallen scientists burn because to go to their aid meant certain death.

Horrified, Gabe mumbled under his breath while shaking his head, "Something terrible like this has happened before in the ancient past because I recall reading it in the Bible, in Samuel 1, chapters 4-8 and then again in Second, Samuel chapter 6." Gabe's whispering was abruptly interrupted, when someone who shouted in amazement, "My God look!" As he pointed to the green plasma floating above the ark, which quickly diverted everyone's attention away from the two smoldering bodies.

Miraculously, enormous images were beginning to form within the green laser plasma, faintly at first then larger and more distinct.

Slowly the outline of a very thin, bearded, longhaired being, about one hundred feet tall and dressed in a long robe was plainly visible. His arms dangled slightly away from his body and he held in each of his outstretched hands, a much smaller figure, both clothed in long flowing robes.

Suddenly everything was dead silent and the image of the three beings started to rotate slowly inside the green plasma-like beam as if they were a hologram. As they turned, their faces were solemn and dark. Deep-set eyes flashed a silvery sparkle and their clothing glistened an eerie pale green in the laser light.

I began to detect a sound within my head,....... a faint ghostly voice, Turning towards Sol and Gabe who were standing there with surprised looks on their faces. I pointed to my ears and they did the same, while nodding their heads in a yes motion, proving that others could also hear the voice. The language at first was garbled and sounded similar to a record being played at a very slow speed then changed into what I thought was Hebrew and eventually into something, everyone seemed to understand, regardless of his or her native tongue.

The communication, which seemed to arrive telepathically and sounding strangely similar to a computer generated musical hymn, began this way,

"I am the great I *AM* and He who you earthlings call *GOD*, and the father of your fathers. Hear me now and take heed. I have caused to be many things and many worlds, but never have I created anything as I did mankind here on this small planet. You, my creations are made in my image and are unique in the Cosmos. When I departed your world eons ago leaving only my spirit, my children were united as one.

Unfortunately, they became divided when one of my fallen angels, Lucifer entered their camps and through him, SIN caused man to rebel against my word and his fellow man. Their speech was no longer discernable to one another, war and hatred replaced peace and the planet was in turmoil. Now however, all twelve of the tribes have once again come together in unison and co-operation and have used the pathway, they collectively activated by the power rings to contact me. The rings I had left behind so long ago to one day, when all the tribes were assembled in peace, be placed into my transmitter and a signal of unity be sent. I would then keep my pledge to return here to your earth. It has been thousands of your earth years, but that day has finally come.

My communication may be short from the mercy seat of the pathway transmitter because your signal is very weak. Your planets once vibrate atmosphere has been polluted by gases from your machines and has lost much of its power. So listen intently to my instructions and do my bidding exactly.

The time has come for all those who have sinned against his fellow man, and who have not kept my words, as written by my disciples in what mankind calls the Bible, to be judged by me. Now all those must face their day of judgment. I will send my *SON* in the flesh and who is *MYSELF* in human form, once again to your planets surface. He will arrive in glory and in a method where the entire planet will know of his coming. He will have with him a multitude of what mankind calls *ANGELS* and with them will be, a righteous man named *ENOCH*, who will help my *SON* persuade the rulers and kings on Earth of the error of their ways.

The planet and all its inhabitants will have twenty-three earth years to prepare for my son's coming, but *HE* will journey only three space years, so preparations must start now. As my son is journeying to your planet, there will be time enough for those who have sinned against me and my holy word to repent of their sins and be saved from obliteration and in so doing will then reside in the kingdom *HE* creates here on earth. Above all things, Peace must prevail and all nations must come under the jurisdiction of the old testament of your bible because this was my holy word given to Moses here on this high point of earth.

I warn those who do not listen, my angels will have with them the necessary means to eliminate from the face of this small planet, any nation or people not committed to peace, tranquility and unity.

I chose to put my creation, Mankind, Male and Female alike, here on what you humans call Earth. It was ideal in every aspect for the survival of the species I caused to give life. Humans have flourished on this small world but so has *EVIL* and *SIN*. *LUCIFER*, who was once one of my angels, but had fallen from grace after he enticed the first male and female creations to defy my words was flung down into the molten center of the planet, as punishment for that act of rebellion, to be entombed there for all eternity.

He, the one who mankind calls *THE DEVIL*, out of spite to me and because he is no longer one of my blessed ones, has worked hard deep within the bowels of the planet and sent his viscous venom into people's thoughts causing all sorts of vile misdeeds. Murder, lies, bigotry, adultery, wars and desecration of one of my holiest of offices here on Earth, the priesthood, who Lucifer has infiltrated and caused its pedophile priests to violate the vows they made to the church and to ME.

Even though I could extinguish the entire planet with a simple wave of my hand, as I did the ancient cities of *SODOM* and *GOMORRAH*, I choose not to do so. Instead, I deem it now time for a new beginning to my grand experiment, *HUMAN BEINGS*.

MANKIND, on his own merits and to demonstrate how much knowledge he has gained, must now prepare a new world. A world of bliss and happiness without the evil influence of the Devil, who cannot escape the boundaries of earth.

A small planet, similar in many ways to earth, is in orbit within a solar system around my bright and shining star Sirius, and is the perfect and ideal place to transfer my seed. So now, all those assembled here who were chosen by me, even before you were in your fathers loins, are challenged to fulfill this quest and with the knowledge

I have given thee of space flight, and genetics, I charge thee to prepare a ship. Man it with only those on this holy mountain who I have now purified of all SIN by just being in my presence and who are now in a state of grace and are incorruptible by Satan. All these will leave your planets surface and travel into interstellar space and create a new race of men on this far off frontier. The new men you create will be in my image and exactly in the order of the words I left ages ago with *MOSES*, who outlined them in Genesis, of your book, the Bible.

Mankind has been in wonderment of the Cosmos for eons and gazing skyward.... looking......searching,..... always *UPWARDS*.... to the heavens, for a sign to come from outer space. While all throughout time, the silent, disassembled signal was here on earth, waiting for you humans to find it, then working together in peace, assemble the pathway, and sent the signal UP to me, which in turn, would bring me *DOWN* once again to Earth and mankind.

Now prepare your ship, and then journey to the star Sirius with my blessing. Find the orbiting planet most like Earth and create there, *MANKIND'S SECOND GENESIS* without *EVIL*.

Now that my twelve tribes have once again united in peace, I tell you to take heed, listen to my warning, and turn thee away from SIN. For I tell you the time of

MY Son's second coming is soon, watch for the signs and be ready, for HE is coming."

Just as the final syllables of God's voice entered my head, I saw the images in the green laser vanish. Suddenly, the green beam somehow began scrambling the light spectrum, and instantly changed itself into a beam the color of blood. The Ark of the Covenant surrounded in a huge pinkish cloud begins to slowly lift off the ground, as did the two still smoldering bodies of Doctor Ben-Gurrie and Rabbi Archer. The tent began to shake and it became airborne in the cloud. The whole complex, tent, Ark, bodies, everything, continued to raise higher and higher and the red shaft of light seemed to be like a powerful tractor beam sucking itself back up into space and taking the holy artifacts and bodies with it. In the blink of an eye, there was nothing discernable in the night sky except a small red dot, then that too vanished completely.

Everyone stood there, motionless, speechless and breathless, in awe of the spectacle we had just witnessed, a spectacle that truly was the most significant event in the history of mankind, God speaking directly to man, announcing the end times are upon us.

I do not know what came over me but I was dumbfounded, as if in a catatonic state and did not move a muscle for a long time, long enough for the night to turn to dawn. Suddenly the sun, in the form of a huge golden disk, burst forth over the crest of Mount Sinai and illuminated our small group in its brilliant glow. We stood there silently on that chilly deserted mountaintop, where the only thing moving, other than the mind blowing thoughts running feverously through our brains, was a small whirlwind spinning a few grains of sand.

I heard Gabe say, "Oh! My heavenly father, what has just happened?" Then looking skyward toward a bright star he exclaimed, "Can you believe it, the ancients were right all along about Sirius being connected to God." As ever, the scientist looking for proof, he continued speaking, "One thing is for sure, without the Ark as hard evidence no one will ever believe our story that something this profound to mankind actually took place."

As he spoke, I noticed over where the tent had stood, there remained a battery of freestanding back-up computer terminals, which had not been drawn into space with the ark. I yelled aloud to Gabe, "The computers! They could have recorded something."

The two of us raced over to the terminals and switched on the sound tracks hoping to hear God's voice once again. Listening intently, we heard nothing but the sound of static; the back-up computers had not recorded one single syllable or sound we could use as evidence.

Looking around at us weary band of observers, several had fallen to their knees and were in deep prayer, Gabe said, "The world will just have to believe us about the second coming of Christ, in fact they *MUST* believe us….. all,"………Gabe hesitated and counted our grim faces then continued saying,….. "*ALL TWELVE* of us males and females. We are the new *DISCIPLES* who will spread the word, and to all those nations who say we lie, we will reply in God's Holy words, "Blessed is he who believes without seeing."…………..… *BELIEVE US, HE IS COMING*!"

THE BEGINNING, of the SECOND GENESIS of MANKIND

EPILOGUE

Second Genesis of Mankind

The year is 2017. I am in deep space, aboard Earth's first Star Cruiser, "The Shalom." My name is Zack Heikel one of the ship's science officers. The vessel has a gross weight of fourteen million tons and is the size of a large city. Its origin having been spawned in a clandestine American government program some fourteen years ago with the intention of secretly exploring new worlds. The craft is on a navigational flight path that is aiming it directly at the Triangular Constellation. It has been five years since we left the gravitational pull of Earth and it would be another three before reaching our final destination, the planet Sirius. Our mission, one in which at times seems almost impossible for the human brain to comprehend, is to create a race of human beings on that planets surface, using as a blueprint, God's holy word taken from Genesis in the Bible. The expedition began in a most unthinkable way eight years ago on the top of Mount Sinai.

Having been touched in a physical way by the Devine, I was driven to study genetics and after graduating from a prestigious university with a master's degree, I became part of a super secret CIA project called Enigma. The project's goal, if successful, could change the course of history and had as its lofty ambition, nothing short of trying to decipher the mysteries and strange codes written in the Bible or hidden in other artifacts. Twelve of us scientists had put together three pieces of ancient antiquities, which had been unearthed, and accumulated over many years from various places the world over.

Although mind-boggling in nature and once thought to be only myths, they were nevertheless real. I still remember how astonished I was when I first saw all three relics and could scarily believe my eyes, but there they were, The Holy Grail, The Twelve Rings of Gods Lost Tribes and the most holy of all, The Ark of the Covenant. Using instructions written in Biblical Hebrew from an ancient text, which we at the time believed God himself had left on Earth millenniums ago, assembled all these components secretly at CIA's headquarters in Langley, Virginia. We then proceeded to the Sinai Peninsula and the mountaintop as directed in the old manuscript to test the machine. Miraculously using the enormous amount of static electricity in the Earth's atmosphere as a power source, the Ark of the Covent came to life with dazzling brilliance and suddenly shot a tremendous laser beam deep into the cosmos. Not aware of the power of the Ark or the meaning of what the Ark actually was designed to accomplish, we were utterly struck numb when it contacted......... our Creator, God. He came down to Earth within the beam and materialized, taking form in an emerald green hologram, which was focused on the Mercy Seat that sat atop the Ark. God's message, was short but very direct. He was pleased that Mankind had finally after eons of warfare came together in peace, found and assembled the Ark and signaled him that they were ready to move forward in Man's evolution. However, he was forthright in saying that man had fallen short of God's expectations and had committed sin after sin against his fellow man and the holy words left by Him with Moses, these sins certainly perpetrated by the evil influence of Satan.

God announced that his son, Jesus Christ would be returning to Earth and with the help of another righteous man Enoch, he would sit in judgment on the nations of the world and bring about a thousand years of peace on Earth before the end times would be completed.

God also charged us twelve who were on the mountain that night with another mission. In order to demonstrate to the Almighty, mankind's knowledge of the sciences, we were to transfer his seed, human beings onto the surface of another planet, by re-creating them perfectly in his image through genetic engineering. This time the new species would not be plagued by the evil influences of the Devil, who God had confined to the bowels of Earth.

I am not alone on this massive ship; there are eleven other scientists as well as one hundred and forty four thousand humans, all with a distinct part to play in this evolutionary changing event of replanting God's experiment Mankind, onto another planets surface located in a far distant galaxy. This transplantation would be giving man a second opportunity at achieving the near God-like state which God himself had intended for all humans.

1932795

Made in the USA